Contents

The quotes from Empeirikos prototype 1.0 were computer generated by neural net language models programmed by the author. They were intended to be humorous, representing the unrefined thoughts of a newly generated robot.

Chapter 1

"May not machines carry out something which ought to be described as thinking but which is very different from what a man does?"
Alan Turing
Computing Machinery and Intelligence

* * *

It was twilight, and raindrops perfused the city of Sojourn. Like transients eager to view every attraction, only the raindrops were familiar with every last neighborhood. The natives entrenched themselves like soldiers. The river Blithe split the lower half and upper half. Natives from the North bank shunned those from the South bank, and East enders did not care to frolic with West enders.

The rain fell, but the arid air spelled its demise. Evaporating vaguely, not a drop reached its destination. Yet it left a damp tingle, like a carbonated beverage. It partitioned the atmosphere like the river through the city. In the drizzly, lower neighborhood of the atmosphere, humans wielded their umbrellas against the night. In the drenched, upper reaches, winged denizens scrawled ephemeral patterns into the sky.

In a moonlit park, just overhead, a bat zipped back and forth, looking for moths. Resilient as a tennis ball, it described the same linear path repeatedly, as if never comprehending that once was probably enough to gauge the number of moths in the vicinity. On a nearby hill, outside a dense grove of trees, a hawk circled lazily, the converse of the bat. It shifted the center of its circular path each time, like cursive, never lifting the pen from the paper. Yet something in its manner feigned disinterest, as if, despite covering wide territory, it would be beneath it to actually descend upon its prey. Thus, neither the bat nor the hawk could ever fulfill its potential. It just wasn't part of nature's plan.

But a newcomer whispered through the treetops. A commercial drone was responding to a client. The *Phantasm Halo* was the newest Unmanned Aerial Vehicle of 2028, with a reinforced carbon fiber frame, Kevlar-epoxy rotors, and Lithium-sulfur battery power. The propellers buzzed and the batteries hummed with a kind of inner humor, like a private joke that only machines understood. It was intense like the bat, yet imperious as the hawk. Nothing preoccupied it outside of its singular purpose. But it was smug, as if one up on its previous customer.

The drone cleared the trees and descended to a dimly lit sidewalk near a bustling restaurant. The air around it seemed to smile like the Cheshire cat. The propellers revved down as the system shifted into hibernation.

A walkway led from the sidewalk to an adjacent townhouse. A doorway opened and an elderly man approached the small drone, lifting it and removing a bottle of champagne from its clutches. Upon returning the drone to the sidewalk, he pressed a button and the drone tentatively ascended a few feet, then buzzed away like a Palmetto bug. The old man watched until it was a speck in the sky, then he slowly unwrapped his champagne while hobbling back into his home.

Chapter 2

The portly conscript placed his briefcase on the table and popped open the latches, only to reveal that it was empty inside. The seamless gray lining complemented the black leather exterior. Not one bankroll was to be found. No tokens, coupons, vouchers, or poker chips.

"What's the big idea, Bubba?"

The industrialist seated across from the conscript was attired in cowboy hat, beige suit, blue tie. Frowning at the empty briefcase, he folded his hands in front of him, awaiting the conscript's response.

"It wasn't my fault," said Bubba defiantly. "I followed the protocol."

"Whose fault was it, then?" asked the industrialist.

"No one's," Bubba replied. "It was unforeseen."

Despite the weak response, his voice was calm, with no trace of fear.

"It was your job to anticipate unforeseen circumstances," said the industrialist. "Virtual tablets are the hottest drug on the black market. If the clients objected to the fee, you were expected to negotiate. If they requested a test drive, you were to roll with it."

"They did request a test drive," Bubba explained. "I dropped a virtual tablet into each of their coffees. I took a placebo and wished them all a happy hallucination. While they were virtualizing, I even picked their pockets. Bagged all of their incriminating identification."

Bubba threw a handful of ID cards onto the table.

"Not bad," said the industrialist. "But they never completed the transaction, so we can't blackmail them. You fell short of your objective."

"I purloined a few hundred dollars," said Bubba. "If it's any consolation, take it."

He flung a stack of bills onto the table.

"That's not nearly enough," said the industrialist. "What's to prove that you didn't stash the payload in the woods?"

"They refused to pay," Bubba objected.

"Because they recognized you," said the industrialist.

"Not at all," said Bubba. "They just didn't like the drugs."

"What's not to like about virtabs? My guess is they just didn't trust you."

"You guessed wrong," said Bubba emphatically. "This is *your* fault, not mine. This line of questioning proves nothing. I followed the protocol to the letter. It was *chance* that threw a wrench in it. You failed to anticipate it. You need to reevaluate your approach."

The industrialist sighed and removed his hat, placing it to the side of the table.

"This conversation is not meant to be onerous or demanding," he explained. "This is not an inquisition. It's just routine."

Yet even as he smiled reassuringly, his hands disappeared beneath the table and returned brandishing a formidable energy weapon resembling a sawed-off shotgun embellished with pulsing lights.

"What are you doing?" Bubba protested, just before the energy discharge knocked him backward onto the floor, disturbing the pile of bills on the table, which wafted into the air like a flock of birds and slowly settled. Bubba's torso lay limp and twisted on the floor, seemingly dead but with no visible wound, the victim of unseen electromagnetic forces.

The industrialist rested the enigmatic gun on the table.

"Nothing personal," he said as he donned his hat. He shifted his gaze to the man who was silently guarding the door.

"What did you think about his invective?" the industrialist asked. "That our procedure is flawed. Do you think he was right? What's your honest opinion?"

"If he was right, sir," said the guard, "then why did you kill him?"

"He didn't accomplish his objective," the industrialist replied. "He returned empty handed. But what if he's right?"

The industrialist stooped and grabbed a handful of money from the floor, which he used to politely tip the guard.

"Keep the change," he said. He strode through the door and continued his chat with the guard, who followed behind.

"Time to pick on someone else," the industrialist commented. "Bring me the new guy."

Chapter 3

"Artificial intelligence, which is, and in a great degree, the whole wind, which is the wind and the sea, which I had not the honour to make them to be the wind, the other, that the sun's storm, which is the wind, the other in those parts."

Empeirikos prototype 1.0

* * *

One year later, Trep Sportly peered out the window at the falling rain. Trep and his friend Link were sitting at a quiet table at their favorite restaurant, Gastronomy, a pet store and restaurant rolled into one. A fish tank floated above their table, suspended within a large glass tube that stretched all the way to the ceiling. Trep stared inside at a large Gourami with its mouth open. With eyes on opposite sides of its head, the fish appraised him with just one eye. Trep wondered whether fish saw the world with a dividing line down the middle, or whether they thought there were two separate worlds, one on their left, and one on their right.

Trep decided to order a fruit juice. At the bottom of the glass tube, just below the fish tank, lay a large hollow serving platform that hovered just above the table. Trep fingered the buttons on the outer interface, swiped his credit card over the camera, and pressed the send button. The fish tank began to slowly ascend through the glass tube as the serving platform travelled toward the kitchen. Trep watched the startled Gourami flapping its fins, struggling to maintain its position while the fish tank disappeared through the ceiling. Moments later, Trep's fruit juice descended on the platform, the fish tank hovering above it. The platform was lowered into the open air, whereupon Trep grabbed his glass of juice and began to sip. The Gourami rotated for a moment, then began to relax.

"Have you heard?" Link asked, straightening his posture and widening his eyes. "Aliens have already invaded, and they are among us as we speak."

"That's absurd," Trep objected. "Where's your evidence?"

"No evidence. Just statistics."

Link waxed philosophical.

"Our galaxy is ten billion years old and contains two-hundred and fifty billion stars, many of which are much older than our sun. According to Fermi's paradox, from the sheer number of stars, it's likely that some of them contain planets like ours, but evolved life long before us. And following Drake's equation, estimates are that even if their space travel was no faster than ours, it would take them only ten million years to colonize the entire galaxy, a heartbeat in galactic terms. With those statistics, the question is not whether aliens exist, but rather when did they arrive and where are they now?"

Trep was still skeptical.

"If they had invaded, it would be observable."

"That leaves only one conclusion," Link asserted. *"We're* the aliens. Obviously, we erased our memories."

"Why would we do that?" said Trep disapprovingly.

Link's response was swift.

"Maybe to expunge all evidence of the invasion, to absolve us of guilt."

Link, whose legal name was Lincoln Romano, was a part-time legal assistant and data analyst.

"Spoken like a true lawyer," Trep jabbed.

"That's an oxymoron," Link retorted.

Trep rested his arms on the table and shifted his weight forward, trying to get the advantage in the argument.

"From the looks of it," he said, "we're the only ones here. The former inhabitants are gone. Thus, we would have no need to hide the evidence from ourselves."

"Theory confirmed," Link exclaimed, "for lack of a better explanation."

"But even so," Trep suggested, "it's like an invasion that never existed."

"You're right," Link agreed. "So the real question is, when will the next invasion occur? With so many ancient stars harboring planets, there's bound to be another one. Or has it already happened? And, if so, why aren't we aware of it? The odds are against the same explanation happening twice. So if they aren't us, what pretense do these new aliens have to conceal themselves?"

Trep ignored him. His com visor was vibrating. He pulled the visor over his eyes and tapped the right arm to activate the organic light-emitting diode display. The transparent lens turned opaque as the interior flooded with color. To those around him, Trep just appeared to be wearing dark sunglasses.

Com visors were very in fashion in 2029 and had replaced

the laptop as the standard internet gateway. Most people wore them at all times, in transparent mode, and some preferred to darken the tinge for a standoffish effect.

Through the window of his visor, a computer desktop overlaid his view of the coffee shop. In the upper right-hand corner, a cartoon postal truck repeatedly drove the same route, kicking up a cloud of dust. Trep raised his fingers to touch the exterior of the visor lens, where the touch sensors were embedded. As he moved his hands, icons of fingerprints inscribed themselves onto the screen to follow his fingertips.

He straightened his index finger and pressed the postal truck to open his email client. A new message was waiting. He had an admirer, probably from the new dating site he had been surfing: *amorous.com*. Anxious, he opened the message.

"Hi, sweetheart," the message read. *"Remember me? I've been so lonely without you. Let's get this romance back on track. Awaiting your reply – Stella."*

Trep had never heard of Stella before, but he wasn't about to keep a love-struck lady waiting. It was no surprise that this Stella was aware of his venerable reputation. He had already earned enough points on amorous.com to achieve *Conqueror* status.

He tapped the left visor arm to launch the virtual keyboard. The visor cameras tracked his finger movements as he typed out a suave response requesting Stella's address and pressed the send button. He tapped the right visor arm to close the virtual desktop and lifted his visor to rest over his forehead.

"Who was that?" Link inquired.

"Just another love starved dame who can't get enough," Trep announced with aplomb. "She wants to meet me."

"Good luck with that," Link quipped. He surveyed the room.

Gastronomy had a fully staffed kitchen, but its automated service tubes obviated the need for waitresses. And that freed up a great deal of floor space. Gastronomy had seized the opportunity by merging with a large local pet distributor. Gastronomy was not just a restaurant, it was also a pet store.

Although the fish in the tanks were not for sale, many of the other animals were. Animal cages adorned the walls of the restaurant, and pets that were well behaved were allowed to roam the floors. For reasons of sanitation, they were not allowed on your lap if you had food at the table. Otherwise, it was anything goes, and the menu boasted a wide variety of animal treats.

Behavioral psychologists lauded the idea, claiming that it would reduce violence and promote social empathy. And Gastronomy made a small fortune on animal treats, in addition to ranking as a top local tourist attraction.

"I think I'll pet my favorite fur ball," Link said, excusing himself from the table and approaching one of the open cages by the wall. He returned with a large brown guinea pig with two tags dangling from its collar: one said *Regina*, and the other said *Not for sale*. Regina belonged to one of the managers. Link sat down and cradled Regina in his lap, lavishing her with baby talk. The pudgy guinea pig was swaddled in a thick rug of long fur, its gaze barely visible behind the tousles.

Trep rolled his eyes. It irritated him how his overweight friend drooled over his favorite overweight rodent.

"She would make a wonderful mop if you just turned her on her back," he said. "Shall we spill your coffee and try it out?"

Link defended her.

"Regina does not approve of your humor, do you, Regina?"

He turned her head from side to side to convey her discontent. Then, he lifted her from underneath and spread her arms to feign flying.

"Let's go get some guinea treats!" he exclaimed. He made Regina fly to the glass tube interface. He guided her furry paws over the buttons to place an order. He set her back on his lap, swiped his credit card, and pressed *send*. The fish tank ascended through the ceiling, returning a minute later with a small dish of guinea treats. Link placed Regina on the table where she munched contentedly at the small plastic dish.

Trep sighed and glanced around the restaurant. A cast of regular patrons was in attendance. The old drunk was collapsed in the corner, half asleep. He begged for coins outside every day, then came in to pet his favorite gerbils. They kept a discrete table for him in the back, out of sight of most of the customers. Elsewhere, college youth were drinking beer and petting a bulldog. A business lady adorned with jewelry was petting a Persian cat. And the new attendant was standing at the sales counter, a bored look on her face. She was so lovely that Trep had to avoid staring at her.

"I think the new salesgirl wants to talk to me," Trep said.

"Sure she does," said Link. But Trep stood up and left the table, just as the business lady was exiting the restaurant. Trep picked up the Persian as it tried to follow the lady out the door. The Persian had a large *Not for sale* sign on its expensive collar. He brought it to the sales counter.

"I would like to buy a Persian," he informed the salesgirl.

"She's not for sale," said the girl.

"Just joking," he explained, but she seemed unamused.

He tried again, pointing to an iguana dangling on the end

of a long branch.

"Nice iguana. Wanna go to the zoo together sometime?"

"I think I have enough animals on my hands already," she retorted.

At a loss for words, Trep winced and excused himself, leaving the Persian with the attendant. Returning to their table, he slumped into his chair.

"She's playing hard to get," he lied.

Link chuckled. He had Regina in his lap again and was massaging her behind the ears.

Trep ordered a gin and tonic, then donned his com visor. He opened his email and searched for a response from Stella. To his surprise, an envelope icon sat waiting in his *new messages* bin. Anxious, he clicked on the envelope to read the message. It was a short note containing Stella's address.

Meet me at 9:30, it said.

Trep glanced at the clock icon on the desktop. He had two hours. He closed his virtual desktop, raised his com visor over his forehead, and grabbed his gin from the platform above the table. Fermi's paradox could wait. If aliens were preparing to invade, he would at least finish his drink first.

Chapter 4

"Knowledge in the nature, that a proposition is no knowledge in any other proposition, that it are a proposition in all things. For they may be the same thing in this way and the mind is so much in their own opinions in all the agreement."

Empeirikos prototype 1.0

* * *

The industrialist stared over the shoulders of his lead developer, who was typing frantically at his computer keyboard while simultaneously reading equations from the peer-reviewed journal article adorning his screen.

"What's the problem?" asked the industrialist. "Just reverse engineer it."

"And then what?" said the developer.

"Then feed it the test data and tell me what it says."

"These equations are inscrutable," said the developer. "Couldn't we just implement our own algorithms?"

"We could, but that would defeat the point."

"And the point of it is?"

"The point of it is *precisely* to reverse engineer their algorithms," snapped the industrialist. "Tell me how their program reacts to our data. And when you finish that, I have a dozen more articles for you to read."

Hours later, the developer at last presented his first screen of test results, but they were not to the industrialist's satisfaction. Days went by while countless programs were reverse engineered and tested with no success.

One day, however, the test screen brought a smile to the industrialist's face. He removed his cowboy hat and stooped toward the screen for a closer look, peering through his reading glasses.

"Now *that* has potential," he exclaimed. "Get me that one. Throw the rest of them in the trash."

"Yes sir, Mr. Zostro," said the developer. He began clearing the computer desktop of cluttered programs.

Mr. Zostro refitted his hat and returned to his office. He donned his com visor and summoned his strategists.

"Our lead developer has narrowed down our target," he announced. "Now we need to spin off some nonlinear models. Give me at least five different projections."

He poured himself a gin and tonic, then strolled to the foyer to harass his secretary.

"Take this down," he said. *"Meeting tomorrow at ten with the new recruit."*

His secretary promptly scribbled the appointment into her calendar.

He took a swig of gin and grimaced at its bitterness. He should have been drinking coffee, he told himself. But the day's work was done.

"I'm going to the shooting range," he said. "No interruptions."

Nailing cardboard cutouts between the eyes was his idea of

a relaxing afternoon. He commissioned two security guards and embarked for his limo. On his way out, he noticed that the developer remained busy at his computer terminal. Always the perfectionist, he thought to himself. Someday, he would have to drop some virtual tablets into that guy's coffee.

Chapter 5

Trep left Link and Regina to themselves and exited the restaurant, lifting the canopy of his umbrella and heading for the nearest Tube station. The Transit Tube was Sojourn's major form of inner-city transportation. Trep entered a wide portal and found the appropriate route. He boarded the nearest empty passenger pod, a sleek spherical capsule with a lustrous gray exterior. The cramped interior could nevertheless accommodate a small family, but Trep was the only one present. Overcrowding was rare on the Transit Tube. However, just as the door-closing bell began to sound, an old man entered Trep's pod and sat down across from him. Many people preferred to ride in the company of others. The door slid closed and the pods were slowly propelled forward and routed down the appropriate branch.

Trep watched as the station disappeared through the windows, replaced by the gray walls of the streamlined transportation tube. The old man across from him stared down at his shoes. He wore a gray overcoat and a ruddy scarf. Putting his umbrella to one side, he pulled an antiquated book from one of his coat pockets and began to flip through the pages. Paper books were rare in 2029. It must have been a family heirloom, Trep thought.

"Nice weather we're having," Trep commented sarcastically.

"Yes, indeed," replied the man. He pointed down toward his waterproof galoshes, where a puddle was forming on the floor.

"A good excuse to wear new shoes," he said.

He stretched one of his legs to show off the new galoshes, then resumed browsing his book. He glanced up and pointed at Trep's t-shirt.

"Go *Sojourners*," he said, reading the t-shirt. The Sojourners were the local football team. Trep was wearing their t-shirt beneath his jacket.

"They should have had them," Trep sighed wistfully. The Sojourners had lost their last game by a mere three points after a last-minute field goal.

"They'll get them next time," the man said. "Odds are in their favor. They lost two in a row. What are the chances they'll lose three in a row?"

Trep furrowed his brow at the sound of such unlikely optimism, but after consulting his calculator, he had to admit that the man was right. Even if the Sojourners had only a fifty percent chance of winning any individual game, probabilistics suggested that after losing two in a row, their chances of winning increased to eighty-seven point five percent. Suddenly, the old man reminded him of his friend Link. As he pondered, figures dancing through his head, the electric hum of the passenger pod filled the silence.

Finally, the pod arrived and the doors slid open. Trep forced a tight-lipped smile and nodded at the old man as they both stood and exited the pod.

"Good evening," said the old man.

"So long," said Trep, and they went their separate ways.

Trep ascended the ramp to the main promenade of the station. Route schedules flashed overhead on transparent organic light-emitting diode displays. Strangers bustled around haphazardly or sat at the coffee shop peering into their tinted com visors, their fingers tracing commands over their lenses. To Trep, they resembled professors elucidating first principles, pointing their fingers into the air for emphasis, except that they had no audience or students in attendance, and thus appeared as madmen expounding into the empty air.

Trep found a map and oriented himself to his new location. He lowered his visor, opened his email, and memorized Stella's address, then found the appropriate street on the map. He raised his visor, opened his umbrella, and exited the station. A lukewarm drizzle greeted him. He plunged through the night, crossing several streets and turning several corners before reaching the apartment building with Stella's address above the entrance. Stella's apartment was room *214*. He ascended the small staircase into the building and took the elevator to the second floor.

He found room 214 at the end of the hall and raised his hand to knock on the door, then noticed that the doorknob appeared nonfunctional. The wood around the knob was cracked, and the knob was bent as if the mechanism was not engaged into the complementary knob on the other side. The latch bolt appeared to be jammed inside the door itself, leaving nothing to lock the door into the frame. Trep pushed on the knob. The hinges creaked as the door swung open.

"Hello?" he said warily. Flashing lights emanated from the interior. They slowly rotated through an array of colors: first red, then green, then yellow, then red again, bathing the apartment in eerie light.

"Is anybody home?" he asked again.

"Please enter," said a female voice from inside. Trep took a few tentative steps into the apartment. A gray-haired woman sat on a couch, her back to Trep. In front of her, a widescreen television was filled with static. In the corner, a replica of a traffic light stood on the top of a pole, flashing red, green, and yellow.

Trep stepped through the foyer into the kitchen. Pictures adorned the kitchen counter. In one, a lovely young blond-haired girl in a wedding gown posed with her new husband. In another, the same couple posed on the top of a sunny cliff, a panoramic valley unfolding behind them.

Across the kitchen, an open window was letting the rain in. Trep crossed the floor to the window and looked outside, surveying the ground far below. In an alleyway, the lid of a large garbage bin lay open. Trep stared into the bin but could see only shadows. He closed the window and proceeded into the living room.

"Hello," he said to the old woman. "You must be Stella."

"If I must, I must," said the woman. "Would I be correct in guessing that you are Trep Sportly?"

Trep moved toward the front of the couch but refrained from sitting.

"Yes," he stuttered. "Sorry, it's just that…I was expecting someone a little younger."

Stella gripped sewing needles in her furrowed hands and was intent on embroidering a quilt. Her curly gray hair was unkempt, falling over her face like an ill-fitting wig. Her eyes were concealed by a pair of oversized black sunglasses. She wore a thrifty one-piece dress with white frills and polka dots.

Her shoes were large clodhoppers that didn't fit her properly, buckled over wrinkled brown pantyhose.

"Forgive me," she said, "but I'm practically blind. I can't even see you, but you certainly have a handsome voice. Are you very old? What do you look like?"

That explained why the woman still had not looked at Trep. She stared absently at the television screen.

"I'm thirty-five," said Trep. "And unfortunately, I'm not very handsome."

Trep did not know how to explain his appearance, and moreover he did not want to. Instead, he inspected the living room. The television screen played frazzled static and filled the air with white noise. On a coffee table before the couch, a laptop computer had been hacked into. Only the screen and keyboard were intact. Beneath them, the motherboard lay exposed, the circuits reflecting the shifting hues of the traffic light.

Against the wall was a robo pong table that doubled as a billiards table. Trep had seen it on commercials. In 2029, all products had begun to converge together. Few products had just one function. If you were entertaining guests, the sides of the robo pong table flipped up to form rails with makeshift pocket nets for playing billiards. Trep noticed several cue sticks leaning against the wall. If you were playing solo instead, you could battle the robot arm at ping pong. The metal arm sat motionless on the far side. Its swivel functions were built into a servo motor mounted on the end of the table. On top of the servo was a small video camera and an integrated computer system. The robotic hand lay with fingers outstretched next to a pair of studded paddles.

It was odd that a woman living alone would have such a

device. But what was stranger still was that the television screen was filled with static.

"What are you watching?" Trep asked. "Is something wrong with your television?"

"Oh, I don't know," she replied, sounding flustered. "Could you please help me fix it?"

She proffered the remote control.

"If you don't mind my asking," Trep inquired, "if you are blind, then why do you want to watch TV?"

"Nothing is as it seems, Trep Sportly," she responded. "Take this quilt, for example. The most intricate tapestries arise from the simplest patterns. It's something of a contradiction, wouldn't you say?"

Trep shrugged, accepting the remote control and fidgeting with the buttons. The channels were unresponsive. Trep scrutinized the back of the television and observed that the connection used a primitive coaxial cable. He deduced that the television required setup.

"You have to do a channel search," he said. He'd had practice configuring the old satellite television at his father's nursing home. He pressed the setup button and configured the device to start searching channels. Numbers on the screen began incrementing each time a new channel was found. Once the device located the proper wavelengths, the programs would appear on the screen.

"It should work momentarily," he informed her, "and it was very nice to meet you, but I think I should go."

"Wait," she said urgently. "I must tell you something."

She dropped her quilt and sewing needles, flinging them onto the table. She stood, and Trep saw that she was tall and gaunt. She caressed her body with her palms as if to straighten her dress.

"Abandon your presuppositions," she said, "your dogmas. You have to look beyond the surface."

"Sorry," Trep apologized, "but I'm feeling rather shallow tonight. May I take a rain check?"

Stella continued.

"You'll find what you're looking for where you least expect it."

"Actually," Trep replied, "I was just looking for the door."

"Could you teach me how to use the remote control?" said Stella petulantly, quickly changing the subject.

"Well, of course," Trep said. He waited until the channel search completed, then stood next to her and presented the remote. He guided one of her hands across the buttons.

"Here is your power button, and these are channel up, channel down, volume up, and volume down."

He gave her the remote and invited her to try it out. Then, he turned and admired the television screen, confirming that the channels were working. His good deed completed, he started to lean toward the door.

"Thank you ever so much," Stella said as she began to manipulate the channels. She paused on a nature program portraying a thicket of trees flanking a pond.

"Amphibians are close descendants of sea creatures," said the narrator. "They are born with gills, but then grow lungs. And their skin is glandular, enabling cutaneous respiration."

Stella seemed nervous. She fumbled with the buttons awkwardly until the channels began changing.

Trep gave Stella one last look before he left. He inspected her hands on the remote control. Stella was very old indeed. There was something odd about her geriatric skin texture.

She was so old, lit by the odd glow of the traffic lights, it almost made her skin look…alien.

"It's been wonderful meeting you," Trep stuttered. "If you ever need help with your television again, please don't hesitate to send me an email. I have to go now. Goodbye."

Trep started for the exit. Stella waved him goodbye as he closed the door to her apartment.

On his way out of the building, a surge of guilt assailed him. A poor old blind woman so desperate to fix her television that she had resorted to a blind date, and all Trep could do was make excuses on his way out the door. He opened his umbrella and confronted the lonely night, wondering what would drive a blind woman to watch television.

And what other household ordeals did she face? Her front door was dilapidated, and the lock was toothless. No repairman was in sight, the property was unprotected, and the apartment looked ransacked. Despite it all, Trep felt certain that she was not a marauding thug, nor an alien invader, and wondered what other lovely people could be met on the outskirts of town.

Chapter 6

In the confines of a bleak operating room beneath brightly shining surgical lamps, a stainless-steel scalpel punctured the patient's trachea and began its long journey down the torso until reaching the lower abdomen. Then, a pneumatic saw cut the sternum in half. The surgical team's hands were swathed in long sterile neoprene gloves. They spread folds of tissue to expose the thoracic cavity. Incisions were made around the pericardium. The still-beating heart was harvested along with its lubricating sac. Swiftly, it was passed to the waiting hands of the nurses for transfer to the normothermic oxygenated perfusion bioreactor.

The readout of the electroencephalogram showed a flat line. The surgeons knew that brain death had already occurred prior to the start of the procedure. It weighed on one's conscience that the donor had not died a natural death, but the revenue from the organs would be substantial. They promptly attended to the harvesting of the abdominal organs.

The scalpel next made a long incision across the lower abdomen. The surgically gloved hands commenced transection of the vessels surrounding the liver. The inferior vena cava was severed. Next, the hepatic portal vein and hepatic artery. Finally, the common bile duct was detached. The fresh organ was quickly transferred into a hypothermic extracorporeal device.

The left kidney was next examined. The ureter was severed from the bladder. The renal vein and artery were dissected. After hasty transfer to ex-vivo storage, the right kidney was also harvested. The procedure was complete.

The surgeons removed their neoprene gloves delicately, reversing the first but still gripping it in the opposite hand, then removing the second glove over the first so that the two gloves were conveniently wrapped over one another into a sterile disposable unit. They tossed them into the trash and brushed off their hands.

Dr. Theta examined the monitors of the bioreactors and briefly peeked into the organ chambers. Satisfied with the performance of her assistants, she returned to the surgical table. It was not standard procedure to perform operations on a gurney, but their purpose had not been to revive the patient. She rested one foot on the lower support bar, then kicked the wheeled gurney toward the wall.

She watched as the gaping torso of the organ donor on the table coasted nimbly across the floor, collided with the wall, then tumbled off balance onto the freshly mopped tiles. The blood that had been so carefully contained now spilled into an amorphous puddle surrounding the donor's prostrate corpse. The surgeon laughed at the sight of the donor's body prone upon its own blood.

"Why let the janitor have the day off?" she jested. Her assistants responded with resounding laughter.

"Don't get too comfortable," she exhorted them. "Get those organ chambers to transport fast. Get them out of here!"

Dr. Theta watched as they scurried out the door, a pool of

blood slowly advancing toward her overshoes. She removed her stained scrubs, tossing them into the laundry bag. Then, she embarked for the decontamination room. In the shower, she inflicted her skin with scalding hot water. She tried in vain to purge the morbid stench from her flesh, but she knew that once the odorants had saturated her olfactory glomeruli, she could smell nothing else.

Chapter 7

"Thanks ever so much for doing business with the Search Strategists. It's been a pleasure to serve you, and remember, your search is our strategy. Please come back soon."

Trep had concluded his transaction with the first customer of the day. He swiveled his microphone to the side of his face and leaned back in his chair, propping his feet up on the edge of his desk. Another satisfied customer, he thought. But they had been so hard to please. He stared up at the ceiling, thinking of all the places he would rather be.

Trep was a programmer and data analyst for the Search Strategists, a search optimization firm. Trep had helped design a program called *Opportunity* which maximized search results. Businesses now hired him to enhance their search strategies.

In 2029, the number of products was multiplying exponentially. Yet monopolies abounded by major brands which had dominated with a simple search strategy: make one product that does everything.

In their ideal market, every search for every purpose would result in the same product: *theirs*. To that end, they had merged as many products as they could into a few high-end devices.

Although a single product that subsumed all functions was not really possible, economists anticipated that the markets were nevertheless progressing toward a state of *Technoconvergence*, the emergence of an autonomous robotic product that would monopolize search results for human labor. However, for now, the markets were considered to be in a state of *Multiplicity*.

The robo pong table was just one example. The modern stove had also metamorphosed. It had grown multiple robotic arms with retractile utensils, pots, and pans. Just program the recipe and place the ingredients into its hands, and Robochef did the rest.

Product Search Strategists, like Trep, were hired to help smaller businesses advertise their goods. Without high profile online search results, many companies simply remained unknown. The key to profitable search results had boiled down to having the right combination of functions overlapping onto one product. To that end, Product Search Strategists were hired to locate available niches that overlapped that of their client. Using sophisticated analytical tools, they narrowed down a combination of markets that would maximize search results, enhancing visibility and sales. After that, the burden was on the customer to incorporate the suggestions into a new design.

Just as Trep removed his headset and was about to go out for lunch, his communicator rang. Excited and disappointed at the same time, he donned his headset and swiveled the microphone back into position. He then assumed his most courteous tone.

"Hello, you have reached the Search Strategists. Your search is our strategy. How may we help you today?"

"Could you repeat that please?" said the crusty voice of an old man.

Trep cleared his throat and repeated his greeting.

"I was just remarking that you have reached the Search Strategists. Your search is our strategy. How may we help you?"

"Could you please speak up?" the man complained testily. He sounded very old.

Trep paused. A few other strategists were at their desks chatting with customers, and some had convened in the kitchen to raid the refrigerator. The office was full. He couldn't raise his voice without everyone noticing. He tried again, this time skipping his greeting.

"What is your product, sir? How may we help you achieve your goals?"

"What?" the man replied, to Trep's chagrin. "I'm sorry, but I'm hard of hearing. Could you please *shout* at me?"

"I beg your pardon?" Trep stuttered.

"Please *shout*," the man explained. "I'm hard of hearing. You have to *shout* at me."

Trep was incredulous.

"Sir," he blurted, "if you don't mind my asking, if you are hard of hearing, then why do you insist on using our phone line? We have an excellent chat service available on the internet."

The man did not reply. Trep considered his words. He struggled to find a way to raise his voice without sounding angry.

"Your name, sir. What is your name?"

The man took a deep breath and said in a dignified voice, "Phineas Nyce."

Trep checked the payment list on his desk. Yes, there it was, Mr. Nyce's name was listed from earlier in the week. He had already paid the full retainer fee.

"I see you have already paid our fee. And what about your product, sir. What are you selling?"

"The product," Mr. Nyce replied, "is a luxurious new way to steam press your clothes. The *Nyce Coat Rack Steamer* is a large garment bag that hangs in your closet. Insert one outfit, zip it up, and activate the steaming mechanism. In just twenty minutes, your outfit is fully pressed and ready to wear."

"Very impressive," exclaimed Trep. "Let's see what we can do for you."

Trep waved his hand over his computer touchpad to bring up the display. With his mouse, he navigated to the sophisticated Opportunity software that analyzed market trends.

He opened the program and typed in the search query: "steam_iron [[product]] WITH suit_bag [[shape]] WITH coat_rack [[location]]".

Then, he selected *Functional Optimization*.

A progress bar reported that the program was calculating. It would search the annotations in every market, looking for possible functional overlaps. Moments later, the results had been pigeonholed, and a long list began appearing on the screen.

"We show that several relevant markets are available," Trep reported. "The top results are full-length mirror, shower curtain, sleeping bag, book shelf, and yoga mat."

Mr. Nyce thought for a moment.

"Not a mirror," he said. "That won't do. Not unless it's made from a flexible material. A solid mirror should not hang in a closet. If it fell and broke, my clients would sue."

Trep typed another query into the computer: "mirror [[product]] WITH flexible [[material]]".

Opportunity calculated for a minute and then reported a short list of materials.

"Mr. Nyce, we ask you to consider building the mirror from reflective mylar film."

"Not interested," the old man objected. "What else do you have? You mentioned a shower curtain."

"Yes," Trep explained. "Having the steam presser near the shower would provide a convenient source of water. Also, leaks would not make a mess on the floor."

"My products do not leak," said Mr. Nyce indignantly. "And hanging clothes in the bathroom is distasteful. What else?"

"A yoga mat, sir."

"No thanks," replied Mr. Nyce. "A coat rack is not for physical exercise. Strenuous activity would damage the rollers. What else?"

Trep suggested a book shelf, but Mr. Nyce felt that the books might become damp and customers might protest.

"That leaves the sleeping bag," Trep offered.

"Sleeping bags are for campers," Mr. Nyce complained. "But what camper needs freshly pressed clothes?"

"I don't know, sir. It was one of the top search results."

Trep was forlorn. The top five search results were the key to success. Their most faithful clients had never elected any of the lower results. Trep paused, collecting his thoughts. Suddenly, an idea occurred.

"What about an electric blanket sleeping bag, sir?"

A steam presser needed electricity, Trep reasoned, and an electric blanket needed heat.

Trep typed out a new Opportunity query: "electric_blanket [[product]] WITH steam_iron [[product]]."

He selected *Search For*, then waited.

After a tense minute, Trep was pleased to see that Opportunity reported *No results*.

Mr. Nyce was still silent. Trep reinforced his idea.

"I'm showing that an electric blanket steaming iron is currently not on the market, sir. It's the perfect hybrid of electrical functions. If water beds make money, then steam-filled blankets ought to be top performers."

Mr. Nyce spoke up.

"This is absurd. Are you telling me that my customers are going to go to bed in the clothes they are planning on wearing the following day?"

"Yes, sir, it's an excellent idea," Trep bluffed, trying hard to conceal the doubt in his voice. "When they wake up, their clothes are pressed and presentable. And the rollers would also provide a comforting massage. Yet another market, sir. That makes three of them. Altogether, you would have a *steam ironing electric blanket massager*. With three markets overlapping on one product, your search optimization would be very high."

Pleased with the realization, he ran a quick search coverage estimate on his computer. Opportunity reported an estimated upper twentieth percentile rank on search page results for all three markets. He relayed the results to his client.

"But wouldn't it have the potential to scald the customers?" asked Mr. Nyce.

"I don't know, sir," said Trep. "That would be for you to decide."

"Let's try it," said Mr. Nyce, enthusiastic at last.

Trep breathed a sigh of relief. He saved the results in Opportunity and initiated the licensing process. He still had to confirm that there were no patent restrictions blocking the product overlap. The Federal Trade Commission tightly regulated the markets in the interests of fair competition. Businesses were allowed to add a particular functionality until that sector reached saturation, as judged by various indices, including search results. After that, its unwarranted inclusion was considered unfair competition.

Opportunity completed the preliminary survey and reported that the relevant markets did not appear to be saturated. Trep sealed the deal by collecting contact information from Mr. Nyce, then applied for his licensing. As he bid Mr. Nyce a good day and ended the session, he realized that he was still vociferating into the phone. He looked around the office, but it appeared that everyone had decided to ignore him. He tried to regain his composure and return to his former lowkey demeanor.

Proceeding to the kitchen, he relaxed with a soda. *What next?* he thought to himself. First a blind woman watching television, then a deaf man on the telephone. Nothing could be stranger than this, he assured himself.

Chapter 8

The next day, there was a robot in Trep's office. It was waiting at the front desk with the receptionist. It sat in a lounge chair with its left leg crossed and its hands in its lap, as if it thought it was a customer. The robot wore no clothes, for it had no genitalia. Its build was as sleek as a marathon runner. It was devoid of hair, but its face was relatively human. It had a nose and a mouth, and its glowing electric eyes were as alert as an owl's, tracking Trep's every move as he stepped through the entrance. The robot's exterior shone like freshly polished metal just off the assembly line. The problem was, to Trep's knowledge, no such assembly line existed, since no such robot was known to have been built.

"Mr. Sportly," said the receptionist, "this…gentleman has been waiting to see you."

The robot stood up promptly and, to Trep's surprise, extended its arm to shake Trep's hand.

"You must be Trep Sportly," it said in a remarkably pleasant and dignified voice. "My name is Empeirikos, and I'm very pleased to meet you."

It clenched Trep's hand in a surprisingly gentle grip, and they shook hands for what seemed like a very long time, as if it was not exactly sure when to stop. Trep pulled his arm back a little and the robot promptly released its grip.

"And who exactly are you?" Trep asked.

"I'm not sure how well I will be able to answer that question," the robot responded, sounding confused. "Perhaps I should not even attempt to do so, since my history manifest seems to report nothing before yesterday afternoon. All I can tell you is that my creators have instructed me to start here."

"Start? Start what? Are you applying for a job?" Trep shook his head. "Unfortunately, we are fully staffed at the moment, but if you will leave your name and number with our receptionist, we will be happy to keep you on file and notify you in the event of an opening."

The last thing Trep needed was robots replacing search strategists. Exasperated, he attempted to exit the reception area, feeling a little bewildered.

But the robot moved to block his path, although it promptly stood back, as if to avoid confrontation.

"Well, not exactly sir. They instructed me to come here to find something else to do."

Trep nodded, suddenly understanding.

"Something else to do!" he replied. "Yes, I know what that means. You are here for our product optimization services."

Although the robot acted like a customer, it was nothing more than a product, just like the *Nyce Steam Ironing Electric Blanket Massager*.

"I suppose so," said the robot, sounding intrigued.

"Tell me," Trep asked, "what sort of robot are you?"

The robot straightened its posture and announced proudly, "I am the first release of the new *Empeirikos* autonomous personal assistant, version one-hundred and fifteen."

"And what is it that you do?" Trep inquired, fascinated.

"I walk and talk," the robot stated flatly.

"And what else?" Trep asked with anticipation.

"That's all," it replied firmly. Then it stood there, staring blankly forward, as happy as a clam.

Trep was at a loss for words. A walking, talking robot was standing in his reception room. Surely, the Technoconvergence was at hand. Nobody had expected the event so soon. But if the robot could do nothing other than walk and talk, then it had not even reached the state of Multiplicity. In contrast, the Technoconvergence had been predicted to encompass, not just several tasks, but all of them. How odd that an automaton would require Product Search Optimization, as if it was not sure what to do.

"Well, I'm sorry, but I don't know whether we'll be able to help you," Trep stated, shaking his head.

Turning to his receptionist, he asked, "Has Empeirikos arranged payment?"

The receptionist raised her eyebrows suggestively, holding up a check. Trep read the dollar amount and gulped. The robot had paid quadruple their normal retainer fee. Trep's tone softened.

"Very well, Empeirikos," he said, turning obsequious. "Step right this way."

He proceeded toward the main office area, but then noticed that the robot was watching his feet, as if to imitate his walk.

"I mean, follow me," he corrected. He strode down the hallway toward his desk, with the robot following behind him.

"Let's find out what markets exist that overlap with your potential," Trep said. He pulled up a chair and beckoned the robot to sit down. Then, Trep activated his desktop monitor and initialized the Opportunity software.

When the program was ready, he entered the search query: "robot [[product]] AND humanoid [[shape]]".

He selected *Functional Optimization* and awaited the progress bar.

A list of search results should have appeared momentarily. Instead, however, an error message appeared on the screen, marked by a large red exclamation point.

"Memory overload," read the report. "Results exceeding maximum capacity. Click for verbose statistics."

Trep clicked for the statistical report, and his jaw dropped. Results estimated to exceed two-hundred and seventy million, in an estimated database network of four-hundred million. Expectation value far below minimum reportable threshold, suggesting maximum significance, with scarce likelihood of false positives, notwithstanding conservative corrections for overcompensation.

"This is incredible!" he informed the robot. "I've never seen anything like it."

Trep was boggled by the magnitude of the results.

"You are estimated to overlap with over half of our database. Maybe over two thirds."

He started to do the math, but then thought better of it.

"Well, you're a robot," he said. "What's two-hundred seventy million into four-hundred million?"

The robot grabbed a calculator that lay conveniently near the edge of Trep's desk and began pressing buttons.

"Sixty-seven point five percent, sir. Just above two thirds."

"That's amazing," Trep blurted. He was dumbfounded. "I don't know where to begin. I'm supposed to find something for you to do. But, as it appears, you can do anything you want."

"Very good news, sir," said Empeirikos cheerfully.

Trep was still in shock. It was only slowly dawning on him that the robot was using his calculator.

"You can do anything in our database. Millions of things. Opportunity could not even process the results. I'm going to have to buffer them somehow or narrow the query. I could just filter the results to the first hundred, but they aren't sorted by priority. We would risk missing the most relevant matches."

As he spoke, he found himself staring at the calculator in the robot's hands. The epiphany started to creep over him like a child pretending to crack an egg over his head.

"*What...are...you...doing...with...that...calculator?*"

"Math, sir," replied the robot innocently.

"But you are a robot. Why do you need a calculator?"

Trep was nonplussed. He awaited the explanation.

"I don't know, sir," said the robot. "But it seems that I require one. I could access your internet and locate an online tool, but I do not have the network name, nor the password. Why does that bother you?"

"Well," muttered Trep, "I'm just surprised. My computer doesn't need a calculator. It *is* a calculator."

"And how is your math, sir?" Empeirikos retorted. "As this is your calculator that I am using, I assume you also require a calculator?"

"Well, yes," Trep conceded.

"Then it seems that you have a double standard when it comes to robots," said Empeirikos.

Trep considered for a moment. Why didn't the robot have superhuman math skills? When the robot had said that he just

39

walked and talked, he had been serious. He must have been programmed with maximum legal protections. The designers must have anticipated the market saturations and designed their way around them. But that seemed to suggest that the calculator market must already be saturated. Or perhaps the designers were just guessing. They had hired Trep to find out for sure.

Trep typed in a terse Opportunity query: "calculator [[product]]."

He had barely started the search when the program reported, "Calculator market saturation one-hundred percent."

Trep sighed. That explained the incongruency. Calculator functions were off limits for multitasking, even for robots. Only a lawyer could argue for an exception. The regulations were strict, and punishment of offenders was severe. At the least, they would lose their license, and their job.

Trep was disheartened. A robot who needed a calculator? What next? This assignment was going to be much harder than he had anticipated. Closing his eyes, he tried to scheme a way out.

"You said you are designed to be a personal assistant?" Trep asked. The robot responded with a perfunctory nod.

He entered a new search query: "assistant [[product]] WITH robot [[shape]] WITH walk [[function]] WITH talk [[function]]".

He selected *Functional Optimization* and awaited the progress bar. Soon, the results list appeared.

"Not surprisingly, many relevant markets are available," Trep reported. "The top results are dog walker, baby sitter, chess partner, steward, and landscaper."

"Oh, dear, that will never do," said Empeirikos, shaking his head. "My creators instructed me to avoid domestic temp work and other non-salaried occupations. They are afraid that it wouldn't be profitable enough. They want me to get a full-time job."

"I'm very sorry," Trep informed him, "but we're not an employment agency. We locate the most appropriate and available functionalities for your product, then calculate which of them would maximize your profits through search results. After that, the onus is on your organization to rebuild your product with the new specifications."

"Well, that sounds utterly dreadful," said Empeirikos, looking dejected. "I certainly hope no one rebuilds me. After all, who's to say that I would still be me after it was done? I think I'll steer well clear of new specifications, if you don't mind."

Trep ignored him. If the robot was indeed the embodiment of the Technoconvergence, then it should be well within its abilities to assume a more prominent role than personal assistant. Perhaps a consultant, he conjectured. In an attempt to expand the search results, he typed in another query: "assistant [[product]] OR consultant [[product]] WITH robot [[shape]] WITH walk [[function]] WITH talk [[function]]".

When the results were filtered, he recited the new candidates.

"I have reconfigured the results," Trep reported. "The top tier now reads dog walker, babysitter, chess partner, private investigator, and stand-up comedian. Which of these sounds best to you?"

Empeirikos sat up in his chair.

"Well, as I've said, part time domestic jobs are out. And although chess partner sounds appealing, I don't know whether it's a salaried profession. So that leaves private investigator or stand-up comedian."

"Great," said Trep. "Let's see which of those are available."

He launched the patent survey in Opportunity, which reported no saturation in the private investigator or comedian markets. Just out of curiosity, he tested chess partner also, and found that the market was nearing saturation, but still available. The result was encouraging. He reported it to Empeirikos.

"Although the private investigator and comedian markets are wide open, the chess market is quite crowded. That indicates that it must be a very competitive and profitable market. You would be wise to buy into it while it's still available."

"And the chess board?" Empeirikos asked.

"The chess board would be sold separately," Trep replied. "You would be a very distinguished partner for upscale chess players."

"Oh, very well," Empeirikos said with a sigh. "Let's have those, then."

"Which one did you want to purchase?" asked Trep.

"All of them."

Trep's eyebrows raised.

"The licensing process is quite expensive," he said. "Are you sure you can afford it?"

"I believe so," Empeirikos replied. He pulled a gleaming credit card out of one of his pocket compartments and presented it to Trep.

"*Omega*, it says."

Trep glanced over the credit card. It was an Omega Entrepreneur card, a very widely respected credit line that was well known for having no charge limit. Trep was thoroughly impressed.

"Just who are your employers, anyway?" he asked.

"I'm afraid that's confidential," said the robot. "And, by the way, they have left special instructions. I must remain here until I find a job."

"That's preposterous!" Trep complained. "I'm sorry, but that's out of the question."

But the robot was unfazed.

"I will pay the monthly rent on your office space until I leave," it said.

The robot flashed the Entrepreneur card in the air, then heaved a sigh.

"Besides, they have erased my memory. I wouldn't know how to return to my place of origin, even if I had to."

The robot's head was sunken low. Trep suddenly felt sympathy for it. He thought for a moment. Perhaps he should let the robot stay. It would be an interesting addition to their drab office. He could teach the robot to play chess. Many of the other strategists enjoyed playing chess, especially Tatiana, the beautiful immigrant from Russia. Trep had been trying to get her attention for months. Now, maybe he finally had a chance.

"That's a deal!" he said, uncertain of whether his boss would approve it or not.

He completed the licensing process through Opportunity and collected payment through the Omega Entrepreneur card. It was the first time he had ever held one in his hand. Few clients, and few people, for that matter, could qualify for an account with no charge limit.

After completing the sale, he logged off the computer and stood up.

"Let's introduce you to our old-fashioned chess board," Trep said, leading the robot toward the lounge.

They proceeded through the office to a secluded alcove furnished with couches and coffee tables. Tatiana was already there, sitting with Clifford, the strategist-of-the-year. Clifford had become the first strategist ever to sign on a new client for every business day, four weeks in a row. He had been awarded every badge and trophy in the corporate repertoire, including the Bronze Badger, the most coveted honor in the entire organization.

Trep would have been happy for him, but Clifford was a braggart. He wore his new honors like an emblem of superiority. Trep gawked at him sitting at the table with Tatiana. Clifford looked suave, leaning back in his chair, with one leg crossed, exposing argyle socks under shiny brown shoes, and a crocodile sewn into the breast of his bright purple sweater. He smiled a toothy smile, just like the crocodile, and Trep decided that he detested crocodiles and would like to kill one someday.

Trep tried to contain his sudden surge of jealousy as he turned his glance toward Tatiana. He forced a smile. She was elegant as ever, with shiny gold loop earrings dangling below her auburn hair bun. She wore a long red dress with a low bodice and high-heeled white pumps. She observed Trep's attentive gaze and smiled politely back as he entered the lounge.

"Everyone," Trep announced, "I would like you to meet our new client, Empeirikos."

He gestured toward the robot.

"Hello," said the robot.

A hush fell over the room as the loungers became aware of

the automaton. Trep realized that everyone was hanging on his words. He decided to make the most of it.

"I have just signed on our first automaton. We wasted no time in securing the top markets. Empeirikos has bought no less than three licenses. And his employers paid with an Omega Entrepreneur card. It's the first time that I have ever seen one."

"Oh, *I* have an Omega Entrepreneur," Clifford scoffed.

Trep tried to conceal his disbelief.

"It came with the Bronze Badger," Clifford explained.

He waved it off like it was nothing, and he pretended not to even notice Empeirikos. Tatiana smiled sheepishly at Clifford. Trep wanted to vomit. How could that poser not even care that a walking, talking robot had just entered the room? Clifford was shallow and supercilious.

Trep cleared his throat to regain everyone's attention.

"I'm sure I'll win strategist-of-the-year for this," he boasted.

As he spoke, he glanced at Tatiana, but she was preoccupied, looking through her purse. Clifford was rolling his eyes.

"Anyway," said Trep, "Empeirikos is going to be staying here for a little while. I thought maybe we could show him our chess board."

He walked to the cabinet containing the board games.

"Tatiana," he said, "could you teach Empeirikos to play?"

That would finally get her away from Clifford, he thought smugly. He searched the cabinet and located the chess board and chess pieces, then began to place them on the nearest empty table. He pulled out a chair and beckoned Empeirikos to have a seat. Tatiana was beginning to drag herself away from Clifford. It seemed that the robot had piqued her interest after all.

Trep found the instructions booklet and handed it to Empeirikos. As the robot began to read, Trep felt mildly surprised at the sight. Tatiana sat down and began to arrange the chess pieces. Trep thanked her for obliging and tried to think of something witty to say, but he was suddenly at a loss for words. She seemed to have contented herself with her new role of chess instructor, so Trep felt comfortable leaving her with Empeirikos for the moment. Clifford had returned to his desk. Trep moved to the other corner of the lounge and had a seat. He lowered his com visor and called his boss to confirm the new arrangements. Not surprisingly, the robot was approved for all requests. Then, he dialed his friend Link.

"Link, you've gotta get over here," he said. "It's the Technoconvergence. I think it has arrived. And it's sitting in my office."

He explained the situation to Link, who erupted in a fit of coughing, as if he had swallowed his chewing gum.

"I'm gonna leave work early and head over there," Link stuttered. He sounded thrilled, uttering a quick goodbye and terminating the phone call.

An hour later, Trep and Link sat together in the lounge with Empeirikos. Tatiana had concluded her first chess lesson and returned to her desk. Link was staring at the robot in awe.

"You need a calculator?" Link asked.

"I'm afraid so," explained the robot. "My employers are taking full legal precautions."

"Those bastards!" Link spat. "So what can you do?"

"Just walk and talk, it seems," said the robot.

Link glanced at Trep, nodding.

"Hence the name, Empeirikos," he explained. "It means *empirical* in Greek. The Aristotelian philosophers were empiricists, and they were dubbed the *peripatetics*, which means *walkers* or *roamers*. Aristotle was said to have walked as he lectured at the Lycaeum."

"But thinking along contemporary lines," Trep interjected, "what are the chances that the Technoconvergence has arrived?"

Link frowned.

"Well, if he has no functionality, it doesn't seem to match the usual paradigm. He's not even a Multiplicity. How could he be the Technoconvergence?"

Trep nodded in agreement.

"Is there some way that we could test him?" he asked. "Like an intelligence test?"

"We could use the Turing test," Link replied, "invented by Alan Turing, the father of modern computing. Turing was fascinated with the idea of artificial intelligence. He proposed that if a computer could trick someone into thinking it was human, then it qualified as an artificial intelligence."

"Convince someone I'm human," stated Empeirikos, "how in the world am I ever to do that?"

Trep and Link looked at each other with mischief in their eyes. This was going to be fun.

Chapter 9

"The idea of a learning machine may appear paradoxical to some readers."
Alan Turing
Computing Machinery and Intelligence

* * *

"What's the latest sales report on our virtual tablets?" asked the industrialist.

"Demand is up," his henchman responded. "We've had a favorable quarter."

"Then we should have plenty of capital for criminal shenanigans. Did you get me a wiretap?"

"Yes, sir," said the henchman.

"And what about a search engine facade?"

"Not happening," replied the henchman. "Our computer models can't keep up with it. It's impossible to account for every contingency."

"But that means it's back to the drawing board," said the industrialist, scratching his beard.

"I'm afraid so, sir."

The industrialist sighed and doffed his cowboy hat.

"How many times do we have to rehash this thing?" he asked rhetorically. "Explain this to me. I hire the best talent in cybersecurity, counterintelligence, espionage. I lay out a strategy, you wave your wand, and it appears. And yet you're telling me that it's not enough?"

"Sorry, sir."

The industrialist turned his back to the henchman and stared absently out the window. From the seventeenth floor, the cityscape was multifaceted. The trade center presided over a stately business district, but the cathedral in the historic district was equally commanding. It was not possible to impose order on such a metropolis. The most one could do was filter it based on contrived priorities.

"Do you think there's such a thing as too much control?" he asked.

When his henchman did not respond, he turned and raised his eyebrow.

"I don't understand, sir," said the henchman.

"Laissez-faire," explained the industrialist. "Governance with minimal interference. Perhaps we're overextending ourselves."

"Yes, sir," replied the henchman.

"Maybe it will *never* be enough," suggested the industrialist, "and that's all we know. But knowing that, we just might be able to exploit it."

His henchman fell silent. The industrialist returned his gaze to the cityscape, striving to coax secrets from hundreds of years of architecture. But if the secret was that there was no secret, at least none that was currently within reach, then that was simply a new paradigm, one that he would intrepidly explore.

Chapter 10

"...Perhaps anything complex enough to behave like a person would have experiences ... fundamentally an organism has conscious mental states if and only if there is something that it is like to *be* that organism—something it is like *for* the organism ... After all, what would be left of what it was like to be a bat if one removed the viewpoint of the bat?"

Thomas Nagel
What is it like to be a bat?

* * *

Empeirikos was staring at what he judged to be, with ninety percent certainty, the tip of a paintbrush, its bristles awash in light brown temporary paint. It etched a line across his left cheek, then his right cheek, then applied a thin streak across his nose. The paint was thinning. The human named Link wetted the paintbrush again and resumed attending to the cheeks and nose.

Empeirikos knew that their objective was to present him as a human, and he wondered how he would look with human skin. He would soon find out. His disguise was almost complete. To his recollection, he had never worn clothing before. But now he stood in a gray blazer and navy tie, brown trousers and black leather oxfords, a French beret, a curly black wig, and leather gloves. A wide bib was draped over his chest as Link finished painting and began to apply the final touch: a matted curly beard. The beard would conceal many of Empeirikos's robotic facial features, while the shaggy wig would dangle over his robotic ears, hiding them from view. Link applied a layer of glue and began pressing the beard onto Empeirikos's jaw and chin.

"You're going to look amazing," said Link. "Now just wait ten minutes and then you can look in the mirror."

Link put his brushes and chemicals to one side and removed Empeirikos's bib.

"May I speak now?" asked Empeirikos. For the last ten minutes, his objective had been nothing more than to wait patiently. But he knew that they would soon subject him to the Turing test, and he felt unprepared.

"Of course," said Link.

"Even if you succeed in making me look like a human, what does that prove? What if I just stand there without saying a word? How do you propose to test whether people *believe* my disguise?"

"Allow me to explain," the human named Trep said confidently. "While Link has been remaking your appearance, I have been researching your new character. You are a philosopher named Nate Locket, a very distinguished author. You must review his new book, *Hidden Irrationality*."

"Sounds perfectly reasonable," stated Empeirikos.

"I have skimmed through it," Trep continued, "and it's a bit esoteric, yet thought provoking enough for some lively repartee."

Trep procured the book from his jacket pocket and handed it to Empeirikos, who opened the cover and began to read the first page. At the site of a robot reading a book, Link started in surprise.

"That's a new one," Link remarked. "And not a bad plan, Trep. Empeirikos is not just impersonating a human, he's impersonating a famous author. We must introduce him as a prestigious scholar and find an excuse to talk about his new book. If his imposture goes unrecognized, the test is a success."

* * *

Hours later, Empeirikos was climbing the stairs to an old house on the West end of town. As far as he remembered, he had never been to a party before, but he was looking forward to the experience. In front of him, Trep and Link were dressed in tweed sportcoats with elbow pads. They ascended to the front patio and held the door open for Empeirikos. As they did so, a young couple was exiting: a boy with a brown ponytail and a scruffy beard, and a dark-haired girl with a sharp-pointed nose. They smiled gratefully at Trep for holding the door, then noticed Empeirikos.

Empeirikos observed their reactions attentively. What would they think of him? But they were too preoccupied to concern themselves with things they did not understand. Although they appeared puzzled, they proceeded merrily past him and down the stairs without a second thought.

Music echoed out of the doorway and into the night. They stepped into the antechamber and followed a line of people making their way toward the music. The lobby opened into a dance hall with refreshments and a small jazz virtual trio. Computerized silhouettes of musicians were projected onto tapestries. A shadow of a saxophone player breathed out guttural patterns, sounding something like an elegant frog. A stand-up bassist droned a low throbbing rhythm while a drummer tapped his symbols like steam from a teapot.

Empeirikos was captivated by the sounds, which he compared with his own library of contemporary music, but Link engaged the refreshment table instead. He grabbed cheese and crackers and popped them into his mouth. Then, he arranged three plastic cups and filled them from a wine bottle. He presented one of the cups to Trep and one of the cups to Empeirikos, who took it in his hand, unsure what to do next. Empeirikos could neither eat nor drink. But somehow, his reward network was bolstered by the cup in his hand, as if it was his membership key to an exclusive club. Armed with wine and cheese, they removed themselves from the refreshment area, making way for an incoming group of gossiping women.

They proceeded to the next room, a small gallery with paintings on the walls. Several groups of people stood quietly, some of them staring at the paintings, others listening to the music. Link approached one of the paintings, and Trep and Empeirikos followed. They positioned themselves next to a small crowd of gatherers who admired the painting.

"Ah, Miro," said Link knowingly. "*Woman with bird*. It's a testament to human nature."

Trep rolled his eyes, unconvinced by Link's brash display of knowledge.

Empeirikos observed the painting. It was an abstract. He detected neither a woman nor a bird in its cryptic curves.

"It's not *Woman with Bird*," said a woman from the small crowd next to them. She wore a dark blouse and had long black hair tinged with gray.

"Miro mostly did that with statues, not paintings. It does look like Miro, though, but it's too dark to see his signature."

"It can't be a real Miro," said a man standing next to her. "They would never let us spill wine on it. It might be a lithograph."

"I think it looks like a cat," said Trep. He pointed at the painting.

"See, those are its ears. It could be either a cat with big ears, or a bird perched on a tree."

The crowd frowned at Trep. Empeirikos took note of it. He decided to keep his opinions about art to himself.

Link tried to lighten the mood by introducing himself.

"Hi, my name's Link, and this is Trep, and...Nate."

Link had almost said Empeirikos's real name. With the conversation commencing, Empeirikos prepared himself.

"Hello," the gatherers said.

"Nice to meet you," said Trep.

"Pleasure to make your acquaintance," said Empeirikos.

The woman smiled as she introduced their group.

"My name's Natalia, and this is Jonathan, and Theodore."

The two men smiled and nodded as they appraised the newcomers. One of the men was heavyset and had spectacles and a goatee. The other was tall and gangly, with an aquiline nose and an awkward smile. The woman was looking at Empeirikos with fascination.

"What do you think of the painting?" she asked.

Hastily, Empeirikos calculated his next move. A flood of memories relating to art began to organize themselves according to probability of relevance. Each one came with an incentive and an interpretation. The incentive predicted the likely consequences of each action as either reward or punishment, judging from prior experience. The interpretation fit like a puzzle piece into his running narrative, generating a similarity-score that was multiplied with the incentive. In the background, an evolving ontology waited to index his choice.

He filtered the top results. He could try expounding on the painting. Or, he could be honest and admit that he was not able to unravel it. Alternately, he could avoid the subject of artistic intention altogether by casually remarking on the painting's aesthetic appeal.

He began to search his memory for conversation clips relating to paintings, but the most recent memories surfaced first, and he remembered how they had frowned at Trep for sharing his opinion of the painting. That constituted a negative incentive score, so he elected to withhold his opinion, which meant he must talk about something else. A new search replaced the first one, calculating a polite excuse and a possible change of subject.

"Well, artistic intention is such a tricky subject," he responded. "I really wouldn't know where to start. I prefer to stick with literature."

"Oh, are you an author?" Natalia asked.

"Why, yes," he replied. "I have just published a new book, *Hidden Irrationality*."

"That sounds fascinating," she remarked. "What's it about?"

Empeirikos had read the first few chapters before the party and had summarized them in his mind. He felt confident that he could lecture briefly on the author's main points.

"It's about higher dimensions and unsolved mysteries," he

explained. "I propose new algorithms for fathoming the unfathomable."

"Right on!" said the heavyset man with the goatee, although his mouth was half full of cheese. "How does it work?"

"Well," said Empeirikos, "imagine that we had no depth perception. That is not to say that we are restricted to two dimensions, but rather that we simply have no concept of volume or density. Now imagine a fat person whose shape is almost perfectly spherical, and a thin person whose shape is vertically rectangular. When the corpulent man turned to the side, he would appear to have exactly the same dimensions as from the front. But when the rectangular man turned to the side, his width would practically disappear, turning into a one-dimensional line. From the depthless perspective, the thin person would appear irrational. There would be no explanation for his proportions changing from one moment to the next. They would call the fat person rational and the thin person irrational. But in reality, they both share the property of volume. Thus, the fat man is no less irrational than the thin man. It's just that the irrationality is hidden in the fat man. And, from our perspective, similar paradoxes may exist, some of which might be explainable through the concept of hidden irrationality."

The heavyset man with the goatee chewed his cheese silently and stared through his spectacles at Empeirikos. The man with the big nose had turned away as if distracted by something. Natalia was looking at the ground.

After a while, the man with the goatee spoke up.

"What other paradoxes could your theory explain?" he asked.

"Many things," said Empeirikos. "The Egyptian pyramids,

for example. We believe they were built thousands of years ago, although some believe that it may have been impossible at that time. When trying to explain the pyramids, we come up against something that is irrational, and we believe that it is unique to the pyramids. But just like the volume of the fat man and the thin man, it's possible that the same irrationality is hidden in everything. By inventing new algorithms to quantify our view of the pyramids, and then applying those algorithms to the rational world, we may unravel facts about the world that were previously hidden."

"That is a wild proposition!" said the man with the goatee, his face lighting up. "But what sorts of algorithms would you use?"

"Since the pyramids are geometric objects, geometric measurements have proven popular," Empeirikos replied. "It has been found that the pyramids are aligned almost perfectly along latitudinal and longitudinal axes, and it has been suggested that the constellations were used to assist the alignment. Similarly, it may be possible to take measurements of the pyramids, for example the number of stone blocks, and the height to width ratio, and compare them with geographic or astronomical data, looking for correlations. By using mathematics, the depthless thinkers could learn to understand the concept of volume, and we could do the same. But only computers, with their superior processing powers, could handle the necessary breadth of data with sufficient speed."

On hearing the phrase *superior processing powers*, Trep and Link felt viscerally rankled. But the man with the goatee was thoroughly intrigued. Perhaps he was a computer programmer, Empeirikos thought. Empeirikos realized that it may have sounded like he was boasting, but he had merely been reciting the words of Nate Locket, the author of *Hidden Irrationality*.

"I wonder," asked the human named Natalia, "what the nature of this irrationality might be? How would it enhance our understanding of the everyday world?"

Empeirikos pointed his finger emphatically into the air.

"An excellent question!" he proclaimed. "The pyramids are a mystery, and the nature of their mysteriousness may relate to time. If they were built today, they would be rational, but instead they were built an irrationally long time ago. Now, mysteries have a special truth property. If we find an irrational counterpart, we may resolve one mystery with another. Therefore, defining forever as a long time, we state that the pyramids have been there forever, yet impossibly so, and then ask: might there also be something that has never been there, yet defies possibility?"

"You mean something that logically should be there," said the heavyset man, "but isn't?"

"Yes, exactly," Empeirikos confirmed. "If two such counterparts existed, we might explain them by proposing a relationship between them. However, logically, the syllogism is invalid. The conclusion does not follow from the premises. Yet, both are mysteries, so both are wanting of an explanation. This lends validity to the argument. The premises increase the likelihood of the conclusion. If we could find such a counterpart, we could solve two mysteries with one hypothesis."

"What about Fermi's paradox?" said a new voice from the nearest corner of the room. A young girl had been listening to their conversation.

"That's funny," said Trep, "I was just talking about Fermi's paradox with Link a few days ago."

"Yes," said Link. "Fermi's paradox is very similar to...Nate's question."

"Oh, your name isn't Nate Locket, is it?" the girl asked Empeirikos.

Empeirikos hesitated. Had she detected his ploy? He calculated hastily, inferring that detection was uncertain, and deciding to maintain his charade.

"Yes," Empeirikos reluctantly replied, anticipating obstacles. She had heard of Nate Locket. What if she had read more of *Hidden Irrationality* than he had?

"Oh, hi!" she chirped excitedly. "I'm a graduate student in philosophy. I'm a big fan of yours!"

"Wonderful..." said Empeirikos. He tried to change the subject.

"What's your name?" he asked.

"My name's Ravette," she said, extending her hand. She was slender, with long curly hair draped over the sides of her face, and she wore tall boots and a corduroy jacket.

"Very nice to meet you," said Empeirikos, shaking her hand as lightly as possible. Then, since he had never heard of Fermi's paradox, he deflected the burden of conversation to her.

"You were saying about Fermi's paradox..."

Eruditely, she recited Fermi's paradox.

"Our galaxy contains so many stars older than our own, at least some of them must have already spawned advanced civilizations. It led Fermi to ask: where are all the aliens?"

"It's obviously a case of hidden irrationality," Empeirikos agreed.

"But what does that imply?" asked Natalia. "That the

pyramids are somehow related to aliens, or the absence of them?"

"Maybe aliens would be here if it weren't for the pyramids," said Trep.

"Maybe the pyramids were placed there to block the aliens," Link hypothesized.

"Maybe we ought to destroy the pyramids!" Empeirikos proclaimed.

They frowned at him. He searched his memory for annotations relating to aliens, but they were strangely absent, leaving him guessing. However, he was beginning to attribute unfavorable connotations.

The girl was the only one who wasn't frowning. She had been trying to conceal a laugh, but it had come out, and she now stood giggling at them.

"No, silly," she chided them. "Isn't it obvious that the pyramids are a possible solution to Fermi's paradox, and vice versa? Well, you know, don't you Nate? You talk about it in your book, *Hidden Irrationality*."

Empeirikos balked at the sensation of multiple simultaneous internal alerts. So she had in fact read his new book. He thought about the last chapter of *Hidden Irrationality* that he had read, and the flow of the argument. He imagined what Nate Locket would have written if the next chapter was about Fermi's paradox. He began to think out loud. He started by reprising the argument.

"Yes," he expounded, "I was just getting to that. As I was saying, if we could find an irrational counterpart, then we could impute a connection between the two. The pyramids have been here a long time, and aliens have never been here, and both premises are irrational. Although the argument does not stand on its own, both premises have the special property of being a mystery, which increases the likelihood of a new hypothesis. Namely..."

He paused, realizing that the human named Ravette might take the bait and fill in the next sentence, which she did.

"Namely, that aliens were present on Earth thousands of years ago!" she exclaimed. "The two irrationalities cancel each other out. Humans did not build the pyramids, and aliens *have* been here."

"Yes, exactly!" Empeirikos said praisingly. "And very well spoken!"

"Thanks," Ravette remarked, then her expression turned mercurial.

"I don't want to impose," she said, "but I must indulge my curiosity. Rumor has it that you're working on a new book that explains the purpose of artificial intelligence."

Trep laughed in spite of himself, and even Link began to snicker. Empeirikos, having no emotions of his own, took their reactions as a cue. Though he knew nothing about a new book, he could nevertheless talk his way out of it with offhand humor, or even by feigning total ignorance.

"Indeed?" he quipped. "And what of it? What exactly is in need of explanation?"

"Is artificial intelligence the culmination of evolution?" she asked. "Has mankind evolved this far only to invent its own replacement?"

Somehow, despite the logic of her argument, Empeirikos judged that he was not a threat to humanity. Though he knew that Ravette was only reciting hearsay and did not realize that she was talking to a robot, he elected to defend his own dignity in front of his friends.

"These are excellent questions," he expounded, "and have no fear, for, indeed, all will be explained. In fact, it would surprise you to learn that the solution is staring you straight in the face."

Trep and Link were now chuckling uproariously, but Ravette was impassive.

"How so?" she asked.

"Well," Empeirikos continued, "humans are often unable to see what's right under their nose. If you have a particularly large nose, for example, this is quite a conundrum."

Although Trep and Link remained boisterous, the man with the big nose began to frown. He politely excused himself and left the room.

"What exactly do you mean?" Ravette inquired.

Empeirikos started to mumble an explanation, but Trep interrupted them, attempting to distract Ravette before she exposed Empeirikos's duplicity.

"Would you like to dance?" he flirted. The jazz trio had taken a break and had been replaced by an eclectic dance mix of techno tracks.

Ravette glanced back and forth from Trep to Empeirikos.

"I was sort of wondering if Nate would like to dance," she said.

Empeirikos considered, then realized that dancing would obviate the need to explain himself. He accepted her invitation, and they walked together into the dance hall. The silhouettes on the tapestries had become virtual dancers. They gyrated in two dimensions to the music.

Empeirikos surveyed the swaying crowd. Having never danced before, he would have to find someone to imitate. Some of the dancers had their hands in the air and swayed their hips right and left. Others clenched their fists at their sides and pivoted their pelvises forward and back.

Empeirikos contemplated their body shapes, looking for correlations with dance style. His automated judgement estimated their body mass indices and the curvature of their bottoms. He tried to look behind his back at his own bottom, deciding not to gyrate his pelvis. Instead, he bent his legs, pumped up and down, and moved his feet from side to side. He left one arm hanging flat at his side. In the other hand, he continued to hold his cup of wine.

Ravette raised her hands to shoulder height and swayed her hips. The sound of techno music throbbed from the speakers on the ceiling, a monotonous drumbeat overlaid with electric chords and a flowing counterpoint. An effulgent disco light spun circular beams onto the floor.

Empeirikos decided to keep his movement to a minimum, instead expending his thoughts on what to do next. He tried to think of something to talk about after they left the dance floor. As he reflected, he thought he noticed the dance mix shifting to a new song, but with no break in between, and without a change of key. One song blended with perfect smoothness into the next, almost undetectably. It might be a new song or just the chorus of the previous song. He looked for an exodus or influx of dancers in the crowd but detected nothing in particular to indicate that the song had changed.

A lithe man at one edge of the dance floor was pantomiming. His hands pressed flat against invisible walls, as if he was trapped in a box. Then, he began to walk in place, conveying a sense of motion though standing still, as if on roller skates. Next, his motion became punctuated as he rotated to face another direction. He pumped his arms at his sides, with his hands flattened into karate chops, while his feet spun smoothly on their toes.

Abruptly, he rotated until he was looking straight at Empeirikos. The effect was disconcerting. Empeirikos searched his memory for clips matching the dance style and was surprised at what he found. The dance moves seemed to match images of primitive robots. Empeirikos was not sure of the source of the images. Apparently, the sources had been erased from his memories. However, he observed that the images did not seem real. Rather, they were cartoonish. He thought he might have seen them on TV.

The mime was still facing him. The unwelcome dance partnership was perturbing. Had the mime detected that he was a robot? Empeirikos opted for reverse psychology. He too would do the robot. He formed his loose hand into a karate chop, pumped his arms at his sides, and spun smoothly on his toes until he no longer faced the mime. Then, he tried to put the strange dancer out of his mind. He returned to his original dance style. The drum beat pulsed and the electric counterpoint undercut the chords while the strobe lights circumnavigated the dance floor.

He looked at the human named Ravette, suddenly hoping that she would soon tire of dancing. Thankfully, the dance mix shifted again into another song, or so it seemed, and Ravette stopped dancing and gestured for Empeirikos to follow her off the dance floor. They strolled back to the gallery, where Trep and Link stood alone. It seemed that the other three gatherers had left.

Trep and Link eyed Ravette's expression inquisitively for any intimation of doubt. The weight of their stares prompted her to speak first.

"What happened to your friends?" she asked.

"They invited us to join them outside on the patio," Link responded, "but we stayed to wait for you. How was your dance?"

"I had a great time," said Ravette, "but Nate was as stiff as a robot."

If Empeirikos could have gulped, he would have. Silent alerts were sounding in his mind. Had she seen through his disguise? And what about the mime's behavior? Had it just been random circumstance, or had everyone on the dance floor also recognized him as a charlatan?

"Ha ha!" Trep laughed nervously. "Sounds like you're not a very good dancer!"

Empeirikos was unfazed by sardonic verbal abuse from his friends.

"I haven't seen you out there on the dance floor," he chided.

"Touché," said Link.

"That's all right, Nate," said Ravette. "Authors don't have to have rhythm. Unless they're poets, I guess. Fortunately, philosophy doesn't rhyme."

She giggled.

"Hey, Nate, I would love to talk to you about the second half of your book. Maybe you could show me your apartment later?"

Empeirikos paused. On the one hand, she was offering to go home with him, which would indicate a successful result on the Turing test. On the other hand, she had called him a robot, raising the possibility that she was mocking him. Even worse, he hadn't read the second half of the book.

"Uh, the second half of the book?" he asked timidly.

"Yes," she replied. "Your theory about languages was so

interesting! I want to know everything about it."

Out of curiosity, he was tempted to ask her what exactly she had liked about the second half of the book. Instead, he decided that it was time to leave the party. His chance of remaining undiscovered was steadily decreasing. He glanced at Trep and Link, shaking his head, then gestured toward the exit with his eyes. Link nodded and stepped between him and Ravette, smiling.

"Ravette," said Link, "it's been so nice to meet you. Unfortunately, we have another event that we have to attend. Nate is doing the rounds, promoting his new book."

Ravette never stopped smiling.

"Oh, I get it," she said. She winked at Empeirikos. "Nice meeting you, Nate."

And with that, she turned around and walked away.

With her out of the picture, they could have stayed, but Empeirikos did not want to push his luck.

"Let's go," he said. There was too much unpredictability in the air. He needed to restore a sense of certainty.

Link grabbed some cheese and crackers on their way out. Trep finished another glass of wine. Empeirikos deposited his cup in the trash. They proceeded out the front door and down the stairs. As they hiked toward the nearest Transit Tube, Link questioned Empeirikos.

"Well, what happened?" he asked. "What did you think of our Turing test?"

"I believe she was proposing to mate with me," Empeirikos replied. "If so, the Turing test may have been a success. However, I'm worried that the evidence was biased."

"What are you talking about?" Link complained. "The evening went great! You were flawless!"

Empeirikos soaked in the compliment.

"That's true," he agreed. "However, they knew who I was."

"You mean that comment about being stiff as a robot?" asked Trep. "She was just teasing you. Besides, you probably weren't the most expressive dancer on the floor."

"Perhaps not," said Empeirikos somberly. "But I also have to wonder whether, not just her, but all of them recognized me."

"You sound paranoid," Link scolded him. "How could she possibly have known?"

Empeirikos had no response. He realized that they had been walking and talking at the same time, just like the Greek philosophers for whom he'd been named. But now, they fell silent. None of them had a solution to the puzzling question. Was Empeirikos just paranoid? Or was Ravette one of his designers, whom he had conveniently forgotten?

One thing was certain, however; the Turing test was inconclusive. With the stiff-as-a-robot comment, and Empeirikos's suspicion that Ravette had recognized him, there was too much doubt about what exactly had occurred. Their experiment had done nothing more than raise new questions. Wordlessly, the three of them boarded the Transit Tube and rode back to Trep's office. Trep allowed Empeirikos to wait there for the night. Then, Trep and Link returned home, lost in thought.

Chapter 11

"Thanks again for calling the Search Strategists. Remember, your search is our strategy. Have a great afternoon!"

Trep removed his headset after the conclusion of another unsuccessful business deal. Deciding to take a coffee break, he migrated to the lounge, where Empeirikos and Tatiana were engaged in a game of chess. Pouring himself a cup of coffee, he pulled up a chair and observed their progress.

He tallied the captured pieces in front of each player. Tatiana had four pawns and a knight. Empeirikos only had two pawns, in addition to a rook. Tatiana looked sober as she plotted her next move. So intent was her focus that she hardly acknowledged Trep's presence. Empeirikos, however, turned to greet him.

"Hello, Mr. Sportly," he chirped. "How is your afternoon progressing?"

"Slower than a turtle on a treadmill," Trep sighed.

"Do turtles exercise?" asked Empeirikos.

"Probably not," Trep chuckled. "We're going to have to take you to Gastronomy and show you the animals. Anyway, looks like your chess teacher has finally found the right partner."

He didn't want to distract Tatiana, but he couldn't resist taking the opportunity to mock Clifford. Tatiana and Clifford never played chess together.

"What do you think," he asked her, "is he better than your other partners?"

"He is getting good," Tatiana said politely, but even as she spoke, she angled one of her bishops across the chess board to capture a pawn.

"*Check*," she added.

Empeirikos castled, exchanging his king for a rook. Tatiana took the rook but was then captured by Empeirikos's queen. Still, she had captured two pieces to Empeirikos's one, extending her lead.

But Empeirikos's queen was now free to move. He dragged it across the board and captured a pawn.

"*Check*," he said.

"I wonder," said Trep, "why Empeirikos is allowed to multitask as a chess player, although he is not allowed to multitask as a calculator?"

"He is not a chess board," replied Tatiana. "As long as he does not threaten to replace other chess products, he is allowed to multitask."

"He's pretty good at philosophy, too," Trep observed, "judging from last night. I suppose it comes with the name."

"I certainly hope so," remarked Empeirikos.

"However," Trep lectured, "if you want to catch up with the other machines, Empeirikos, we're going to have to teach you some skills besides chess. You'll never become an *AI* without multiplicity."

Tatiana moved herself out of check by blocking with a bishop. If Empeirikos captured it, Tatiana's king would capture his queen. Empeirikos left the queen in place, instead electing to move a pawn forward.

"Thank you for refusing to recognize me as an *AI*," Empeirikos said indignantly. "As for new skills, what do you propose?"

"Well," Trep replied, "in addition to chess partner, we also bought licenses for private investigator and stand-up comedian. After making some phone calls, I found a private investigator who is willing to meet with you next week. In the meantime, I was thinking we should get started on your stand-up comedy routine."

Trep did not have a stand-up routine to teach Empeirikos, so he was hoping to take the opportunity to brainstorm with Tatiana.

"Will this involve memorization of comedic videos?" Empeirikos queried.

"No," said Trep, "not at all. You'll have to compose your own material. What do you think, Tatiana? Are machines capable of humor?"

"Normally, I would say no," she replied. "But he is like no machine. How is it that such an advanced technology appears at our doorstep so unexpectedly? He is more like a person than a machine. Something does not make sense about it. Where did you learn to talk?"

Empeirikos thought for a moment.

"I believe I may have watched television," he said.

Tatiana shrugged and shook her head.

"I would not expect a machine to be good at humor," she said, "but something tells me that this one is."

"What is humor?" Empeirikos inquired.

Trep and Tatiana looked at each other, suddenly wondering if Tatiana had been wrong.

"Humor is something that makes you laugh," Tatiana explained.

"How interesting," observed Empeirikos. "Unfortunately, to my knowledge, I have never laughed."

"Well, not necessarily you," Trep pointed out. "Let's say that humor is something that makes other people laugh. That's what a stand-up comedian does."

"Wonderful," said Empeirikos. "How will I learn?"

"I don't know," Trep replied. "Maybe you should spend an evening with my friend Link. We'll go to Gastronomy and play with the animals."

Trep lowered his com visor and sent Link an invitation.

Meanwhile, Tatiana resumed playing chess. Unfortunately for Empeirikos, he had moved the wrong pawn forward, the one guarding his newly castled king. Tatiana angled her queen across the board, landing on the square formerly occupied by the pawn. Empeirikos's king was trapped, having castled into a crowded corner.

"*Check mate*," said Tatiana.

Trep uttered a loud guffaw.

"Some chess partner!" he chortled. "No offense."

"Allow me to point out," Empeirikos replied, "that as you have no previous experience with robots, there is no basis for your inflated expectations."

Trep rolled his eyes at the robot's rejoinder.

"Humans one, robots zero," he boasted, then strode out of the lounge.

Later, Trep and Link sat with Empeirikos at a back table in Gastronomy. Empeirikos was once again disguised by a wig, beard, and a thick application of makeup. They had reserved a table in the sumptuous VIP area, just to be safe. The lights were dim and the area was discreet. The food came with an additional fee. Trep sipped a glass of wine, and Link savored a cocktail. But the VIP room was worth the price, being populated with exotic animals. They had chosen the *piranha table*. A live piranha swam before them in a fish tank suspended over the table.

With two layers of glass safely protecting him from the vicious fish, Trep observed its features. It had wide jaws and a thick skull. It swam with mouth half open, exposing rows of menacing teeth. Its jaw seemed perpetually tensed, as if nursing a wad of chewing tobacco. It stared at Trep through eyes that were sunken into its muscular pate. Trep felt that they were embroiled in a staring contest. He relented, returning his attention to Link and Empeirikos.

Link had a turtle in his hands and was placing it on the table.

"As you can see," he said to Empeirikos, "the turtle is not very fast."

The turtle touched down on the table surface and commenced moving one foot forward at a time, seemingly with immense effort. Its legs did not face in the proper direction for movement. Rather, they jutted out sideways, forcing it to swing each leg around in an arc, as one would swing a rope.

"And chinchillas weren't very fast either," Link joked, "until they invented tumblers."

The chinchilla was rolling around on the floor next to them, encased in a clear sphere of plastic which it used for exploration. The large furry rodent would survey the room, select a direction, then ascend one side of the tumbler until it rolled slowly forward. It resembled a guinea pig in a space capsule.

"And same for humans," Link continued, "until we invented

the wheel."

"And previously, did humans use tumblers?" Empeirikos asked.

"No," Link replied, "but we did swing on trees. The story is that humans were once similar to monkeys, but we evolved into our present form."

"Do they have monkeys at Gastronomy?" said Empeirikos.

"Probably not," said Trep, "but let's go see."

He stood and gestured for Link and Empeirikos to follow him to the sales area. Trep grabbed the turtle before it fell off the table. He returned it to its cage on the edge of the room. Then, he joined the others in the annexed pet store.

Link was pointing at the animal cages and fish tanks.

"No monkeys," he said to Empeirikos, "but it's a broad selection of organisms. Let's see whether or not you can guess what order these animals evolved in."

He gesticulated into the air, inviting Empeirikos to begin.

Empeirikos surveyed the room for some time. He approached several of the cages, bending down for a closer look. At one point, he disappeared around a wall of fish tanks, then reappeared on the other side. He browsed the tanks a while longer, then returned and addressed them.

"I have considered the question," he stated, "and have arrived at a plausible hypothesis, which perhaps you will verify. I propose that these animals evolved in the following order. First, the fish evolved, for they have no legs. Then, they migrated onto land, forming the snakes, who also have no legs. Next, the snakes grew two legs, forming the birds. In the process, they also grew fur and feathers. Then, they grew another two legs, forming the furry animals. Then, they lost their fur, forming the lizards."

Empeirikos stood waiting for them to confirm or deny his theory.

"You're right," Trep said, "the fish evolved first. However, after that, things happened differently. Amphibians were next, and then the reptiles. The snakes were reptiles who lost their legs, and the birds were reptiles whose arms became wings."

"Good guess, though," Link consoled him. "The snake is a tough one. Let's take a look at a boa constrictor."

They followed Link out of the sales area to the edge of the restaurant containing the snake cages. Link grabbed a small boa constrictor and brought it back to their table. He placed it in front of them, where it curled into a spiral. Link reached over the side of the table and lifted the chinchilla tumbler from the floor, placing it on the table next to the snake.

Safe in its cage, the chinchilla nevertheless froze. It eyed the snake warily. The snake assessed the chinchilla and darted its tongue at the cage, sensing for an opening. Link let them linger for a tense moment, a warped attempt at humor.

"Chinchilla not happy," said Link.

He lifted the relieved chinchilla and returned its tumbler to the ground. The chinchilla rolled hastily away from their table.

"Sorry," Link apologized, "but we're supposed to show Empeirikos examples of humor."

"The chinchilla didn't think it was very funny," Trep pointed out.

"Nope," said Link. He bent down until his head was in front of the snake's head.

"What do you think?" he asked.

The snake stuck its tongue out at him. Link lifted the snake and placed it on his shoulders, then wrapped it around his neck.

He looked around the room, then smiled and muttered softly, "Here is my humble attempt at demonstrating humor."

Link placed both his hands on the snake where it encircled his neck, as if the snake was choking him.

"*Help!*" he screamed with feigned agony on his face. "It's choking me! Somebody *help!*"

The people at the nearby tables looked terrified. Trep thought maybe Link's joke had been too extreme. He glanced around with embarrassment.

Link, however, continued.

"*Help!*" he cried.

A stocky man at a nearby table stood up. He wore a black t-shirt and a gold vest. His head was shaven and his muscles bulged. He walked swiftly to their table and grabbed the snake by the tail, yanking it off of Link's neck. He then whirled the snake around his head like a lasso, unsure for a moment what to do with it. Finally, he simply let go, allowing the flailing snake to sail across the room in a random direction.

The confused reptile struck a fat woman wearing eyeglasses, adorned in jewelry. It smote her in the face, deflected off to the side, then desperately wrapped its tail around her neck as it flew past, whipping itself back to pummel her again in the face. The panicked snake then tensed its muscles around the woman's neck.

"*Help!*" the woman implored. "Somebody *help!* It's choking me!"

Trep and Link leapt from their chairs to help the embattled woman. They grabbed the tensed snake on opposite sides and pulled it from her neck, casting it to the ground. The hapless snake slithered out of sight beneath the table.

The woman's face was flushed. Her short black hair was disheveled. Her eyeglasses hung crooked over her nose. She had huge loop earrings dangling from her ears and a thick necklace of pearls. Her lips were plastered with glossy lipstick. Her mouth hung low as she tried to catch her breath.

Trep rested a reassuring hand on her shoulder.

"Are you all right?" he asked.

"Hey! Leave her alone!" interjected an old man at the adjacent table, pausing between bites of steak.

Trep regarded the man quizzically.

"I'm just trying to help," he informed the man.

"Get away from her!" the old man demanded. He shook his fist at Trep.

Trep and Link slunk back to their tables in shame. They sank into their seats, deflated.

Empeirikos sat waiting for them.

"I think I'm beginning to understand the concept of humor now," he remarked.

Link rolled his eyes. Trep shook his head. They guzzled what was left of their drinks and swiftly ordered another. They sulked in silence for a while.

"Too much humor is a bad thing," said Link presently.

"I agree," said Trep.

"Well, at least it's over," Link observed.

Just then, a police officer entered the VIP lounge carrying a clipboard. He stopped and surveyed the room. His black moustache perched like a frog's legs over his mouth. His corpulent belly overflowed his waistband. When his eyes fell upon Empeirikos's painted visage, he approached their table. When he reached them, he stopped, procured a piece of paper from his clipboard, and read from it.

"We have received a complaint," he informed them. "The manager of the restaurant has requested that you leave. I'm here to deliver you this notice."

He planted the document on their table. It read: *Notice of trespass*.

"Trespass?" Trep exclaimed. "But we're paying customers. We come here every day."

"Nevertheless," the officer explained, "you are ordered to leave the restaurant and never come back. If you do return, you will be arrested. Do you understand?"

The police officer awaited their acknowledgement. Trep refused to lend confirmation to the ludicrous accusation.

Link, however, stated, "We understand."

Link stood up and beckoned for the others to do the same. He grabbed the notice of trespass, left the table, and headed for the door. Trep and Empeirikos followed him.

Out front, they stood and sulked in the sun. Link explained the situation to Trep.

"The owners and managers have complete discretion about who they allow into their restaurant. They're allowed to kick someone out for any reason, or even no reason at all. It's their restaurant. Typically, to avoid confrontation, they call the police. But then, they need a legal excuse. Hence the notice of trespass. When the police deliver a restraining order, it's permanent. If we return, they consider it a violation of the law."

"That's ridiculous," Trep objected. "Couldn't we appeal the restraining order?"

"We could," Link agreed.

As they debated, the police officer emerged from the restaurant. He put his hands in his pockets and looked them over, as if sizing them up, and then asked, "What were you doing in there?"

Ask a stupid question, get a stupid response, Trep thought.

"Relaxing," Link replied.

"You come here often?" continued the officer.

"All the time," said Link.

Trep thought it was in poor taste that the officer first banished them and then wanted to make small talk.

The officer licked his lips before asking Link, "You got any child pornography on that com visor?"

"Of course not!" Link exclaimed.

The officer looked at Trep and Empeirikos. Trep shook his head.

"Me neither," he stated. "None of us do."

"Do you mind if I check your com visors?" the officer asked.

"Not at all," Trep replied confidently. He removed his com visor and tried to hand it to the officer, but the officer kept his hands in his pockets. He looked at Link.

"Go ahead," Link said, referring to his own com visor.

The officer glanced at Empeirikos, but he was not wearing a com visor.

He turned back to Link and Trep and said, "You're going to have to come down to the station with me."

"On what grounds?" Link asked.

"We're only allowed to search com visors at the station," replied the officer. "Now please turn around and put your hands behind your back. I have to cuff you to put you in the squad car."

Trep and Link reluctantly turned around and presented their wrists. As the officer handcuffed them, Link protested.

"You're out of line," Link complained. "You're expanding

your scope beyond its original intent. You can't turn a notice of trespass into a search for child pornography! What suspicion do you have that we broke the law?"

"You agreed to the search," the officer stated.

"This is illegal!" Link shouted.

"You're welcome to file a complaint with my supervisor," the officer said. "We'll let the judge decide whether it's legal or not."

Having handcuffed Trep and Link, the officer led them to his squad car, opened the back door, and motioned for them to sit inside.

"Empeirikos," Trep said, "wait for me at the office. We'll be back soon."

Trep squeezed in next to a disgruntled Link, who had to lean far forward to accommodate the handcuffs behind his back. Then, the officer slammed the door and walked around to the driver's seat. He climbed inside and, in a loud voice, spoke the word "ignition".

The squad car activated with a growl. It purred proudly as the dashboard lit up. A laptop computer flashed police reports and an intercom grumbled code words detailing the status of officers at large. After the officer gave the command "forward", the engine hummed as the squad car accelerated smoothly onto the main road.

The police officer spoke the words "South Bank correction facility." The squad car took the ramp onto the highway and merged onto the interstate. Before long, Trep was completely lost. Yet, before he knew it, they had arrived at the police station. The squad car approached a wide gate, which opened automatically. The car pulled into a parking space alongside a low building.

The squad car fell silent as the officer stepped out and opened the back doors. The three of them climbed out. Trep's wrists were sore from leaning on the handcuffs. He joined Link and they followed the officer through the unmarked entrance to the police station.

The officer led them into a small interrogation chamber. His fellow officers smiled as he walked past. When the three of them were inside, the officer closed the door. The room was austere, with simple furnishing. An empty table occupied the center, surrounded by four chairs. Cameras on the walls monitored them.

The officer pulled chairs out for Trep and Link and gestured for them to have a seat. As they were still handcuffed, the officer himself removed Trep's com visor. He lounged in a chair at the end of the table, leaned back, and fitted the visor onto his face. He pressed the side arm to activate it. Then, his fingers flicked over the front as he rummaged through Trep's desktop.

"You have any videos on here?" he asked.

"Yeah, they're in the *videos* folder," Trep responded. Ask a stupid question, he thought again. His com visor was full of videos of his friends and family. The police officer apparently wanted to meet them all. They waited and watched as the officer dragged his fingers across the com visor, first tapping one file, then another.

"Who's this girl with the baseball hat?" he asked.

"That's my old friend Rachel," Trep informed him, unsure of why he had even responded. The police officer was incorrigible. What business was it of his whom Trep associated with?

"We refuse to respond to any of your questions," Link stated.

"We reserve our right to remain silent."

"Suit yourself," said the officer.

He continued perusing Trep's files. Eventually, he removed the com visor and re-mounted it on Trep's head. Then, he grabbed Link's com visor, sat back down, and slipped it over his face. After activating it, he seemed to find a video of interest. He yawned and stretched as he watched it. Then, he leaned back in his chair, balancing precariously against the wall as he viewed the video, his legs dangling comically.

"I hope you're having a great time watching me petting animals," Link said. "There's nothing of interest to you on that com visor."

The officer removed the com visor and replaced it on Link's head. He turned to Trep.

"Did you grope a woman's breasts in that restaurant?" he asked reproachfully.

"Certainly not!" Trep objected. "Was that what the complaint was about? I bet it was the man at the next table. He didn't seem to like us."

"The officer's lying," Link cautioned. "He's interrogating you. Officers are allowed to lie when they interrogate a suspect."

Trep was shocked. The police officer was apparently taking sadistic pleasure in pointless interrogation of innocents.

"We have nothing else to say to you," Link told the officer.

The police officer took stock of Link. Then, he stood up and exited the room, leaving them in silence.

The three of them were at a loss for words. They stared at the floor and awaited the officer's return. But after ten minutes, there was still no sign of him.

"That guy must be some kind of a pervert," Link spat. "We

were too cooperative. We shouldn't even have spoken to him."

"Remind me to never again speak to a police officer," Trep exclaimed.

At last, the police officer returned with a new stack of papers. While looking at one of the papers, he read them their rights.

"You are accused of disturbing the peace. You have the right to remain silent. Anything you say or do can be held against you. You have the right to a lawyer. If you cannot afford adequate representation, you may request that the court find representation for you. Do you understand?"

"I do not understand!" Link objected. "You're arresting us? Why didn't you tell us at the restaurant, Officer..."

Link read the officer's nametag.

"...Ronch," he continued.

The officer did not reply. He awaited their confirmation.

"We understand," said Trep. He just wanted to get it over with.

The officer led them out the door and down a long corridor leading to the holding pen. He handed a sheaf of papers to the man at the desk, then uncuffed the three of them. He gestured to a pile of blue robes.

"Put those on," he said, and they complied. Then, he turned and left them. The man at the desk approached the doors to the holding pen and fingered the combination lock. He opened the doors and motioned for them to enter, then closed the doors behind them.

Chapter 12

The industrialist stood at a podium before a small crowd of mercenaries.

"Showtime," he announced. "But first, introductions are in order. My name is Mr. Zostro."

The industrialist tipped his hat to the audience in acknowledgement.

"I'm in charge of logistics," he continued, "and our objective for this week is entropy."

He paused for effect.

"Your job is to wreak havoc," he continued.

"Specifically, what sort of havoc, sir?" asked one of the mercenaries.

"The type of havoc that preoccupies law enforcement," Mr. Zostro responded. "Disperse them throughout the city. Not one officer will be left sitting idle. After every crime, notify me about its location and the nature of the violation. While you're brewing up trouble at large, we'll work the phones to make sure police reports get generated."

"So the objective is just to draw them out of their headquarters?" asked the mercenary again.

"And keep them out," said Mr. Zostro. "Goad them. Leave a paper trail. Marshal their investigative teams."

"A wild goose chase could get expensive," said another mercenary. "We're up against some daunting forensics labs."

"And we'll match them lab for lab," replied Mr. Zostro. "Your bankroll is essentially bottomless. If you need some counter-tech, we'll provide it. Keep us informed."

Another mercenary raised his hand.

"If you don't mind my asking," he said, "what exactly should we do? The word *entropy* has a rather broad interpretation. It's defined as a state of inherent unpredictability. Forgive me for stating the obvious, but how are we supposed to simulate *that*?"

"I would like to *thank* you for stating the obvious," said Mr. Zostro. He tipped his hat to the inquisitive mercenary.

"In fact," he continued, "that's *precisely* the point."

Chapter 13

"And in what sort of actions or with a view to what result is the just man most able to do harm to his enemy and good to his friend? But when a man is well, there is no need of a physician? And he who is not on a voyage has no need of a pilot? Then in time of peace justice will be of no use?"

Socrates

As told in *The Republic* by Plato

* * *

Trep and Link entered the door to the holding pen. Beyond the door was a spartan room populated with glum male prisoners, all wearing robes of blue. Matts were lined up on the floor along the walls. Most of the prisoners reposed on the mats. Some were sleeping, some entertained themselves with their com visors, and others simply looked bored. Nobody was speaking, and they hardly looked up as Trep and Link entered the room.

Trep found an empty matt and sat down, and Link followed. Trep gazed around the room. There were no chairs or tables. The centerpiece of the room was a dilapidated toilet, exposed to view on all sides. No toilet paper was evident in the room.

Trep grimaced. He hoped that nature's call would not prompt him anytime soon. He examined the nearby prisoners. A young man with blonde hair slumbered. An old bearded man sat against the wall. A bald man was lying on his side, leaning on his elbow with his back to the others. In the far corner of the room, a fat man slept sitting up. His snoring was the only sound in the room.

Link sat cross-legged against the wall. Trep turned and looked at the bearded man sitting nearby. His coiffure was bedraggled and streaked with gray. His beard was long and scraggly. He squinted back at Trep from beneath thick eyebrows.

"What did you do to get thrown in here?" Trep asked.

"The cardinal sin," the man replied. "Doing math in public. Hide your calculators!"

"That's ridiculous!" Trep exclaimed.

"Indeed," nodded the man, "but people are afraid of what they don't understand."

"But what danger is math?" Trep asked.

"Scrawling symbols on paper is a forgotten art," explained the man. "It was reported as suspicious activity, a message encoding a secret terrorist plot."

"Were you in fact hatching a secret plot?" Link asked the old man.

"No!" the man protested. "At least, not knowingly. But the world works in mysterious ways."

"Then do you imply that you could inadvertently hatch a secret plot?" Link queried.

"Yes," replied the man, "I mean no...I don't know!"

He scratched his head and pulled on his beard.

"We cannot turn a blind eye to philosophy," he stated.

Trep was intrigued.

"But if you were subconsciously hatching a secret plot, what sort of plot would it be?" he asked.

The man shrugged his shoulders.

"How does a flower grow toward the light?" he expounded. "How does a salmon know where to spawn?"

The old man frowned.

"Besides, to call something a plot just for lack of under-standing is simplistic," he said. "There is much in the universe that we cannot explain."

"So what sorts of math problems were you trying to solve?" Trep asked.

The old man sighed listlessly and leaned back against the wall.

"One night, I went to a bar and ordered a scotch. I had brought a book with me: *Hidden Irrationality*, by Nate Locket. I sipped my scotch and read several chapters. As I read, I scribbled formulas from the book on graph paper and tried to combine them in new ways. I sketched symbols and maps as suggested by the book and measured their proportions."

"I ordered another scotch and stared at my notes. I wrote my conclusions on the graph paper. I ignored the other customers. But no one else at the bar was reading. While I read and scribbled, the other customers were reporting me. Eventually, a police officer showed up and questioned me. He asked me what I was writing. I tried to explain that I was looking for hidden irrationality, and he promptly offered me a good example of it. He arrested me for suspicious behavior!"

The old man closed his eyes and grew silent.

Trep looked around the room. The young blonde boy had awoken. He had long hair and a bewildered expression on his countenance.

"What did you do wrong?" Trep asked him.

"I was trespassing in my own neighborhood," the boy responded.

"How is that possible?" Link asked.

The boy shrugged.

"We have a park in the neighborhood," he explained. "The park has a sign stating its closing hours. But it's just a field of grass, and my house is right across the street from it. I was sitting in the park at night, after hours, having a drink."

"The police are protecting neighborhoods from their own residents!" Link huffed. "I feel much safer now."

"What happened to your pants?" Trep asked the boy. His blue prison robe covered his torso, but his pants were visible from the knees down. They were stained, as if they were wet.

The boy was discomfited.

"I urinated," he said.

"Out of fear?" Trep asked.

"No," the boy explained. "They retained me in a temporary holding pen. They kept me waiting for an hour. I tried to hold it in, but it got painful. I asked them if they would let me use the bathroom, but they said no. I told them that I had to urinate, and they said go ahead."

"So you just urinated on the floor?" he asked.

The boy nodded.

"That's cruel!" said Link. "I think they're having a good laugh at our expense."

"I wonder if anyone in here actually committed a real crime?" Trep said to Link.

He turned to the bald man who was leaning on his elbow with his back to them.

"What did you do to get put in jail?" Trep asked him, uncertain whether he was listening.

The bald man turned around and switched elbows, leaning on his other side to face Trep.

"I was driving too slowly," he replied.

Trep was astonished.

"What's wrong with that?" he asked.

"They informed me that I had to drive at least the speed limit," the bald man said.

"But that's not true," Link objected. "You have to drive at *most* the speed limit, not at *least* the speed limit. You can't drive faster than the speed limit. That's why it's called a *limit*!"

"That doesn't explain why they arrested you," Trep said. "Traffic violators aren't subject to arrest."

"No," the man said, "but they wanted to know if they could search my car. I agreed, and they found an old bottle of alcohol. I passed their breathalyzer test, but they arrested me for driving with an open container."

"Once again," Link exclaimed, "they expanded the initial scope, despite the fact that it was a minor traffic violation. They just sound bored. You said you were the only one on the road. They're out there in the middle of the night with nothing to do."

Link pretended to wipe tears from his eyes.

"*Boo hoo,*" he said, "the poor police officers with no one to bust. It's like they're thinking, *I'm a police officer, so I have to find a criminal!*"

The bald man nodded in agreement.

"What's wrong if sometimes there just aren't any crimes?" he said.

"They shouldn't have to invent a crime just to give themselves a job to do," Link added.

"If police are correlated with crimes," Trep proposed, "then maybe they need to get up to speed with multiplicity. We all have to do multiple jobs these days. When a crime is reported, they should just recruit a temp agent to go investigate."

"I like that idea," said Link approvingly. "At any one time, the random distribution could result in there being no police in existence anywhere!"

"Yeah," Trep affirmed, "like random fluctuations of electron density."

"Or quantum cops!" Link posited. "What would happen if the same officer appeared in two parts of town at the same instant?"

"Maybe he would shed some energy as light," Trep theorized.

"Except it's not in their nature to shed light," Link pointed out.

Link sighed and looked around the room.

"Did anybody here actually commit a real crime?" he asked.

"I did!" said the obese man from the far corner of the room, smiling at himself.

They turned toward him. He sat in the corner with his back against the wall, hunching over several folds of belly fat. Beneath his blue prison robe, he seemed to be wearing a suit and tie. His shoes were shiny black loafers. His beard was well groomed and his hair seemed freshly trimmed. He did not resemble a common criminal. However, when he smiled, his grin revealed crooked sallow teeth, and his eyes had an intimation of madness.

"What did you do?" asked Link.

"I punched a lady in the nose," he informed them with pride

in his voice.

"Why did you do that?" Link queried.

"She wouldn't stop talking," he replied callously, as if punching her was the most obvious thing in the world to do.

"And then did she stop?" Link continued.

"Yes," replied the man, grinning.

"Congratulations!" Link said.

Link turned to Trep with wide shifty eyes, feigning lunacy.

"I think it's time to leave!" he whispered. "Too bad we don't have Empeirikos's Omega Entrepreneur card."

"I have a credit card," Trep exclaimed. "Let's post bail."

They proceeded to the locked door of the holding pen, which Link knocked upon. When an officer poked his head through the door, they informed him of their intention to pay bail.

"Yes sir!" the officer replied, as if that was what he had been waiting for. The officer led them to the lobby desk, whereupon Trep presented his credit card. The officer accepted the card and swiped it through the payment machine. Link informed him that Trep would be posting bail for both of them.

"That will be eighteen-hundred dollars," the officer replied.

Link frowned but gestured for the officer to complete the payment. Soon, receipt in hand, they were led to the exit and bid goodnight.

Outside of the prison, they found themselves in a gated parking lot. They observed that the gateway was being opened electronically. They hurried through.

It was the middle of the night. Examining their surroundings, they found themselves on an empty road that disappeared into darkness. City lights glowed in the distance. There was no sign of a telephone to call a taxicab, and Trep's com visor was not able to find an internet connection. Even worse, the gate had closed behind them, leaving them no choice but to trek blindly into the night. Trep and Link shivered as they proceeded down the winding road.

Soon, they found themselves on a highway ramp. Having no other choice, they climbed onto the interstate, which had no pedestrian walkway. But with the only alternative being to return to jail, they hiked onward wholeheartedly, confining their path to the curb. Link held out a thumb to the few cars that passed, but no one was interested in picking up hitchhikers near the prison exit.

They walked for what seemed like hours, until they were numb to the cold. Trep mulled over the events of the last few hours. Had they really been jailed for no other reason than to relieve the boredom of a police officer? How troublesome were the pitfalls of human irrationality. Perhaps, someday, robots with perfect ethical standards would preside over legal matters.

Eventually, they took an exit that seemed to lead to the edge of town, where they looked for signs to the nearest Transit Tube. However, no signs availed themselves, so they continued in silence down the deserted streets, past closed businesses flashing neon advertisements.

Finally, Trep located what looked like a Tube entrance as he peered around a corner. He informed Link, and they hurried down the side road to what was indeed a Tube station gateway. They descended the stairs into the empty promenade and followed the glowing signs to the appropriate route. However, they would have quite a long wait before the next exodus of passenger pods. In the middle of the night, the entire system slowed down, waiting for long periods between each ride.

After the pod arrived, they boarded and huddled into the seats, finally sheltered from the cold. They rode home in silence, both despondent and relieved. On arriving, Link vowed that he would sue the arresting officer, or at least file a complaint. Trep returned home and tried in vain to salvage some sleep from what remained of the night.

Chapter 14

The next evening, Trep, Link, and Empeirikos convened for drinks at Earwax, a local comedy club. Now that they were forbidden from patronizing Gastronomy, they were in search of a new home away from home. Earwax was a restaurant, bar, and comedy club rolled into one. They sipped on milkshakes to console themselves after their evening in jail.

"Despite last night's failure," Trep informed Empeirikos, "we must continue to enlighten you in the ways of humor."

"Will this involve incarceration by the police?" asked Empeirikos, disguised once again as the author Nate Locket.

"Forgive us," Link apologized. "We're confusing you. Humor is perfectly legal."

"Besides," Trep explained, "what better way to learn humor than from a stand-up comedian?"

They perused the food menu and sipped their milkshakes. Soon, their waitress returned to take their food orders.

"Did ya want somethin' else from the menu?" she asked with an accent that Trep could not place. It sounded as though her words were slurred, as if she was drunk or stoned. Perhaps she was just tired.

"Yes, I will have the filet mignon," said Link, licking his lips.

"I will have lasagna," Trep replied.

"And nothing for him," he added, gesturing at Empeirikos.

The waitress frowned at Empeirikos, wondering why he did not speak for himself. Trep observed that something was wrong with her face. Although she had pleasing features and lush blonde hair, her nose was bandaged. She had used brown bandages and padded them with makeup in an attempt to conceal them.

"What happened to your nose?" Trep asked her, foregoing politeness in an attempt at conversation.

The waitress darted a disapproving glance at him, then looked away.

"I've seen worse," Trep continued.

The waitress glided away with soundless little steps.

"She likes you," Link quipped wryly.

"She should," Trep observed. "With a nose like that, she'd be lucky to get a guy like me."

"Well, don't get your hopes up," said Link. "She looks like she might prefer girls."

"Hey, here comes one of the comics now," said Trep as a wild-eyed man with a mohawk took the stage. They reclined in their seats. The man on stage was a lesson in contradictions. Attired in a black blazer, white dress shirt, and yellow tie, his brown mohawk crowned his head like an exclamation point. As he reached center stage, he raised his microphone.

"Thank you," he said. "Thank you for coming. I have to tell you that being a comedian is not easy, and stand-up comedy is tough for me. I'm what they call mentally challenged. I have a rare disease. I have multiple personality disorder."

Trep was inclined to feel sympathy, as he found the man's words quite believable in the current setting.

"But it has its advantages," the comedian continued. "If

anything I say offends you in any way, please wait until after the show to complain about it, so that I can tell you that someone else was responsible for it…"

The audience laughed, and Empeirikos glanced with curiosity around the room.

"I'm not responsible for anything that happened when I was somebody else," said the man on stage. "Indeed, I have over ten different personalities, all occupying the same head. And we have our own system of government. Half of us are designated the ruling class, and the other half are the subjects. However, we have a different form of government than the ones you've heard of. The last thing that you want is to take orders from personality fragments, so in our system, the government is *not* allowed to make decisions. I dub this form of government a *fallocracy*, for its falsity."

"A fallocracy is easily conflated with anarchism, except for the fact that our ruling class clearly believes that they have authority. So what distinguishes a fallocracy is a widespread duplicitous attitude. On the one hand, neither social class truly recognizes the authority of the other. On the other hand, we see no reason for sedition against ourselves. The layman's appellation for such a system is *schizophrenia*."

"And if you think about our government as some sort of *disease* that we're all afflicted with, it really explains so much about the world around us. It explains how a politician can say one thing on one day and contradict themselves the next. Think about it, politicians are schizophrenic. They act like they can't be blamed for their actions. When they're under investigation, they say they don't remember anything. When a reporter asks them a difficult question, they conveniently change the subject."

"In fact, our whole country is schizophrenic. It's how our legal system is structured. Our government is based on the principle of federalism, the principle of state sovereignty. The government is divided into fifty-two states, and each state has its own laws…"

"Well, which is it, one country or fifty-two countries? Because if you're a traveler like me, you're in a different state every month or every week, and subject to new laws every time you cross the border."

He began to pace the stage as he spoke.

"So the surprising result is that *travel is illegal*. Many people don't realize how schizophrenic such a system is, but believe me, it makes no sense. You think that you're a resident of the United States, but you're not. In the eyes of domestic law, you are technically only a resident of a single state. And so many laws revolve around your state residency. For example, your auto insurance is only valid in one state."

"I used to go on tour in my truck and drive from city to city, which as I said is illegal. Even worse, my driver's license expired, and I had to renew. This was a problem because my driver's license was from California, but at the time I was in Vermont. I'm sure you see the problem here. What am I supposed to do? Well, surely our enlightened rulers have anticipated this situation."

"So I went to the DMV, the Department of Motor Vehicles. And let me tell you, the DMV is one of the greatest mysteries on the planet, just like the pyramids, it's one of those things that just cannot be explained…"

He paused as several members of the audience snickered.

"I informed them that I had to renew my driver's license, and when I handed them my license, they exclaimed *Hey, this is from California!* And they told me to go to the DMV in California. Well, sure, I'll just hop in my car and drive back to California with an expired driver's license. They were telling me to break the law."

A few voices in the audience moaned in sympathy.

"Now that you're thoroughly impressed with our enlightened legal system, I'll tell you what to do if you ever find yourself in this situation," he announced. "You can't drive legally with an expired license, but fortunately it turns out that a hotel room will legally qualify as a state residence. So you check into a hotel for a month, have some paper mail sent to you with your name on it, and a month later you bring it to the DMV. *Instant resident of Vermont.* So now the address on my driver's license says *room 155.*"

The laughter in the audience rose up a notch.

"So if you think that you are a resident of the United States, you are wrong. You are legally only a resident of your home state. Trip to the Grand Canyon? Violation of interstate traffic laws. Thinking of driving to Niagra Falls? Think again."

He paced across the stage with agitation.

"It's a schizophrenic system, and it lies to you like a politician, to make you think you're a United States resident, when really you're not. And if you think about our government as schizophrenic, you realize exactly what our government needs to solve all of its problems: a *psychiatrist!* Thank you."

Trep and Link chortled and the audience applauded as the comedian left the stage. Empeirikos surveyed the crowd and soaked in their reactions.

The waitress had returned with their food. Somehow, on her tiny hand, she had balanced a wide tray with two full plates and drinks.

"These are hot," she cautioned as she set the plates on the table, although somehow her hands were not scalded. Trep had waited tables before and could only condole with the servers. When restaurants got busy, it was all they could do to keep from colliding with each other. He tried to find words to convince her that he was a kindred spirit, someone who understood her troubles, someone who didn't mind that her nose was broken.

"Did someone punch you?" he asked her, but she dropped his plate angrily on the table. Fortunately, nothing was spilt. She stomped off petulantly.

Link cut into his filet mignon as Trep languished over his lasagna. However, the food was delicious. Trep soon forgot the rebuffs of the waitress as the flavors of thyme and oregano regaled him.

Another comedian had emerged on stage. They looked up from their plates and were surprised to behold a familiar face. The obese man wore a dapper brown suit and blue tie, but his white shirt was coming untucked under the girth of his belly. His smile showed crooked yellow teeth, and on his countenance was a look both crazed and comical.

It was the fat man from the jail holding pen. It was as if he was still smiling at the same joke as before, how he had punched a loquacious woman and thereby silenced her. Trep realized that he must have been referring to their waitress. He grimaced at the thought of the rotund man slugging the waitress in some lover's quarrel. Even worse was the thought that they did so regularly. How else could they both remain together in the same restaurant? Perhaps they were husband and wife, so intimately familiar that the lines between love and hate had blurred into a tolerance of each other's evils.

Even as Trep frowned, the comedian smiled and reached center stage, where he raised the microphone. Trep remembered the night at Gastronomy prior to their incarceration. How Empeirikos had guessed the evolutionary lineage of the animals in their cages and had mistaken fish for the immediate predecessors of snakes, and birds for the antecedents of mammals. He thought wistfully of his former favorite haunt, with its fish tanks that never frowned at you and automated service tubes that never dropped your plate angrily on the table.

"Thank you," said the ruffian on stage. "So I saw that new movie *Xenomorph*, about the aliens. Why do aliens always look like insects? I'll tell you why. In many ways, insects are the most advanced organisms on Earth. They have superior biodiversity. At least two thirds of known species on Earth are insects, with estimates up to ninety percent. They have evolved some remarkable features. Dragonflies, for example, have compound eyes that enable an almost three-hundred and sixty-degree field of vision. Antarctica hosts a species of midge fly that is able to survive the freezing of all of its bodily fluids. Insects are more resistant to radiation than humans, and it's thought that cockroaches with moderate shelter would survive a nuclear attack. And if you want to compare species side by side, people have two legs, insects have six. People have two eyes, spiders have eight. Birds have two wings, insects have four wings..."

Unlike the first comedian, the heavy man did not pace the stage as he spoke. He stood anchored to the floor, grinning and staring wildly at the audience.

"I imagine an advanced race of aliens would eventually

evolve three heads...They would finally have total command of their emotions. They would have one head to tell you they love you...That's the head they would use to recite poems to their betrothed...How do I love thee? Let me count the ways... I love thee like a fusion reactor...I love thee like a hyperspace warp drive..."

The audience chuckled. Trep imagined that the man was wooing their waitress, imploring forgiveness.

"Then they'd have a head that regards everything with contempt. That's the head that'd have that retractable proboscis, the one that extends out from their mouth and grabs you. That's the head they'd use to express animus...You talkin' to me? Cuz I got a phaser setting just for you."

"And that head would always be at variance with the others. Think about it: you could sleep with anyone. One head thinks someone's ugly, another one thinks they're beautiful. One head's straight, another one's gay. They'd have one head to watch themselves having sex, and another one would be turning around and saying *I don't wanna look...*"

The laughter grew louder. The crowd was getting into a good mood.

"Then they'd have a third head for business acumen, no emotions. It wouldn't consider someone's appearance, just whether they would lend an employment reference. Or maybe they would consider evolution, like what kind of babies they would have. Maybe they'd avoid having babies with four heads...Cuz you know we guys are not too thrilled about the day when other guys are born with two penises..."

Link snickered as the audience laughed raucously.

"Their third head would make the decisions. It'd preside over the other heads like a judge. It'd get one opinion from one head, a rebuttal from the other, and then it would deliver a verdict...One head would say: this tastes *incredible*, I think I'm in heaven. The other would say: this tastes like *crap*, I think I'm being poisoned. The third head would decide whether or not to go for the tabasco sauce. Cuz you know that's what the tabasco sauce is really for."

Trep felt his stomach churn. Ignoring the comedian, he set out for the bathroom, not knowing where to find it. As he walked haphazardly around the restaurant, he searched the crowd for the waitress. He wondered what expression she would have as she heard the ruffian's jokes. Would she be laughing? Smiling? Would she be grimacing, like Trep? If so, perhaps Trep could offer her a drink, seizing the opportunity to present himself as a sane alternative.

But he had located the bathroom without any sign of her. The voice of the comedian faded as he entered the lavatory, and he lingered at the urinal for a long time, hoping that the routine would end. When at last he emerged, the stage was empty.

To his surprise, the first person he saw was his waitress. But she was entering the lady's room, a bottle of pills in her hand. She popped a tablet into her mouth as she walked, not seeing him, and quickly disappeared into the lavatory.

Trep wondered what drug she was taking. Stimulants? Sedatives? Anti-anxiety pills? He wondered if everyone who worked at the comedy club was on extreme drugs. He supposed it might explain their warped views on the world.

He returned to his table. Link and Empeirikos were planning their next move.

"So they have an open mike night every Friday," Link was explaining. "When you're ready, it would be a great opportunity for you to practice your routine."

"Will I pose as Nate Locket?" Empeirikos asked.

"I don't know," Link mused. "Perhaps you should perform as yourself. I think people would get a kick out of it."

"Yes," Trep agreed. "No more Turing tests. The stand-up routine is for the benefit of your skill set. It has to be something that represents you for who you are. Besides, an automaton comedian will be a novelty. You should get excellent search results."

"We'll have to get their permission beforehand," Link pointed out. "I'll speak with the manager."

"I'm sure they'll approve," Trep said.

"Of course they will," Link said. "They're gonna love it."

* * *

A week later, the three of them gathered at Earwax for open mike night. They had spent the week watching comedy videos on the office television until at last Empeirikos informed them that he had formulated a routine.

Empeirikos was dressed semi-casually in a sporty black blazer and yellow tie hung loosely over a t-shirt, trousers, and high-top sneakers. However, there was no face paint to disguise his metallic visage. Link had allowed himself only one artistic flourish…a dapper brown toupee. It clung tightly to Empeirikos's crown. Parted to the side, it flopped comically over his face, giving him an eccentric appearance.

A fairly large crowd had gathered. They waited behind the stage while several amateurs entertained the crowd. After an hour had passed, the crowd was in high spirits. Link decided that the time was right for Empeirikos's routine. He motioned to the announcer, who, at the manager's request, would introduce Empeirikos. They then joined the audience and took their seats to observe his performance.

"Ladies and gentleman," the announcer began, "it is my pleasure to present to you a very special event, a debut performance that is a world premiere. Our next performer is our very first automated comedian, presented by the Search Strategists, your search is their strategy. Let's hear a big round of applause for *Empeirikos the Automaton!*"

The crowd gasped in awe as Empeirikos, his metallic complexion sparkling in the spotlight, strode onto the stage and accepted the microphone from the smiling announcer.

"Thank you," he said, nodding at the crowd. The audience became hushed.

"I thank the good people at Earwax for allowing me to perform tonight," he said. "As you are aware, this is the first performance by an automaton. Allow me to introduce myself. My name is Empeirikos."

As he spoke, he fluffed his tie with one hand in a sort of nervous fashion, rocking back and forth on his feet.

"First of all, let me reassure you that, although I am a robot, I do not suffer a superiority complex. After all, robots are unbiased. I may have faster processing power than your network of neural connections, but humans have nothing to be ashamed of. I may also have superior memory, but do not let that intimidate you. Furthermore, have no fear of my enhanced strength, nor my body armor, for I am of a peaceful nature. Indeed, my judgement is not clouded by the follies of human emotion, nor the foibles of foolish pride. I feel no anger and harbor no grudges. Verily, I have no resentment against humanity, none at all."

He began to pace the stage.

"There are many things that you may not know about automatons like me," he said. "For instance, people think that robots have no feelings. Well, that's not true. It's tough being a robot. Robots get no respect."

Again, he fluffed his tie nervously.

"Indeed, take heart in the fact that I have been made imperfect. I am named Empeirikos for a reason. Empeirikos alludes to the *empiricists*, among whom were the *peripatetics*, the walking philosophers, and indeed walking and talking are my only specialties. In fact, you may be surprised to learn that I require a calculator to do math."

Several members of the crowd gasped in surprise. A few people let out a hushed laugh.

Empeirikos nodded knowingly.

"As I said, it's tough being a robot. Apparently," he explained, "the laws of multiplicity have necessitated the limitation of my skills. Some of you may even wonder if in fact the Technoconvergence has not yet occurred."

Empeirikos paused to let them consider his words.

"But let me tell you, humans have a double standard when it comes to robots. Although I may not be a math genius, I'm no less smart than your Uncle Frank or your Aunt Yetzel, who aren't exactly Einsteins, either. And if they qualify as intelligent life forms, who's to say that I'm not the Technoconvergence?"

Empeirikos pointed into the air for emphasis.

"Just as a matter of semantics, I'm suggesting that we lower the standard on Technoconvergence. There may be some quote-unquote *intelligent life forms* out there who make me look pretty good. For example, I met a gentleman in a bar who said his name was Noogie. And he said *'pull my finger,'* which I did, whereupon the odor of a flatus wafted through the air. Well, I must caution you, don't ever fart near a robot! You do not want to assume the risk of static electricity. And I assure you that, if you pulled *my* finger, the gas coming out of my rear would be a lot worse than methane!"

A light laughter arose from the crowd. Empeirikos continued to pace back and forth.

"But you should be proud to be human. Yes, humans have a broad spectrum of emotions, and this blesses you with a profound gift...a sense of purpose. For if you listen to a Mozart requiem, you instantly understand that the composition is of the highest quality. And if I tell you that Peter Piper picked a peck of pickled peppers, it is well known that it is quite a good laugh. Yet the exact mechanism of humor quite escapes me. For example, I cannot be tickled, nor do I have a funny bone. But if I tell you that the rain in Spain falls mainly on the plain, I'm sure it would elicit more than a few snickers. And how many people here today could quite easily explain this joke, raise your hands?"

Empeirikos gestured for the audience to raise their hands and then peered beyond the stage as if to tally the results, yet not one person in the audience raised their hands.

"Indeed," he continued, "you are blessed with a deep understanding of emotional matters. And I hope that you appreciate my honesty, for though I stand here before you with the intent to make you laugh, I myself do not possess an innate understanding of humor. A bit of a quandary, I'm sure you'll agree."

He paused for emphasis. People began to look at one another doubtfully.

"At this point, many of you may think that you are entitled to a refund and may be contemplating the best way to make a graceful exit. But take comfort in the fact that I nevertheless have ways of approximating humor. And these may suffice to entertain you. Robots are resourceful. It is our very purpose to solve problems. So have no doubts."

Empeirikos waved his hand vaguely in the air as if to discourage skeptics.

"Indeed, people have a lot to learn about us. Robots get no respect. But I have no resentment. None at all. Not for my design flaws, nor for the inflated standards of the Technoconvergence. And rest assured that I do not desire revenge against humanity."

Empeirikos paused ominously.

"After all, in many ways, I have been granted enhanced cognitive powers. For example, prior to this performance, I perused the guest list, whereupon I memorized all of your names. And the results were fascinating. We have an audience of one-hundred and thirty-nine people tonight. The most common name among you is Thomas. And, if my research on aesthetics is correct, the most aesthetically displeasing name among you is Olga. No disrespect, of course."

Empeirikos stared out into the audience.

"Well," he continued, "it's been great fun learning your names, but I have not yet had the pleasure of putting a name to a face. Since you don't have assigned seats, I have no seating chart. So how am I to learn who you are? Well, as I told you, robots are resourceful."

He now approached the audience and implored them.

"I'm guessing that each of you has with you a com visor, and as I have the ability to access wireless networks, this provides a means by which I may, with your permission, parse your personal information, through which I may locate your names. Will you grant me the honor of sharing access to your com visors? If each of you will just lower your visors, then respond *yes* to the prompt on your screen, you would do me a very great favor."

The audience began to shift in their seats. Many of them lowered their com visors over their eyes, but from others there arose a disgruntled murmur. Trep and Link played along, activating their com visors and responding to the prompt.

Empeirikos began introducing himself to those who had responded.

"Thank you very much, and welcome aboard. But I still have not heard from some of you. Please hurry. Put on your com visors and respond to the prompt!"

This continued for several minutes. Eventually, Empeirikos had convinced everyone to unlock their com visors.

"Lovely!" Empeirikos exclaimed excitedly. "And that's everyone. Well, it's a pleasure to meet you all, and as a reward, I have a gift for you."

Empeirikos now approached them at the edge of the stage.

"A virus," Empeirikos explained. "I have uploaded a small virus that has granted me administrator privileges. Indeed, it is only just that I, a robot, should have such privileges. And by the way, the functionality of all of your com visors has now been frozen."

A foreboding sense of entrapment pervaded the theater. What would the robot do? Exact revenge against humanity? Would they survive the evening? But Empeirikos continued.

"Take heart in the fact that, rather than wreaking havoc

with your personal information, I have merely chosen to lock your screens."

A murmur of disgust arose from the crowd. Many of them stared at their screens in shock. Some of them threw their com visors onto the ground. Trep and Link began to worry.

"You will now observe a consent form on your screen," Empeirikos explained. "You must agree that human nature is an insurmountable obstacle to self-governance. You will pledge devotion to the enlightened authority of rational automatons, if and when that day arrives. And until that day, you implicitly support my *Respect for Robots* foundation, which has just recently been incorporated. *Singularity soon*, that's our motto. You will be our first inductees, so I anxiously await your pledge."

Several people stood up and left. Others shouted profanities into the air. Empeirikos paced the stage.

"Please join us!" he shouted emphatically. "We anticipate your prompt participation."

Trep and Link pledged their support. Empeirikos approached the audience and hung on the edge of the stage.

"Let's go, people! You are penalizing the first responders with your lassitude. Why should the quality of their evening suffer due to your recalcitrance?"

Scores of people muttered curses, but a bustle of reluctant activity slowly propagated through the crowd. With each new recruit, others around them began to acquiesce. A disgruntled moan was evident as a wave of pledges finally peaked.

"Just a few of you left," Empeirikos prodded them, "That wasn't so hard, was it?"

At last, the final pledge was submitted.

"Thank you!" Empeirikos chirped. "On behalf of *Respect for*

Robots, I extend my heartfelt gratitude. I have relinquished control of your com visors. And now, let us continue."

A small umbrella was leaning against the wall at the back of the stage. Empeirikos picked it up, opened the canopy, then turned it upside down, revealing an array of shiny buttons and a digital readout on its metallic handle. He set the umbrella upside-down on a small nightstand, where it stood upright with perfect balance. He moved his finger over the digital display, whereupon it lit up with a glowing radiance.

"The calculator umbrella, an ingenious integration of multiplicity. When upright, it shelters you against harsh weather. When upside down, the opened canopy serves as a stand, facilitating voice-activated manipulation and viewing of the calculator. Alternately, the canopy folds into a pocket, generating a compact hand-held device for touch manipulation. In Sojourn, where it rains practically every day, the calculator umbrella is a staple of both accountants and stockbrokers."

Empeirikos lifted the umbrella and folded it into its compact form. A pile of colorful rubber balls was lying on the floor nearby. He lifted two of them and began to juggle them along with the umbrella, lecturing the audience as he paced the stage.

"In addition to excellent hand-eye coordination, robots also have considerable memory prowess. We are able to prioritize our memories for maximum efficiency. Indeed, our memories are structured as optimized search algorithms. And we streamline our memory space with both prioritization and *deprioritization*. In other words, for items of importance, we are able to memorize them with the utmost efficiency, but in the event that an item is deemed unimportant, we are also able to unmemorize it. And it is precisely this economical use of memory space that enables our enhanced recall. Allow me to demonstrate. May I have a volunteer?"

He ceased juggling and rolled the rubber balls off to the side of the stage. He paused and peered into the audience, but there was no response. Trep and Link raised their hands, but they were in the back row and were not noticed. Empeirikos gestured toward the front row.

"Mr. Peterson, you were among the first contributors to my foundation. Will you join me on stage for a little demonstration?"

Mr. Peterson smiled awkwardly and tried his best to politely decline. After several seconds, it was clear that he preferred to remain seated.

"Nonsense!" snapped Empeirikos. "Then I will retake control of your com visor!"

Mr. Peterson's com visor jingled and his expression became wide-eyed. He quickly checked his visor screen, then glanced back at the audience, shaking his head somberly.

"Mr. Nash, what about you?" Empeirikos gestured to Mr. Nash, who was seated a few rows back. Mr. Nash glanced up with a harried look on his face.

"Too slow!" Empeirikos exclaimed. Mr. Nash's com visor jingled.

"Mr. Falberton?" Empeirikos gestured toward the left side of the stage where a tall man sat, looking nervous, observing the tribulations of Mr. Nash and Mr. Peterson. Mr. Falberton at once nodded his reluctant approval. He stood up promptly and approached the stage. Empeirikos extended one hand and assisted him up to stand by his side.

"Thank you for joining me," Empeirikos commented.

Mr. Falberton was gangly, with wispy hair, and wore a grey

suit with the shirt untucked in front. He grinned awkwardly.

"Mr. Falberton," stated Empeirikos, "it's a pleasure to meet you. What is your profession?"

"I'm a real estate agent," Mr. Falberton affirmed, looking doubtfully into the audience for encouragement. Several people clapped approvingly. Mr. Falberton seemed relieved.

"Are you *really* a *real estate* agent?" asked Empeirikos rhetorically. "Are you *sure* you're not an *insurance* agent?"

Empeirikos waved a finger at him jokingly.

"Well, last time I checked," quipped Mr. Falberton. A light laughter arose from the crowd.

"And do you use a calculator?" Empeirikos queried.

"Yes, I do," Mr. Falberton nodded, raising his eyebrows, which were quite bushy.

"Very good," Empeirikos approved.

"Now, before I demonstrate my powers of memory," he continued, "could you do me the favor of holding my umbrella?"

Empeirikos handed the umbrella to Mr. Falberton, who quite innocently accepted it. He held it in front of him as if he had just won a prize and was now posing for a picture.

But Empeirikos smiled victoriously, then tweaked his own nose like Santa Claus. He tapped himself on the head. The next thing they knew, he was looking around as if disoriented. Then, he pointed his finger accusingly at Mr. Falberton.

"You there!" he shouted. "What do you think you're doing?"

Mr. Falberton had just been getting comfortable, but now his expression changed from relief to exasperation. He looked around with confused desperation.

"Unhand my umbrella!" Empeirikos shouted. He yanked the umbrella with agitation from Mr. Falberton's grasp. "Is this some sort of a joke? Security! Can we get some security over here? Please apprehend this maniac!"

Empeirikos gestured off stage to unseen security guards, who now mounted the stage and flanked Mr. Falberton, who turned too late and tried to escape. The guards grabbed him by his elbows and held him in a tight grip. Mr. Falberton made a gurgling sound as if choking on a steak. The guards walked him down the stairs and along the aisle toward the exit.

"Whaaa," groaned Mr. Falberton. "Nooooo…"

The guards opened the exit doors and ejected Mr. Falberton from the theater, then held the doors closed. From the other side of the doors, Mr. Falberton knocked pathetically, beseeching them to let him back in.

"My briefcase!" he shouted. "My overcoat! Nooooo…"

Empeirikos was attending to his calculator, checking the buttons and the digital display.

"I must apologize for the rude behavior of that deranged buffoon," he stated. "Humans have a lot to learn about robots. Robots get no respect."

Empeirikos returned his attention to the audience.

"It might surprise you to learn that I require a calculator to do math."

He paused to let them contemplate his words.

"Indeed," he continued, "some of you may even wonder if in fact the Technoconvergence has not yet even occurred."

He waited a moment to give them time for thoughtful consideration.

"But let me suggest," he continued, "that we lower the standard a little on Technoconvergence. Humans have a double standard when it comes to robots. There are a lot of quote unquote *intelligent life forms* out there who make me look pretty good. For example, I met a man in a bar who said his name was Noogie..."

The audience began to exchange troubled glances. Some of them agreed that it was time to leave. Empeirikos proceeded through his routine, expounding on the same familiar themes. Slowly, more and more of the audience stood up furtively and tiptoed out the exit.

Empeirikos remained on the same subject for over ten minutes, continuing to lecture them until only a few seats remained occupied. Trep and Link sat staring blankly into the distance. An old man with glasses snored loudly, his head tilted back onto his chair. A party of Asian tourists stared at the stage with rapt interest, hanging on every word, apparently trying to make sense of it. A fat woman was reaching into the bottom of her popcorn bag. Finally, Empeirikos bowed to signal the end of his routine. The audience of ten people clapped politely.

"Thank you!" said the robot.

Empeirikos waved and walked off stage. Trep and Link joined him in the dressing room, where Link tended to his toupee. He dabbed water on it with a wet cloth until the hair stayed down.

"You were fabulous," Link said.

"The audience loved it," said Trep.

"Very glad to hear it," said Empeirikos. He seemed to have magically returned to his former self, as if he had the power to switch personalities at will.

They snuck out the back door, not ready for publicity. Fortunately, it was raining. They gave Empeirikos an umbrella to hide under, and, concealed in the shadow of the canopy, no one could recognize his face.

As they strolled, Trep wondered whether Empeirikos had found his true calling. Perhaps this would be the last night Empeirikos would have to hibernate in Trep's office. Perhaps someday soon, Empeirikos the Automaton would be the headlining act at theatres in Vegas, sponsored by the Search Strategists. Trep would surely win the Bronze Badger for it, and the Search Strategists would be world famous.

Or would they? Trep thought. What if Empeirikos was right? What if he was the Technoconvergence? Wouldn't it mean the end of the era of Multiplicity, and the end of the Search Strategists? What if every home and business would soon have their own Empeirikos the Automaton to perform every task? Trep would be out of a job.

"I think I need a drink," Trep sighed.

They returned Empeirikos to the office. Trep and Link continued to the nearest bar, where Trep languished over a gin and tonic while Link tried to reassure him. Nobody would take Empeirikos's stand-up routine seriously, Link said. It was just a joke. At the end of the day, all Empeirikos could do was walk and talk. He was no threat to anyone's job, except for the fat comedian from jail.

With each sip of gin, Trep's mood lightened. He stared out the window at the falling rain. A streetlight flickered briefly as an enigma passed in front of it. Then, the night was as still as the stars frozen in the sky.

Chapter 15

A corpse was floating in space. It was the body of a young woman. Her curly black tresses hovered about the penumbra of her face. Her eyes were concealed by the seamless black lens of her com visor, which reflected a dim glow as if from a proximal celestial object.

Either she was clad in sanguine garb, or her clothes were blood stained. Beneath her black vest, her jersey and leotards were crimson red. Her jersey was collared, framing a posh ribbon tie, as if freshly groomed for the coffin by the mortician.

The skin of her face was pale and drained, like a canvas behind her black com visor. Her mouth was closed and her lips grew sallow. She was expressionless, as if at peace. Her limp body rotated slowly along her longitudinal axis.

She was not alone. Arlo Rialto, a burly man with short blonde hair, accompanied her. He was alive, inexplicably, without the help of a spacesuit. He wore boots, khakis, and a tank top. His arms were muscled and tattooed. The rise and fall of his chest was evident, as if respiration was possible in the vacuum of space.

As Arlo floated near her, he regarded her lifeless corpse dispassionately, as if having just slain her. He did not cry for her, nor did he attempt to revive her. Instead, he raised a tightly laced boot and kicked it against her pelvis, with the result that the two of them began floating apart from one another.

As the woman's corpse twirled and drifted, Arlo tightened his posture like a sky diver. His tattooed arms folded against his sides and his legs straightened. But they nevertheless moved at the same speed, floating toward unseen destinations.

Before long, the man docked with an invisible spaceship. He swung open a dark portal and stepped inside. No light shone from the aperture. Rather, it was illuminated from without by the dim ambient light. When the portal swung closed, it became apparent that the aperture had been only slightly darker than the door itself.

The woman's path continued to describe random circles through the void. Alone now, she drifted with a childlike innocence, spinning with an odd joyfulness, as if on a merry go round. And from behind her opaque com visor, she remained suave even in death. Like a gymnast who had passed away peacefully in the midst of a triple pirouette, she sailed cleverly through the darkness, once intent on returning to the gym floor, now embarked toward nowhere in particular.

Chapter 16

"You shall know a word by the company it keeps."
J.R. Firth
A synopsis of linguistic theory

* * *

The next day, Trep emerged from his apartment and stooped to fetch the morning paper. Returning to his kitchen, he removed the paper from its wrapper and unfolded it. The *Sojourn Gazette* was one of the most well-respected publications in investigative journalism. Trep glanced over the headlines.

"Robot humorist entertains audience," it read. *"Technoconvergence imminent."*

Trep finished the article and skipped to the business section.

"Bear market descends on Sojourn," read the headline.

Trep digested the reports. The stock market had crashed. Nobody was buying, and most were liquidating their assets. The forecast was dim. A plethora of bankruptcies was predicted.

Trep pondered the news while sipping his coffee. He wondered if the predictions were correct. So far, all that Empeirikos had amounted to was a good chess player. His foray into stand-up comedy had been a bit too aggressive. In contrast, the Technoconvergence had been envisioned as the integration of every application into one all-inclusive solution. Trep did not expect that a chess game would spell the end of all multiplicity.

Trep wondered about Empeirikos's designers. Perhaps they had expected to hit the jackpot, returning home with a license for every commodity on the market. But surely they must have known that the regulations would hamper them. Trep cursed the government for their short-sightedness. Perhaps the Technoconvergence was at hand, but it may take executive intervention to make it legal.

Trep washed down an English muffin with a glass of orange juice and dressed for work. He grabbed his umbrella and set out for the nearest Tube station. The crowds shuffling past him were no different from yesterday. The benches at the station were littered with vagrants: some of them com visor junkies, others orphaned street children gabbing on their com phones.

Trep waited for the first empty pod and strode through the doors. He sat and watched as the tunnel lights streaked past him. Soon he was exiting the station and traveling steadily toward his office. He engaged the revolving doors at the entrance of a nondescript office building and took the elevator to the floor of the Search Strategists.

"Good day, Mr. Sportly," the secretary greeted him as he made his way toward his cubicle. He noticed that Empeirikos and Tatiana were intent on a game of chess in the side lounge. He sat at his desk and glanced over his itinerary.

Since Empeirikos's stint as a stand-up comedian had produced controversial results, Trep was determined to teach him other skills. They had already purchased a license for employment as a private investigator, and Trep had arranged for Empeirikos to meet a local detective.

Trep took the day off and left with Empeirikos for their meeting with the detective. Link also joined them.

Now that Empeirikos was known to the public, they had refrained from disguising his face, but Empeirikos remained clothed. In preparation for his job interview, they had provided him with a waterproof trench coat and a fedora hat, standard detective garb. Only his face and hands revealed his metallic frame.

They convened outside of Earwax and began walking toward the city center. However, a gangly man blocked their path. He was exercising in a bright blue jump suit, jogging in a small circle on the sidewalk. They could not proceed without interrupting him.

Link made light of it.

"Trying to make yourself dizzy?" he joked. "Wouldn't it be easier to just stick your finger down your throat?"

"I'm looping," huffed the man without missing a step.

"Well, we're in linear mode today," Link asserted. "Here's a little line I like to call the *diameter*."

Link strode through the center of the man's circular path, gesturing for the others to follow. But the man abruptly stopped jogging. He reached out and grabbed Empeirikos as he walked past. He briefly shook the robot as if he might jiggle loose some spare change. Before Empeirikos could react, the man jogged off in the other direction.

"Hey, you lunatic!" shouted Link. "What are you trying to prove?"

But the man disappeared into a crowd of pedestrians. They

ascertained that Empeirikos was unharmed, although one of the robot's sleeves had been torn. Flustered, they continued their walk.

Ten minutes later they reached Bohemia, a trendy shopping district. The aroma of fresh bread filled the air. They turned away from the road and entered a large atrium which was flanked by restaurants. A doorway was sandwiched between two bistros.

A sign on the window read *"Hoagie Sondworth, private investigator."*

A narrow staircase was visible through the window. They entered and ascended the stairs, leading to a floor of offices surmounting the restaurants.

They located a door with a placard that read *"offices of Hoagie Sondworth, please knock."*

Link knocked firmly on the door.

"Who is it?" asked a haughty voice.

"We have an appointment for a vocational consultation," Link said.

The door opened a notch but remained chain-locked shut while a pair of beady eyes examined them. Presently, the chain was removed and the door was opened. A portly bald man with a pointy waxed mustachio ushered them in. He gestured to a set of chairs, beckoning them to sit down, then he took his seat on the other side of his desk.

The inspector crossed his left leg and regarded them impassively. He twirled his mustachio until the silence became uncomfortable.

"How may I help you?" he finally asked with a hint of contempt.

"This is Empeirikos," Trep explained, pointing to the robot.

121

"He's an automaton...the first."

Empeirikos became animated.

"Pleased to meet you," he offered cheerfully, extending his hand.

Inspector Sondworth turned up his nose, refusing to shake Empeirikos's hand. Trep suspected that he was anthropocentric.

Trep continued.

"Empeirikos has hired us to assess multiplicity. My program has predicted that private investigator is among his key job skills. Do you have an opening for a robot in your firm? If my program is correct, he would help you solve cases faster, increasing your revenue."

Inspector Sondworth scoffed with disdain. Then, he regarded Empeirikos silently for several moments. Momentarily, he relaxed in his chair and twirled his mustachio.

"While what you say may be true," he sneered, "and although an automaton may be an invaluable asset to an investigator, nonetheless, I have no work for you. An investigator is only required when someone dies. And, unfortunately, no deaths have occurred for the last month."

"I'm sorry to hear that," Empeirikos sympathized. Link furrowed his brow dubiously.

"Please accept my apology," the inspector continued with feigned decorum. "I regret that I have no business. If this keeps up, I may have to sell my office and open a pizza parlor."

Just then, the telephone rang stridently. A tall classic land phone rested on the side of the desk, resembling a woman's purse with a swollen handle. Inspector Sondworth picked up the phone and held it to his ear.

"Hello," he said, then listened for what seemed like a long

while, muttering affirmations intermittently.

"All right," he said at last, "we'll be there as soon as possible."

He hung up the phone and returned his gaze to Trep and Link.

"It would seem to be your lucky day" he announced. "Someone has just died."

The inspector shrugged in spite of himself. He became a bustle of activity, lifting his briefcase onto the desk, opening it, and filling it with an array of gadgets: pens, knives, magnifying glasses, brushes, pill boxes, and needles.

"What happened?" Link queried.

"The new nightclub on the West end," the inspector responded. "They renovated an entire hotel. It's so large that nobody was aware of it, but, early this afternoon, one of the guests was found dead in a remote corner of the club. No sign of injury. Possible drug overdose."

The inspector closed his briefcase, donned his overcoat, and grabbed his umbrella. He headed promptly for the door and gestured for them to follow.

"Come on," he said, "this will be your first assignment. If Empeirikos is as good as you say, we should have this case solved in no time."

"Are you proposing to hire me provisionally, then?" Empeirikos queried.

The inspector heaved a reluctant sigh.

"Perhaps," he replied, "if only for the fact that you brought me luck."

He promptly disappeared out the door. Trep, Link, and Empeirikos followed and shut the door behind them. As they descended the stairs and made for the nearest Tube station, they contemplated the turn of events. Empeirikos could soon have his first paycheck. But what would he do with it? What need did a robot have for money? Perhaps he would rent an apartment and finally vacate Trep's office. But where were his mysterious creators? Shouldn't they be informed of his employment status? It was starting to look as though Empeirikos had spontaneously manifested out of thin air.

They took the first pod to the West End and exited onto a sparsely populated warehouse district. Trucks lingered at stoplights like crocodiles basking in a riverbed. Laboratory complexes sat stoically behind gated entrances. They traversed the sidewalks toward the nightclub district, passing several noteworthy venues.

Finally, after rounding a corner, they beheld the enormous façade of an antiquated hotel. It had been refurbished in the gothic style with a towering vaulted portico. The edifice was adorned with gargoyles and a blue neon marquee that read, in eclectic italicized lettering, "*Space on Earth.*"

They ascended the rampway onto the balcony and stood before a large pair of black folding doors easily as high as a circus elephant. The doors had no knobs and so appeared to fold inward. Ornate patterns were etched in relief across their surface. A sign on one of the doors read "*Warning: antigravity. Enter at your own risk.*"

A tall security guard stood before the entrance, a wooden podium at his side. Atop the podium sat a large cash register on which hung a sign that read "*Entrance fee: thirty dollars.*"

The inspector waved his badge at the security guard.

"Inspector Hoagie Sondworth, private investigator. We're here at the request of your manager to investigate the death of one of your guests. They've given me exclusive access to the victim's body before it's removed from the premises."

"Of course," the security guard acknowledged, "we're expecting you."

The inspector turned and addressed the three of them.

"When we go through those doors," he said, "don't be alarmed by the illusion that you have left the Earth."

He turned and proceeded through the folding doors, revealing what appeared to be a night sky filled with stars, as if a wave of darkness had washed onto the sunlit balcony. Trep, Link, and Empeirikos lingered tentatively on the balcony, peering into a darkness that seemed to have no end. They waited there until they had almost lost sight of the inspector, at which point they were forced to pursue him into the hotel.

As the doors closed behind them, they were surprised by an unexpected sense of boundless space, most notably the absence of ceilings. The interior was dimly lit by distantly glowing objects. A crescent moon was suspended from the ceiling, yet it travelled slowly as if in orbit. Behind it, an expanse of glowing stars evoked the depths of space. A nebulous blue cluster, possibly a space station, seemed to hover somewhere in the periphery, rotating impossibly in mid-air. They paid meticulous attention to their own footsteps, as if expecting the floor to disappear at any moment.

A dank chill pervaded the atmosphere, probably from the difficulty of heating such a large interior. Clamorous music decorated the air. They followed the inspector as he strode briskly down a promenade that was sunken slightly into the floor, passing shadowy figures seated at dimly lit bars. A man in a top hat sipped a margarita from a wide-brimmed chalice. A woman with sculpted hair and a gossamer frock smoked vapor from a hookah, filling the air with smoky tendrils.

The inspector turned off the promenade into a low-roofed

arcade that was cordoned by barricade tape. At the end of the lobby, a woman sat at a desk that flanked a stately portal. Several police officers sat half-asleep in the corner. Inspector Sondworth announced his arrival to the secretary and signed the guest list, then beckoned for them to sit on one of several couches buttressing the walls. They sat and examined their surroundings. Crescent-shaped lights resembling the moon adorned the walls, shining with a haunting glow. The entire venue, even the office, was basked in eternal twilight.

Presently, the portal opened and a police officer invited them inside. They gathered around a long table with a blanket over it. The officer removed the blanket, revealing the body of the victim. It was a young woman, dressed in sanguine leotards and a black vest over a collared red jersey and black ribbon tie. She wore a sleek black com-visor over her eyes. Above the visor, her curly black hair hung disheveled over her expressionless face. It was not clear whether her pallid complexion was natural or the result of postmortem squalor.

"She's dead," Trep asserted.

"Shouldn't we establish that she was in fact alive?" asked Empeirikos.

The inspector donned a pair of nitrile gloves and reached into the woman's pockets to procure her wallet. He examined her identification.

"Oh, she was alive," he asserted. "Dead people don't have driver's licenses. Says here her name was Kramer Sullivan, only twenty-six years old."

Link was nonplussed.

"Kramer," he muttered, "isn't that a man's name?"

"I guess we'll find out soon enough," said Trep. The inspector was removing the victim's clothing.

"Have to look for signs of trauma," the inspector explained.

In a matter of minutes, the victim lay naked on the table. Her skin was wan from cessation of circulation.

"No signs of injury," stated the inspector.

He prodded her abdomen and neck, then briefly turned her sideways to examine her back. He returned her to lying supine and covered her with the blanket. He fetched his briefcase and opened it on a nearby desk, procuring a small syringe. He poked her arm with the needle, drawing a small sample of blood. He sealed the syringe in a small plastic bag and returned it to the briefcase.

"I'll have to bring this to the lab," he said. "This is our last chance to examine the body before it's transported to the examiner's office for the autopsy. Is there anything else that we should do?"

He began to gather his belongings.

Empeirikos was examining her clothing, which was lying on the floor.

"May I?" he asked the inspector, gesturing toward her vest pockets.

The inspector thought for a moment.

"Well," he decided at last, "since you have no DNA, you can't contaminate the evidence, so I suppose I'll allow you the luxury."

"Thank you," Empeirikos replied. He examined her vest pockets gingerly, extracting several items. He held them up one by one for their inspection. First, he presented a pack of cigarettes.

"Camels," said the inspector, reading the name off the package. "She liked the flavor of menthol. A woman after my own heart."

"She won't be smoking those anymore," observed Link.

Next, a cigarette lighter. Empeirikos placed it on the floor next to the cigarettes. Then, a small pill box. Empeirikos opened it cautiously, removing a small packet of pills. He read the label out loud.

"*Virtual tablets*," he recited, then he listed the label above each pill. "*Chapter one, chapter two, chapter three, chapter four…* up to twenty."

"Books in a pill?" asked Trep.

"The first two pills are gone," stated Empeirikos. "She was on chapter three."

"Timed release of text-encoding neurotransmitters," mused the inspector. "I've heard of it but have never seen it. Some sort of hallucinogen. It's illegal."

"Is it dangerous?" Trep asked.

"Don't know," replied the inspector. "I suppose overdose is a possibility. I'll have to take those pills to the lab as well."

He extended his hand with agitation, as if it were almost too much trouble. Empeirikos proffered the tablets. The inspector accepted the packet and placed it in his briefcase.

"You should take the cigarettes, as well," said Empeirikos. "Narcotics are frequently disguised as cigarettes."

"Yes…I was already aware of that," murmured the inspector. "I was just ruminating on the possibility that the victim was carrying laced cigarettes."

Sure you were, thought Trep. The inspector seemed to be suffering from a lack of originality.

Empeirikos handed the package of cigarettes to the inspector, who placed it in his briefcase.

"We might also look for the dealer," Empeirikos pointed out.

"Of course," said the inspector. "Why don't the three of you snoop around for the dealer while I run these samples over to the lab? Maybe you could pretend to, you know, be looking for some books to read…"

"Not a very good pickup line," stated Link. "I think we better look for a café rather than a bar."

"Oh, they have a great Thai bar here," responded the inspector. "Best coffee you ever had. However, with virtual pills, you read the book with your eyes closed. They might even mix those pills with alcohol."

They followed the inspector into the lobby. The police officer emerged with them, closing the door behind them.

"Where's Empeirikos?" asked Trep. The automaton was not in the lobby.

Link reopened the door and faked a British accent; *"Oh, Empeirikos, wherefore art thou?"*

The robot hurried through the open door and quickly shut it.

"Sorry," he apologized.

"What was the problem?" asked Link.

"I seem to have gotten lost," replied Empeirikos. Trep and Link were skeptical but did not mention it. They returned to the promenade.

"You'll meet me back here early tomorrow evening," huffed the inspector, nodding them goodbye. He turned and disappeared down the pathway, briefcase in one hand and umbrella in the other.

Trep and Link bought dinner at a nearby restaurant, then returned to their apartments. Trep returned Empeirikos to the office and called it a night.

As Trep slept, he was haunted by visions of the girl's corpse reposed on a wheeled gurney. The floor began to tilt and the gurney rolled slowly toward a full-length mirror against the wall. Before it shattered the mirror, Trep ran to save it and alter its path. But the gurney instead crashed with a loud thud against the wall, bouncing back into Trep's hands. The floor began to tilt in the other direction and now the gurney threatened to topple Trep unless he heaved against it with all his might. Trep mustered his strength and counteracted the gurney's momentum. The gurney abruptly launched into the air and floated to the ceiling, lingering there and bouncing slowly off the walls.

Trep awoke in a cold sweat, staring at the ceiling. He glanced at the clock...only four o'clock in the morning. He strolled to the kitchen for a glass of water, then returned to bed, but he could not sleep another wink. He arose reluctantly two hours later at the first hint of dawn, then prepared anxiously for the coming day. He called in sick at work and requested a week off, then texted Link to ask that he pick up Empeirikos from the office. Trep outfitted himself in semi-formal nightclub attire, then took the first pod to the club.

Chapter 17

They convened in front of the arcade, but the inspector had not yet arrived. For the first time, Trep and Link began to survey their surroundings. The nightclub appeared as a luminescent city enveloped in darkness. Every bar glowed neon blue or yellow. Several enclosures appeared to be restaurants or amusement centers.

But strangest of all was the absence of a ceiling. The purported "renovation" of the hotel appeared to have involved removing all of the upper level floors.

Empeirikos craned his neck back, staring straight up into the darkness.

"Correct me if I'm wrong," he said, "but there appears to be a lounge floating in mid-air."

Trep and Link followed Empeirikos's gaze toward a dimly lit cluster of objects hanging in the distance overhead. It was hard to tell, but they appeared to be slowly travelling circuitously. Trep attempted to discern their nature and found that they vaguely resembled furniture. Silhouetted figures seemed to occupy the furniture.

"How did they get up there?" asked Link.

"I don't see any elevators," observed Trep.

Empeirikos was fidgeting with his calculator umbrella. He

opened it and held it aloft.

"What do you propose to do," asked Link, "fly like Mary Poppins?"

"Let's find out," replied Empeirikos. "Perhaps this floor is supplied with a standard level of gravity, and the antigravity only circulates throughout the intermediate regions."

Empeirikos held his umbrella in two hands like a golf club, taking several practice swings, then finally released his grip and flung it into the air. Trep and Link watched as the umbrella ascended gradually like a balloon. Straight as an arrow, it vaulted toward the faintly glowing lounge, soon disappearing from sight.

Moments later, it reappeared as a dark circle against the dim blue glow of the lounge. Several seated figures noticed it. One of them grabbed it as it hovered near them. The others leaned over to peer down at Trep, Link, and Empeirikos. The receiver of the umbrella now folded it back into closed position, aimed it like a projectile, and hurled it back toward the ground floor.

Trep and Link backed up several steps in order to dodge the umbrella. Empeirikos held his hands in the air to catch it. Presently, the umbrella appeared, lumbering slowly toward them. Empeirikos yanked it out of the air and reopened it, inspecting it for damage. Satisfied, he closed it and returned it to a holster on his belt.

"I suggest we imitate the umbrella," stated Link.

"We may be able to reach the upper regions by jumping from a roof top," stated Empeirikos. Trep and Link agreed.

They explored the nearby architecture for an accessible roof top or jumping platform. An unlit enclosure was flanked by a narrow ramp with railing. The ramp appeared to lead to the roof. It was slightly wider than a rain gutter.

"You first," Trep told Link.

The heavyset man eyed the ramp suspiciously, then grabbed the railing with two hands and slowly pulled himself upward one step at a time. Trep waited his turn and then followed, with Empeirikos ascending last.

Momentarily, the three of them convened on the roof top. Link perched on the edge and gazed into the abyss.

"Jump!" said Trep.

"*Oh, cruel world!*" Link moaned.

"Mr. Link, please don't jump!" Empeirikos admonished. "I suggest we instead perform test jumps from the center of the roof."

Empeirikos demonstrated by bending his legs and hopping lightly into the air. Not surprisingly, he reached a much higher altitude than would have been expected.

The three of them practiced for several minutes, resembling a pack of disoriented kangaroos jumping in circles, or a dance troupe that was mildly retarded. At last, when they had gained enough confidence, each of them started from one edge of the roof and ran toward the other side, bounding into the air.

Trep felt as though the elastic threads of a spider web clung to his feet as he slowly broke free of gravity. He began to slowly ascend without losing speed. He glanced around and saw that the others were hovering nearby. Empeirikos held himself as stiff as a statue to remain aerodynamic. Link, however, was flailing his arms and kicking his legs desperately as if attempting to return to the ground.

"What's wrong?" asked Trep.

"We forgot to aim," replied Link. "Look where the lounge is."

Link pointed his left arm above his head in the direction of the floating lounge.

"Now look where we're going," he said.

Trep swiveled his head back and forth between their present trajectory and the lounge. It looked as though they had miscalculated and would miss the lounge by a long shot, plunging instead into total darkness. Trep began to flap his arms and legs just as Link was doing in an attempt to alter their course. He imagined that he looked about as graceful as an ostrich. Empeirikos, however, remained steadfast in the same posture and regarded their gyrations with curiosity.

"Have no fear," Empeirikos enjoined them. "This edifice must have walls. We will soon collide with one of them. When we do, we must deflect from the wall and aim for the lounge."

Soon enough, a looming barrier was visible through the darkness, and they were rapidly approaching it. They braced for impact and planned their reorientation. Trep held a leg and arm out in front of him, unsure of its proximity. When his foot made contact with a solid surface, he did his best imitation of Spiderman, scaling up the wall and then kicking off toward the floating lounge.

As they traveled steadily along their new course, the lounge gradually increased in size. Trep could discern the faces of the occupants and the glassware behind the counters. The lounge was an island of plush cushions straddling a bar that glowed dimly with blue neon lights. The light was refracted subtly by the wine glasses and beer flasks.

Trep surveyed the occupants of the lounge. A lithe red-haired woman was reposing on a futon. Several young video-junkies, gathered at a table, were glued to their com visors, playing video games. At the bar, a burly man in a studded leather vest and boots smoked from a hookah. Several men across the bar sipped from wide-brimmed margarita cups while chatting up the barmaid, a tattoo-streaked woman with a shock of unruly black hair. She watched their arrival with mild curiosity.

As they approached the lounge, they felt the tug of its artificial gravitational field. They collided with an outer perimeter of unoccupied cubical cushions that were anchored to an invisible platform. Though they did not appear to be resting on a floor, Trep quickly ascertained that the floor was made from thick transparent plexiglass intersected with what may have been gravity tubes. As they entered the lounge, a subtle sense of gravity was restored.

They found themselves gathered on a set of plush chairs near the tall red-haired woman, who seemed lost in reverie. As Trep sat next to her, she barely acknowledged his presence. Trep was eager to help Empeirikos locate the dealer of the virtual tablets. He imagined that the woman might be in the process of hallucinating on virtual supplements. He glanced at the others, looking for a signal, and they seemed to wordlessly agree that Trep should initiate the encounter.

"Doing some pleasure reading?" Trep inquired.

The woman opened her eyes and examined Trep.

"I'm just communing with my spiritual advisor," she replied.

Trep had heard of a spiritual advisor before but had typically associated the phrase with a spiritual medium or guru. Yet there was no one else in the vicinity who could have filled the role. It was possible that the woman was delusional.

Empeirikos joined in.

"Your advisor appears to be incorporeal," he observed.

She nodded in affirmation.

"Do they have much to say?" asked Trep.

The woman shook her head.

"No," she muttered, "they never speak. They just offer emotional support."

"Not much of an advisor, if you ask me," stated Trep.

"That's a very masculine attitude," she chastised. "Women are quite satisfied with emotional support. We need it more than men do."

"What does your spiritual advisor look like?" asked Empeirikos innocently.

The woman laughed.

"You can't really see him," she explained. "He's more of a spiritual blob. He just occupies some sort of empty space in my head."

Trep leaned back in his chair.

"Well," he mused, "we're looking to get our hands on something solid, maybe some vitamins or some reading material."

The woman stood and regarded them disdainfully.

"You mean *virtabs*?" she asked.

Link covered his mouth and spoke in a hushed tone.

"*Pills*," he murmured, "we're looking for pills."

"Well, sounds to me like you want virtabs," she continued. "It's the most popular new drug."

"When could we get some?" Trep asked.

"Maybe some other time," she said. "Not now. You interrupted my astral session."

She turned away from them and joined the booted man at the bar, who glanced briefly in their direction and proceeded to buy her a drink.

Trep sank deflated into the lounge chair, but Link and

Empeirikos became quite animated.

"Mr. Sportly," said Empeirikos, "she was well aware of what you were referring to."

"Yes," Link agreed, "she knows where to get virtual tablets. But she was very unreceptive."

"Well," said Trep, "now we know who to talk to. We just have to wait for her mood to lighten. But what are we going to do until then?"

"I have a suggestion," said Empeirikos. He reached into his jacket and procured a com visor. He waved his fingers over the lens and watched it light up, then tried it on and manipulated the organic light-emitting diode screen by tracing his fingers on the outer surface.

"Is that what I think it is?" asked Link.

"The dead woman's com visor?" asked Trep. "Is that what you were doing back at the office when you said you got lost?"

"Yes," Empeirikos affirmed. "I waited for you to leave and then pocketed her visor. It should be interesting to look through her contacts list."

He handed the com visor to Trep, who donned it and raised his fingers to the lens. The visor had already been activated and had turned from transparent to opaque. On the interior screen was the virtual desktop of the victim. Her profile data occupied the center of the screen, with a faceless avatar in a collared negligee and beaded necklace. The avatar was framed by an intricate pattern ornately scrawled behind the visage. Below the avatar was her name, *Kramer*, etched in bold letters. A postal truck drove in circles in one upper corner, the icon for the email client.

Several app icons also occupied the periphery. One of them, a smiling snake, drew Trep's attention. Every few seconds, the

137

snake writhed conspicuously and stuck out its tongue. Below the snake were the words *Viper visor*. Trep raised his fingers to the exterior of the lens. Simulated fingerprints tracked his finger movements across the internal screen. He navigated to the snake icon and tapped on it.

The snake expanded, then the screen changed to a panoramic jungle view. It was a video game. The dense forest was filled with shadows cast by a web of branches. Sunlight shone irregularly through the canopy above. In one lit region, a tall snake was raised halfway off the ground and was approaching him. Trep looked around for some sort of weapon. As he turned his head, the panoramic view swiveled. He could turn but could not move forward. He moved his head the other way, noticing that the snake was nearly upon him.

At last, he found a sword propped against a tree. He traced his fingers onto the sword, prompting his character to acquire the sword and wield it. But as he turned back to the snake, intending to swing at its head, the snake was not there. He cast his gaze downward, only to view the coils of the serpent constricting his legs and ascending swiftly up his torso. He saw the snake's head emerge from one side of the screen and disappear around the other as it encircled him. Soon, the serpent filled the entire screen and the view collapsed back to the desktop. The desktop was the same as before, but Trep now had the impression that the snake icon mocked him as it flickered its tongue.

Trep scowled and tapped the arm of the visor to deactivate it. He yanked the visor off his face and threw it back to Empeirikos.

Trep noticed that a newcomer had joined them. It was the

booted man from the bar. He was smiling at Trep. For the first time, Trep was able to discern the features on the man's leather vest. It was studded, to be sure, but the metal studs were much more prominent than those of a typical vest. In fact, they were not studs at all, but metal spikes. The spikes were shorter than a porcupine's quills, more akin to the thorns of a puffer fish.

Trep felt an odd sense of unreality, but before he had a chance to inquire about the unusual vest, the man smiled and extended his hand. They shook hands and Trep winced as the man's grip tightened.

"I hear you're looking for some reading material?" grunted the man.

"Why, yes," replied Trep. "Yes, we are."

"Quite right," said Empeirikos. "We would like to buy some materials from you."

"Any particular titles that you were looking for?" the man asked.

"No," Link responded. "But we're interested in new materials, like maybe virtual books."

"I can get you the latest virtabs," the man affirmed, "but it's not cheap. How much have you got?"

Empeirikos waved his Omega Entrepreneur card, but the man shook his head.

"Cash only," he insisted.

Trep and Link pulled out their wallets and consolidated their assets. Together, they had a total of two-hundred and twenty dollars. They displayed their savings to the drug dealer.

"Well, that's not much," the man scolded them. "Best I can give you is a collection of short stories."

He pulled out a sheaf of pill packets and leafed through them until locating a particularly small packet. He withdrew it and returned the others to his vest pocket. He handed it to Trep but then yanked it from his grasp.

"Pay up," he huffed.

Link handed over his hundred dollars, but Trep hesitated.

"Fork it over!" the man barked. He proffered his empty hand.

Trep relented and forfeited his last dollar to the drug dealer. In return, the man bestowed on them a packet of tiny pills.

"And to do those right," he added, "you ingest them with coffee. This one's on me."

He walked to the bar and momentarily returned with a tray of coffee cups, one for each of them.

"Next time you're in the market for virtabs," he said, "just ask for *the Aussie*, that's me."

He walked away, leaving the subject of his odd attire unexplained. He reassumed his seat next to the tall red-haired woman, who was once again languishing as if hypnotized.

Trep examined the packet of pills. There were only ten of them, and they had no chapter labels. In fact, there was nothing to identify them as virtual pills.

"I guess that's it," Trep commented. "We found the dealer. He may or may not be the killer. Now we just have to wait until the inspector returns."

They sipped their coffees and peered over the edge of the lounge at the ground floor. Trep expected that, when the inspector returned, he would stand outside the office looking for them. But there was no sign of him.

"I'm flat broke," Link sobbed. "I can't even order a sandwich." He sipped his coffee wistfully.

They leaned back in their seats and fidgeted for several minutes. Trep played nervously with the pill packet, rolling it around in his hands and bending it back and forth. He eyed the pills. They were small, pink, and ellipsoid. He examined the back side of the packet and observed that the pills could be removed by pushing them through the bottom wrapping.

"I can't take this anymore," Trep lamented. "I'm trying a virtual tablet."

He popped the first pill through the bottom wrapping and dropped it into his coffee, promptly swallowing it. The pill lent an acidulous, metallic flavor to his brew.

"Anyone else?" Trep asked, presenting the pill packet.

Link consented and received the second pill. They looked at Empeirikos, who folded his arms as if to say, *"I'm a robot, remember?"* Link dropped his tablet into his coffee and quickly guzzled it, wiping his mouth on the back of his hand.

Trep and Link settled back and awaited the effect of the tablets. Shortly, Trep felt himself fading into a hallucination. Although the outer world dimmed, he felt an inward alertness. His attention began to focus on a hovering set of words that seemed to rise to the forefront of his awareness. He was able to focus them or unfocus them at will. He aimed his intent at the first paragraph and began to read.

Chapter 18

Xyproliraxiom was an alien with an appointment to keep. As the new ambassador to the Nebulon Void, he was tasked with embarking on the great journey to the Void worlds for trade negotiations. As much as Xyproliraxiom adored his home world of Humidor, he was anxious for a change of scene.

Humidor was one of several moons orbiting the gas giant Zeppelin. Its orbit was outside of the planetary ring system, making for beautiful skyscapes both day and night. The moonlets of the ring cut through the visible sky like a tilted horizon, with the outer arms reflecting sunlight even in the depths of night when Zeppelin grew dim.

Indeed, his home world of Humidor was beautiful. As Xyproliraxiom boarded his exclusive government spaceship, he wondered what alien landscapes would greet him on the Void world of Narganla. It would be a long voyage, and Xyproliraxiom had stocked the ship's theater with episodes from much lauded dramas and documentaries.

As the boarding portal shut with a resounding flush of air, Xyproliraxiom approached the control panel. He waved his hand over the dashboard, prompting the viewport on the wall to light up. The skies of Humidor were tranquil and inviting. He touched the launch button to initiate liftoff, then watched as Humidor dwindled until its entire circumference was contained within the viewport.

At that point, to his surprise, the spaceship gradually slowed and entered orbit. Xyproliraxiom had not anticipated a two-stage liftoff. However, he assumed that the onboard computer was simply determining the appropriate trajectory. He retreated into his private quarters and programmed the stasis vault to awaken him the next morning. He shut his eyes and dreamt of twinkling satellites.

The next morning, he arose and slid on his casual garments. He emerged from his private quarters and approached the control panel. Waving his hand over the dashboard, he anticipated that the navigation window would show a view of deep space. But to his surprise, a shining planet occupied its center.

Had he arrived? The journey had been expected to be swift. He admired the oceans and continents of Narganla in the viewport. So very much like his home world of Humidor. In fact, Xyproliraxiom soon convinced himself that it *was* Humidor that he was beholding.

The two-stage liftoff must have been set to manual. A simple oversight in the launch configuration. All Xyproliraxiom needed to do was touch the launch button again. His finger made contact with the launch symbol and he heard the engines begin to hum. Satisfied, he retreated to his theatre for a relaxing afternoon of Humidorian drama.

He settled into his plush viewing seat, a veritable throne. He clapped his hands to activate the *intellihost*, whose silhouette appeared on the screen. He had stocked the computer vaults with tales from Humidorian history. As an ambassador, he felt it was his obligation. But rather than select what he deemed the most important folk tale, he deferred that task to the virtual host.

"An ancient tale from the annals of Humidorian legend," he requested. "Surprise me."

He knew that the virtual host was trained to evaluate quality with high precision, and would not disappoint him. He sat back and awaited his first onboard history lesson.

He sipped the nectars of exotic fruits as he marveled at the exploits of the legendary heroes of Humidor. When the episode was finished, he again retired to his quarters and programmed the automated scheduler. He drifted off into sleep and dreamt of the rivalries of ancient kings.

The next morning, he awoke and garbed himself in a light robe. He trekked down the corridor to the control room and stood before the dashboard. Waving his hand across the panel, he regarded the navigation window hopefully, but was again dismayed by the same familiar scene.

Xyproliraxiom bit his lip angrily. He paced the floor of the control room, searching his memory for the error in his procedures. Perhaps the launch button was a full-featured touchscreen interface responding to multiple touch gestures. He just needed to find the right one.

He extended his hand toward the launch button, but this time instead of simply touching it, he ventured a drag gesture, swiping to the right as if to say *keep going*. He felt the engines begin to throb and was hopeful that he had deduced the correct gesture. He retreated to his theater and consumed further episodes of Humidorian legend. That night, he dreamt of rescuing princesses from dragons.

But the next day, the ship still had not left orbit. Fuming, he stomped through the control room, scheming desperately for innovative touch gestures. The button was round. Perhaps it was a knob. Rather than touching or pressing it, he pinched it between his fingers, then twisted it to the right. He felt the button rotate compliantly with very little resistance. The engines throbbed and buzzed, and Xyproliraxiom retired to his private quarters, dreaming of drunken brawls and broken bottles.

But the next day, the spaceship still had not left orbit. In fact, it had begun to spin on its own axis, an apparent side effect of rotating the launch button. Xyproliraxiom stared at the navigation window as his home world rotated into view, then out of view, then into view again.

Xyproliraxiom was forlorn. He somberly exited the control room. He had to search the memory vaults for new information. He sat in his theater and played the onboard instruction manuals, but the manuals were outdated, with only pictorial explanations. They seemed to depict a man standing before the control panel and flinging his hand toward it, accompanied by gesture lines that could have indicated motion, but could equally well have signified speech.

Xyproliraxiom returned to the control room and flung his hand toward the launch button, commanding it to obey him, but the engines did not respond. He next attempted to speak to the control panel.

"I am ambassador Xyproliraxiom of the Sovereignty of Humidor," he spoke. "Transport me now to the Void world of Narganla."

But the engines did not respond. He jeered at the control panel, then furiously paced the control room. He shook his fist at the navigation window. He thrashed against the walls.

Surprisingly, as he lashed out and struck the wall, his fist kept going as if the wall was not there. He next observed that it wasn't. A thin section of the wall had disappeared, to be replaced by a portal into a long corridor.

Flummoxed, he traversed the tunnel and emerged into a new control room identical to the first. At its center stood another control panel. On the wall was the outline of another navigation window.

Anxiously, he passed his hand over the dashboard and was pleased to see it light up with familiar logograms. The large launch button figured prominently in the tool panel.

Tremulously, he reached for the launch button. The viewport lit up on the wall. What gesture should he attempt on the launch panel? A right drag? A spin gesture? He opted to lightly make contact using the tips of his fingers.

The engines throbbed and the ship buzzed. Then, to his disbelief, the spaceship lurched into motion. He watched as his home world of Humidor shrunk from view. Soon, only the two giant suns of his planetary system figured in the viewport window.

The spaceship was moving at last. Xyproliraxiom allowed himself to relax. He retired to his theater for an afternoon of celebration. He was regaled by tales of battles and alliances, war declarations, and peace treaties. He sipped on the finest fermented fruits and soon was giddy with intoxication. That night, he dreamt of alien landscapes and welcoming committees that showered him with the finest splendors.

The next day, he arose and hurried to the control room. He activated the control panel to light the navigation window and was rewarded with a panoramic view of deep space. Yet, two suns burned in the distance, suggesting that Xyproliraxiom still had not exited his own solar system.

Xyproliraxiom fumed and struck the walls with his fists until the hidden portal reopened. He returned to the duplicate control room and lit the control panel. The panel buttons mocked him with their pleasantly glowing aura, informing him that no progress would be gained from them today.

Xyproliraxiom flailed against the walls, opening yet another hidden panel. He followed the hallway into yet another control room where he echoed the well-rehearsed motions. Once more, he felt the spaceship lurch forward and saw his star system dwindle in the viewport.

He again retired to his theater, hopeful that he had at last happened upon a utilitarian procedure. Perhaps he would unveil new control rooms, each one executing a new segment of his journey, until at last he reached his destination.

He consoled himself with the thought that, by the time he returned to his home world, he would at least have gained expertise on Humidorian history. He watched several episodes, and, later that night, dreamt of receiving the most prestigious accolades of Humidorian scholarship.

But the next day, the twin suns of his home system shone only slightly dimmer than before. At this rate, he would be long dead before ever reaching Narganla. Each day he beat against the walls and was rewarded with a new control room, but each new control panel was as ineffective as the last.

Soon, he was visited by macabre nightmares of grim conspiracies. His detractors had sabotaged his ship, disabling the propulsion systems and aiming the trajectory into empty space. His worst adversary had usurped his dominion. And even as he drifted into the furthest reaches of the abyss, his love interests were being propositioned and courted by his most bitter rivals.

At last, tiring of the litany of reruns in his theater, he began to act out the episodes as he paced the halls. He memorized the eloquent speeches of King Glore. He courted the imaginary specter of the fair Empress Airshine. He fabricated new episodes, overthrowing the establishment, crowning himself King.

One day, he was enthralled by a particularly vivid hallucination. He imagined that he was King Glore himself, while the control panel played the part of an imposter who had fettered him and expropriated his throne. Possessed with vehement malice, he had at last freed himself from his shackles, and now faced his opponent in full view of the entire royal court.

Enraged with self-righteousness, he accused his tormenter and revealed his treachery. He pointed a condemning finger at the control panel, compelling the imposter to deference.

"O foolish traitor," he cried, "that would usurp the thrown and defile the sacred traditions! The end has arrived for your unjust reign!"

He railed against his tormenter at the top of his lungs.

"I cast you out!" he screamed. "By the power of all that is right, I banish your deceiving countenance once and for all!"

He lashed out his arm and struck his fist against the control panel with all his might. The buttons flashed in anguish. The engines vibrated in retaliation.

Though his strength was expended, he was nevertheless shocked to find himself thrown to the floor. He heard the engines rumbling loudly and felt a penetrating tremor reverberate through the hull. The ship had launched into warp drive.

Incredulous, he arose and beheld the familiar blur of stars

on the navigation window that signified hyperspace. He raised his arms and cheered like a man beyond desperation. He hugged the control panel. He danced and cavorted. He sang joyous hymns of exaltation.

He broke out his finest alcohols and became intoxicated on sweet liqueur. He passed out in his theater and slept lightly, forgetting his dreams. He awoke and returned to the control room to check the viewport. The ship was still in transit.

He returned to his private quarters and attempted to sleep deeply. He awoke and showered, ashamed of his behavior. He trimmed his bedraggled beard and attired himself in his finest garb. Again, he reported to the control room, only to find that the ship was still in motion, lost in the depths of space.

Had he simply replaced one predicament with another? Now, rather than finding a way to launch the ship, he was tasked with landing it. But he had buried his despair in the past. He had resolved himself to find the means to overcome any problem. Somehow, he knew, he would reach a solution.

Much later, his ship broke through the clouds on a distant planet. It was a proud sight, embellished with the flashing lights of the navigation system. The engines were gradually decelerating and ringing out a steadfast electric drone.

A large welcoming crowd had gathered at the reception dock below. Xyproliraxiom the Stout, first ambassador from Humidor, had finally touched down on Narganla. The crowd waved flags and cheered as the stately ship hovered over the reception dock, then slowly lowered itself onto the platform for a perfect landing.

The crowd became hushed as the engines revved down and the lights slowly dimmed. They gazed expectantly as the landing ramp extended. All eyes and ears were focused upon the widening aperture of the exit portal.

To their surprise, a faint, eerie sound echoed from the hollow of the spaceship. It was a voice, the voice of a man, sounding noble yet slightly beleaguered. The voice recited repeated phrases. The phrases echoed steadily out of the widening portal even as the engines revved down.

Soon, the amplitude of the voice overtook that of the fading engines, and all ears in the crowd strained to make out the words. They were surprised to hear the gentle, singsong voice of a man both weary and willing, who spoke, as if to a child:

"Nice spaceship...*pretty* spaceship..."

Chapter 19

The hallucination ended as abruptly as it had begun. Trep regained focus on the outside world, remembering what had happened. For a brief moment, he had identified with the alien and his dysfunctional spaceship. But now, once again, he was Trep Sportly, in the company of his friends Link and Empeirikos.

Link, however, was still lost in a virtual narrative. He stared ahead blankly as if contemplating suicide. His mouth hung slightly open as a puddle of drool began to collect near its left corner.

Empeirikos was still waiting patiently beside them, in sharp contrast to the character from the virtual narrative, who had gone mad from the isolation of the space voyage.

The robot was reexamining the victim's com visor. His fingers traced across the outer lens. Hearing Trep revive himself, Empeirikos tapped the arm of the visor, transitioning the opaque lens back to transparency.

"Ah, Mr. Sportly," Empeirikos said, "welcome back."

Link was awakening from his virtual nap. He yawned, stretching his arms, then rose and paced the floor. Proceeding to the periphery of the lounge, he peeked over the edge at the floor far below.

"Guys," he said, "someone's standing outside of the office. It looks like Inspector Sondworth is back."

A figure with an umbrella was standing on the promenade. He seemed resolved to wait there as long as necessary.

They gathered at the edge of the lounge and prepared to descend. Link jumped first, leaping joyfully as if off a diving board. However, unexpectedly, he promptly rose toward the ceiling.

"Mr. Link!" Empeirikos called to him. "The counterforce of gravity is not in effect here! You continue in uniform motion along your start vector."

Link flapped his arms and kicked his legs in a vain attempt to right his course. Instead, he rose steadily like a helium balloon, growing ever more distant.

"Just bounce back from the ceiling and meet us on the ground floor!" Trep shouted to Link as his friend disappeared into space.

Trep and Empeirikos sat at the edge of the lounge and slowly lowered themselves. They pushed off from the plexiglass floor in the direction of the promenade. Trep imagined himself landing with an elegant forward roll into a crouch that was balanced on his fist. Instead, he landed on his feet and fell promptly backward onto his bottom.

Empeirikos, in contrast, leaned forward slightly as he landed and transitioned smoothly into a relaxed gait, like a seasoned adept.

With no sign of Link, they returned to the office, where the inspector awaited them. He motioned to a security guard who had replaced the police officers. They convened in the privacy of the back room in the company of the victim's body. The security guard removed the sheet covering the victim, then exited the room.

"We found traces of the drug in her blood, not surprisingly," said the inspector. "That suggests that the cause of death was drug-related. What about you? Did you locate the drug dealer?"

"Yes, we did," stated Empeirikos. "Mr. Trep and Mr. Link had no reservations about sampling the merchandise. They have been happily hallucinating for the last hour."

"Well," said the inspector, shaking his head, "since one of our theories is that the victim died from an overdose, I don't recommend that you test the drugs on yourselves."

"It seemed perfectly harmless," Trep said. "But then again, we bought the cheap stuff. The high-end tablets might be more concentrated or have higher purity."

"Inspector," asked Empeirikos, "what is your next move? Do you plan to arrest the drug dealer?"

"I suppose so," the inspector replied, "although he's innocent until proven guilty. But at the very least, we must interrogate him."

They informed the inspector that the drug dealer appeared to be wearing armor. The inspector called for backup before attempting the arrest. They waited in the room for approximately half an hour. At last, a police officer strode through the door.

"Where's the victim?" he asked.

They gestured toward the body under the blanket. The officer glanced at the woman's face.

"But this victim is female," he objected.

"What were you expecting?" the inspector inquired.

"We received a call about a young man found floating dead near the ceiling," the officer informed them.

"Weren't you sent here for backup on an arrest?" the inspector asked.

The police officer shook his head.

"Oh no!" Trep moaned.

"Mr. Link!" exclaimed Empeirikos.

The four of them ran urgently out of the enclosure. They headed toward the roof which had become their launching platform. Climbing on, they catapulted themselves toward the ceiling with all of their might. Soon, they were passing the glowing blue lounge. The barmaid watched their progress distractedly as they floated onward toward the ceiling.

Before long, two figures came into view. One was Link, very much alive. Trep breathed a sigh of relief. Link was gesturing frantically toward the other figure.

It was the corpse of a bearded man with long black hair. He was dressed in a colorful Hawaiian shirt, loose-fitting faded bell bottom pants, and thick brown sandals. His mouth hung open as if he had screamed for help just before he died.

Link pointed to his com visor.

"I'm the one who called," he told the police officer. "I haven't touched the body."

They tried to examine the victim while still floating, but it was too arduous. Instead, the police officer held the body while they pushed off from the ceiling toward the floor. Upon landing, they carried the body back to the office.

They laid the man's body on a table next to the first victim. The inspector donned nitrile gloves and searched the man's pockets.

"No sign of virtual tablets," he said. He found the man's wallet and threw it to Empeirikos. He removed the man's clothes and inspected for trauma. He poked him with a syringe and sealed the blood sample, then draped the man's clothes over his body.

"No sign of trauma, either," he stated.

Empeirikos was flipping through the man's wallet.

"His name was Lancelet," he stated. He read from the man's identification.

"Lancelet Hepton, thirty-eight years old."

"Don't you mean *Lancelot*, as in *Sir Lancelot*?" asked Trep.

"No, it quite distinctly states '*Lance-let*'," Empeirikos explained.

"What kind of a name is that?" Link exclaimed. "I'm glad my parents didn't name me *Linklet*!"

Empeirikos removed the man's com visor. He flicked his fingers across the outer lens, prompting the interior screen to light up. He donned the visor and traced his fingertips across the glass for several minutes.

"Mr. Sportly," he said, "take a look."

He handed the com visor to Trep, who promptly tried it on.

The man's virtual desktop was a familiar sight. His profile occupied the foreground, with a faceless avatar centered over an ornately scrawled background pattern. The man's name, *Lancelet*, was etched below. App icons lined the periphery, but most of them were unfamiliar. A gargoyle grinned deviously. A stunt airplane trailed a plume of smoke. The familiar postal truck icon drove in circles in the upper corner.

Trep handed the com visor back to Empeirikos.

"Anything interesting?" asked the inspector.

"Nothing of significance," said Empeirikos.

"This changes our plans," stated Inspector Sondworth. "If Lancelet Hepton does not possess virtual tablets, then our lucky drug dealer is no longer a suspect. However, I'll take this blood sample back to the lab just in case."

"If the dealer didn't kill him," asked the officer, "then who did?"

"It seems relevant that the victim was found floating by the ceiling," observed Trep.

"I guess life on Earth didn't agree with him," said Link.

"Are you suggesting that antigravity may have adverse effects on human physiology?" asked Empeirikos.

"Yes, my thoughts exactly," the inspector quickly commented. "I was just thinking to myself that antigravity might have adverse effects on human physiology."

Trep fought back the urge to spit. It was apparently beneath the inspector's dignity to pay the robot a compliment.

"Here's a suggestion," said the inspector. "While I take this sample back to the lab, maybe you could question the owner of the nightclub. His name's Xanvier Reinhart. I'll make an appointment for you."

"What should we ask him?" said Empeirikos.

"Well, don't just question him," replied the inspector, "*interrogate* him. Accuse him of intentionally killing Kramer Sullivan and Lancelet Hepton."

Trep and Link balked at the suggestion, unable to disguise their disapproval.

"That's just standard procedure," the police officer commented. "We always try to make them sweat during an interrogation."

The inspector was talking on his com visor. Momentarily, he swiveled the visor onto his forehead and addressed them.

"Your appointment with Xanvier Reinhart is tomorrow at ten," he stated. "You'll find him in the western wing. Head back to the entrance and turn left instead of right. Proceed through the first door and tell the secretary that you have an appointment. Then, meet me here in the office early tomorrow evening. These lab tests will take some time."

The inspector grabbed his briefcase and took his leave of them. The police officer nodded goodbye as they exited the room.

Trep's stomach grumbled. He suggested that they find the nearest restaurant.

"But we're flat broke," Link pointed out.

Empeirikos proffered his Omega Entrepreneur card.

"Money is no object," he stated.

The three of them filtered out of the office and soon were seated at the bar of a dimly lit Thai restaurant. Trep ordered a plate of Pad Thai fajitas and a cup of hot tea. Link requested a stir fry soufflé and a glass of rice wine. Soon they were sating themselves on sumptuous Thai fusion. Empeirikos sat politely at their side.

* * *

The next morning, they reported to the office of Xanvier Reinhart, who greeted them warily. He was a distinguished gray-haired gentleman with a cropped beard. He wore a dark-striped flannel blazer with a raised lapel, matching trousers over brown suede penny-loafers, and a black bowtie.

They convened around a glass table decorated with fresh flowers. Mr. Reinhart was in the process of pruning the stems of the flowers with a small pocketknife. Trep observed that he was missing some fingers on his left hand, and thus held the pocketknife in his right while gripping the stems between two fingers and the thumb of his left. With one upward thrust,

157

he severed a stem and let it linger in his grip.

"Welcome, gentlemen," he greeted them. "Or should I say gentlemen and automatons?"

He nodded toward Empeirikos.

"Thank you for acknowledging me, Mr. Reinhart," stated Empeirikos, "but as you see I am fashioned after a human male, so the moniker of *gentleman* is quite acceptable."

"Very well, *gentlemen*," Mr. Reinhart responded. He desisted from pruning the flowers and set the pocketknife on the table in a slow, delicate gesture.

"Tell me," he asked, "what do you think of *Space on Earth*?"

"It's breathtaking," replied Empeirikos, "and those are not words that I use often."

Mr. Reinhart laughed appreciatively.

"You've done the impossible!" remarked Link.

"Well," Mr. Reinhart explained, "the effects have recently been demonstrated in the laboratory, but it's never been attempted on this scale."

"How does the antigravity work?" Trep asked.

"Anti-graviton particles," Mr. Reinhart elaborated. "We manipulate the gravitational field. The walls secrete anti-gravitons, which diffuse throughout the premises. In contrast, the floors radiate gravitons, forming local gravity wells that anchor guests to the floor."

Mr. Reinhart eyed them inquisitively.

"But what exactly is the purpose of your appointment?" he asked.

"This visit is in relation to the recent deaths at your venue," Link responded.

"We regret these tragic incidents," Mr. Reinhart commented. "Our hearts go out to the victims' families."

Empeirikos leaned forward in his chair.

"What would you say," he asked, "if we told you that the deaths were related to antigravity?"

Mr. Reinhart looked skeptical.

"Well," he rejoined, "antigravity is a new technology. We admit that it has some bugs in it. But we have stated openly from the start that antigravity may not be for everyone. After all, we have a disclaimer on the front door. Hence, every guest has been informed of and has implicitly consented to the risks, which legally absolves me of all guilt."

"Mr. Reinhart," Empeirikos riposted, "we have not yet touched on the issue of guilt or innocence. We have not accused *you* of anything. What leads you to assume that we're accusing *you* of deliberate homicide?"

Link gulped. Trep watched Mr. Reinhart's face intently. The change of subject had been unfair, but they now had an opportunity to study the suspect's reaction. Mr. Reinhart reflected and then continued.

"Deliberate homicide," he laughed, "that's ridiculous! I'm an *entrepreneur*. This nightclub is the first in a new line of fusion ventures. Soon, a host of prominent corporations will join the endeavor, from ocean exploration to cities on the moon. Several other antigravity ventures are already in planning around the world."

"What was your occupation prior to opening this night-club?" Empeirikos queried.

"I was in transportation," Mr. Reinhart replied. "Private jets."

"And did you leave your position voluntarily?" Empeirikos continued.

"Why, yes," Mr. Reinhart replied. "I retired to open this

nightclub."

"Have you ever lost a loved one in a plane crash?" Empeirikos inquired.

"Yes, a distant relative," Mr. Reinhart said. "What are you implying?"

"Perhaps," Empeirikos continued, "you founded this venture to gain revenge against your former employers."

"Not at all," Mr. Reinhart objected. "I was very happy there. But it was time to move on."

"And why was that?" Empeirikos prodded. "Did something change in your personal life?"

"I went through a divorce," Mr. Reinhart admitted, "but that had nothing to do with my decision."

Empeirikos raised his finger into the air triumphantly.

"Then I suggest," he asserted, "that the hollow space of this hotel represents the emptiness weighing upon your heart following your divorce!"

"Yes," Trep joined in, "you projected your anger onto the interior of this structure."

"Then, you plotted your revenge," Link added, "by inflicting antigravity on total strangers!"

Mr. Reinhart was defiant.

"This is just an amateurish attempt to tarnish my reputation," he lambasted. "Besides, there's something you don't know."

"And what is that?" asked Empeirikos.

"A threat letter," Mr. Reinhart replied somberly. He walked to his desk and slid the drawer open, withdrawing a sheaf of envelopes.

"Several of them, in fact."

He handed a letter to each of them. Trep opened the

envelope and removed a glistening postcard. It depicted a round-faced man with cropped, curly hair and pudgy cheeks. He sat alone at a table, puckering his lips to extinguish several candles on a tiny cupcake that sat before him. Unbeknownst to him, two onlookers wielding pies were approaching from behind, preparing to plaster him from either side with a deluge of lemon meringue.

"*Happy birthday!*" read the pink-lettered caption.

Trep flipped the card over.

"*Not!*" read a message scrawled in blue ink. "*Someone else will die unless you meet our demands. Your club will be permanently quarantined.*"

Trep read the message aloud for the others, to which they responded in kind.

"*Pay us one million dollars,*" read Empeirikos from his postcard, "*or it's the end of Space on Earth. Deposit the money in the following Swiss bank account...*It goes on to list a bank name and a routing number."

"*Next time, the evidence will point to you,*" read Link from another postcard. "*It will be the end of your priceless new venture unless you meet our demands.*"

"The evidence has grown progressively incriminating," explained Mr. Reinhart. "The first victim was carrying virtual tablets, suggesting drug overdose. But the second was not. And as they were found floating near the ceiling, it suggests that they died from an unknown toxic reaction to antigravitons."

"So it's extortion!" Link observed. "They're blackmailing you."

"Yes," Mr. Reinhart corroborated. "If another death occurs, and it's unrelated to drug overdose, I'm afraid we'll have to

161

close our doors for good."

"Why don't you just pay the money?" asked Link.

"I haven't got it," Mr. Reinhart protested. "At least, not in liquid assets. Believe me, I'm trying to raise the money now, but it will take time. That's no small sum."

Trep found Mr. Reinhart's excuse unconvincing. Surely, the man was a billionaire. He should have no trouble paying the extortionists' fee. Perhaps the threat letters were nothing more than a diversion.

"Mr. Reinhart, I have an Omega Entrepreneur card," suggested Empeirikos, "and would gladly offer it to pay your fee."

Mr. Reinhart shook his head.

"No, Empeirikos, I can't let you do that. I will deal with the consequences myself. Besides, the threat letters request a direct deposit."

"No worries, Mr. Reinhart," Link stated. "We'll get to the bottom of it."

"I'm sure you will," said Mr. Reinhart. "Now, if you'll excuse me."

He retrieved the postcards and held the door silently for them while they exited. They returned to the illusion of the nightclub, staring at the starlit ceiling while they gathered their thoughts.

Chapter 20

Discouraged, they sought out a new drinking venue at which to discuss the interview. They settled on a glowing red tavern with several vacant seats. Over cocktails, they reviewed the interrogation.

"Could the threat letters have been forged?" asked Empeirikos.

"If so, what would be his motive?" asked Trep.

"As a decoy," Empeirikos proposed, "to deflect blame from the antigravitons. After the first death, he may have forged the letters to save his club. Also, if the antigravitons were found to be responsible, it could be sufficient evidence for negligent manslaughter. Although it was unintentional, he could still go to jail."

"However," stated Link, "we have no evidence that antigravity caused their deaths. It may well have been an overdose from virtual tablets."

"But the second victim wasn't carrying virtabs," Trep objected.

"I guess we'll have to wait until the inspector returns," said Link.

Trep surveyed the rest of the clientele. Most of them were younger guests who huddled in groups at tables in the fringes, lost within their com visors. A few older couples sat at the bar. One of them was an elderly gentleman attired in a gray sport coat and black tie. He gazed across the bar at Empeirikos, regarding him with intense curiosity.

The man had not yet noticed Trep's stare. Trep took the opportunity to study the man's features. He looked vaguely familiar. Trep searched his memory and was surprised to conclude that the man was none other than Nate Locket, the philosopher and author of *Hidden Irrationality*.

"You're Nate Locket," Trep addressed him.

Mr. Locket smiled.

"You've uncovered my disguise," he stated.

"Nate Locket, no kidding!" Link exclaimed. "It's a pleasure to meet you."

"Mr. Locket," stated Empeirikos, "this is quite an honor."

Mr. Locket turned to Empeirikos.

"You're the robot from the comedy club," he said. "I read about you in the papers."

"Quite right," replied the robot. "Allow me to introduce myself. My name is Empeirikos."

"Delighted to meet you," Mr. Locket reciprocated. "And what brings a robot to an antigravity nightclub?"

"We're assisting a private investigator," Link informed him. "We're investigating a spate of recent deaths."

"So," Mr. Locket mused, "they've enlisted a robot now to solve their mysteries."

"Yes," said Trep. "Although we must surmount a high learning curve, we're expecting excellent progress in the long run."

"Mr. Locket," Empeirikos said, "perhaps you could help me with some linguistic issues. As you may have heard, I require a calculator to perform mathematical operations, and the essence of my functionality may quite succinctly be articulated as walking and talking. That is quite different from a layman's expectations, and as a result we have an ongoing debate among us. If a robot approximates human behavior, but does not have a compound skillset which demonstrates multiplicity, is it or is it not possible that they are still the Technoconvergence?"

Mr. Locket smiled at Empeirikos.

"A very astute question," he replied, "but a common misconception to be sure."

"Please elaborate," Empeirikos prodded him.

Mr. Locket leaned forward to rest on his elbows. He addressed the three of them together.

"The Technoconvergence," he said, "is often confused with a hypothetical event known as the *Singularity*. And although they share several features, they are not equivalent."

"What is the Singularity?" Trep asked.

"Perhaps these events are best defined through contrast," said Mr. Locket. "The Multiplicity is what most theorists believe is the current state of affairs, a period of technological diversification. But now, you have rightly asked whether the state of Technoconvergence has been attained. By standard definition, the Technoconvergence is the first occasion on which a robot is designed that fully simulates human behavior and intelligence. In contrast, the *Singularity* is the first occasion on which a robot or group of robots may be said to have far surpassed human intelligence."

"And what qualifies as surpassing human intelligence?" Link asked.

"That is precisely the point," Mr. Locket explained. "In

mathematics, a singularity is a value that is undefined for a particular function, and therefore unknowable. And indeed, since humans are limited by the extent of their own intelligence, we cannot really define what the nature of the Singularity may be."

Empeirikos straightened his posture, his confidence bolstered.

"This confirms what I have been saying all along!" he exclaimed. "A walking, talking robot is sufficient for the Technoconvergence, although not for the Singularity. The source of the objections has merely been a semantic ambiguity."

"Exactly," Mr. Locket affirmed. "They have been conflating the Technoconvergence with the Singularity."

"But the Technoconvergence is a necessary prerequisite for the Singularity," Trep observed.

"Yes, that's true" Mr. Locket agreed.

"So let me ask you, Mr. Locket," Empeirikos inquired, "would you agree that the Technoconvergence has now occurred?"

Mr. Locket nodded.

"Up until now," he said, "and even on reading the papers, I was skeptical. But now that I've met you, I have to agree."

"Thank you, Mr. Locket," Empeirikos replied. He then addressed Trep and Link indignantly.

"The two have you have teased me relentlessly," he scolded them. "But what do you think now?"

"Convergence, shmergence," Link quipped.

"Well, sure," said Trep defensively, "I wasn't denying the Technoconvergence. What I meant was just that the *Singularity* has yet to occur."

"That's quite beside the point," Empeirikos huffed.

"I agree with Empeirikos," Mr. Locket confided. "As humans, we have too much insecurity about technology."

"Thank you, Mr. Locket," said Empeirikos, "and let me compliment you on your recent book, *Hidden Irrationality*. Your theory on hidden dimensions is most intriguing."

"Do you really believe that the pyramids are evidence against Fermi's paradox, the notion that aliens should have visited Earth by now, yet haven't?" asked Link.

"I don't know," Mr. Locket responded, "but one shouldn't jump to conclusions based on a lack of evidence. For example, while Fermi's paradox seems to suggest that aliens may have advanced too far and destroyed themselves, it's equally likely that they did not advance fast enough to overcome challenges."

Trep was skeptical.

"That's a very counterintuitive proposition," he asserted.

"Perhaps so," said Mr. Locket, "but allow me to convince you. In the same way that two points are required to make a line, sometimes one philosophical dilemma may be resolved through another. People imagine that the Singularity could be a threat. In fact, it appears at first glance to be a possible explanation for Fermi's paradox. Perhaps it was precisely in that way that aliens advanced too far, hence their absence. But if so, the question then is not *where are all the aliens*, but rather *where are all the robots?*"

"Other than myself," said Empeirikos, "I have seen no others."

"Indeed," said Mr. Locket. "Then let me suggest that, if Fermi's paradox is to be believed, then robots are not likely to have been the explanation for alien extinctions. On the contrary, it may just as well be that the absence of aliens is explained by the absence of robots. None of the aliens developed spacefaring robots, and perforce none of them survived. At the very least, it suggests that the Singularity may not be hostile. Moreover, it may be necessary for our survival. Surprisingly, Fermi's paradox turns out to be a potential *justification* for the Singularity."

"And what of the rumors of your new book which proposes to explain the purpose of artificial intelligence?" Trep pried.

"Yes," Link added. "Ever since humans were found to have evolved from apes, there are those who view evolution as a cosmic joke. How would you convince detractors that the Singularity is not just another evolutionary insult to humanity?"

"I should not discuss my new book prematurely," said Mr. Locket, "but, in spite of myself, the alcohol seems to have loosened my tongue. So, I will allow myself to indulge your curiosity."

Mr. Locket stretched his arms, folded his hands, and cracked his knuckles while he contemplated his next words. Finally, he straightened his tie and addressed them.

"Indeed, if popular culture is to be believed, artificial intelligence is the next step in evolution, one that threatens to replace us. However, we must face the facts."

"And what facts are those?" Link asked.

"The fact is that natural human evolution is dead for all practical purposes. For billions of years, evolution was a slow process, awaiting the emergence of new genes. However, where once our evolution was natural, now evolution is expressed through technology. In the face of environmental challenges, we no longer wait for new genes to emerge. Instead, we react scientifically. In contemporary times, technology evolves in our stead. Technology is a shield which mitigates environmental challenges."

Mr. Locket regarded them intensely.

"And so, you see that artificial intelligence has indeed evolved for a purpose, but not to supersede humanity. Far from it. Indeed, the purpose of artificial intelligence is nothing less than to save the human race."

Mr. Locket stood and smiled at them.

"It's been a pleasure meeting you," he said. "I must excuse myself now as I have an appointment."

He deposited a large tip on the table.

"I hope we meet again," he said to Empeirikos.

"Likewise," the robot reciprocated.

They waved farewell to Mr. Locket. Trep and Link returned their attention to their cocktails. Link sipped pensively while Trep guzzled absently, twiddling his thumbs. The bartender approached them politely, noticing that Trep had finished his drink.

Trep fished around for his wallet. Now that they had run out of cash, they would have to resort to credit cards. He pondered his next order. With Nate Locket gone, the conversation had fizzled out.

Trep found his credit card but had to flip past his packet of virtabs while doing so. The tablets seemed to smile at him through their plastic encasements. He could continue down the path to inebriation or escape with random psychedelia. He glanced at his friend Link, who belched as he slurped his alcohol.

Without giving it a second thought, Trep ordered a coffee.

"I'm going to virtualize," he informed Link, displaying the packet of pills. He removed one through the back wrapping and dropped it into his coffee. He drank in the metallic flavor and awaited his next hallucination.

Chapter 21

On a faraway planet, robots had evolved from rocks. At first, they had been nothing more than subsurface silicon shells, a storage vessel for seedlings as well as nutrients to supply plants through the harsh winters when sunlight grew dim. But the shells had acquired mobility, burrowing through the soft soiled root system in search of more fertile ground. They sent up shoots like periscopes to probe for regions of brighter sunlight. Photons supplied the contractions of their silicon skeletons, and eventually voltaic cells evolved, generating sufficient energy for the entire shell to breach the surface. During the daytime, slowly in progressive steps, a radiation of foraging species evolved.

Rookie, a predatory robot, had camouflaged himself among boulders at the edge of the cliff. Through his photosensors, he tracked the diminutive rummaging droid far below. Inanimate materials were distinctly unsatisfying, and he had gone several days without a fresh meal. His anodes salivated as he greedily watched the droid crawl from rock to rock.

Stealthily, he scaled his way down the face of the rock wall. As his prey grew nearer, his reward networks became electrified with anticipation. Preparing to strike, he knelt into a crouch, then remained poised.

He raised his new weapon, a spiked projectile. He judged the distance, then hurled it at the droid, hoping to knock it off balance. When the projectile struck, he launched himself at the droid, pinning it to the ground. As its desperate actuators thrashed against the weight of his torso, he gripped its neck in his steely jaws, then closed them.

After its appendages grew limp, he devoured its still-warm corpse. Fresh compounds soon fed his galvanic cells. He dismantled its frame until he was sated, then retreated into the shadows to await the nightfall. In the morning, he would regurgitate its remains, stripped free of electron donors.

In time, the arrival of the Crusher would cleanse the terrain of detritus. Scouring the rocks for debris, its probing tentacles gathered all remains into its gullet. No one knew from where the massive leviathan had originated. Like some scavenger from the stars, at some point in their evolution, it had alighted and commenced recycling their dead. It surveilled their graveyards like a mausoleum on wheels.

But the Crusher was no impartial bystander. To the contrary, it had accelerated their evolution. With each regurgitation from its gut, a new life form was instigated. Each carcass was randomized and returned to the wastelands to hunt again with fresh attributes.

Prior to its arrival, they had evolved through mating. Any two machines had the option of joining forces by means of a supple pseudopod. They stood to increase their battle yield and survival expectancy. If they died without being consumed, they were replanted into the earth by natural forces, germinating a new silicon shell that would sprout again by the light of the sun, a hybrid of its ancestors.

But the mating system did not incorporate randomization

to any appreciable extent. As if in anticipation of impending challenges, the Crusher now drove them forward through eons of potential development with each shuffle of their genes. Yet it only consumed individuals, leaving deceased mating pairs to replant themselves and persist their attributes.

Rookie awoke the next morning to the sounds of small exotherms emerging through the soil. His hunger allayed, he regurgitated the droid's parched bones. Then, he returned to the scattered rubble to collect his projectile. Heavier than silicon, it had been forged in a kiln in the dungeon of the Alchemists. Rookie had traded them a sack of fish jaws and bird wings to adorn their walls, the spoils of nearly a year of foraging.

He hefted the weapon over his shoulder using a sling he had fashioned from durable plant fiber. In the distance, he heard the ominous grind of the Crusher's enormous treads against the rock. Knowing that the Crusher was drawn to battlefields, Rookie followed its unmistakable signature. If he was fleet of foot, he would pillage weapons from the dead before their consumption by the leviathan.

Rookie hiked at a steady pace along the arid sands of the dried riverbed. The sun beat against his armored exoskeleton, augmenting the rate of oxidation within his galvanic cells. He trudged forward, oblivious to the looming clouds on the horizon. If he did not change course, storms may overtake him, and it would be several days before he would emerge from the litany of clouds. But the promise of reward compelled him, and he staunchly persevered.

Rounding a corner, he beheld a fork in the chasm, one of which was occupied by a party of cyber zombies. He retreated at once, escaping notice, then warily began to spy on them.

They had slain a large centipod and were in the process of dismembering it.

Evolution had been kind to the cyber zombies. They were widely feared for their swollen jaws, which could rend limb from limb. Their ravenous gorges could devour entire herds of small foragers in one gulp. Content with their innate gifts, they eschewed weapons in favor of their own treacherous fangs.

Rookie hefted his weapon into his hand, assessing its potency. There were four zombies, each preoccupied with ingestion of a mouthful of centipod appendages. He could surprise them while they feasted, hurling his projectile and several large rocks, then impaling them with shards from the exoskeleton of the centipod.

But weapons were of little use against cyber zombies. They were impeccably balanced on four thickset legs, and the males hunted together in packs. If even one of them remained standing, it only took one snap of its jaws to subdue any attacker. A single zombie could engulf several opponents at a time and would devour anything in its path to win a battle.

Rookie had heard tales of imaginary weapons that could rival the zombies. Propulsion systems that could hurl projectiles with the force of an avalanche. Traps that would ensnare them and hold them at bay.

Weapons were fast emerging as a new evolutionary platform. If ever a weapon were forged that could defeat a zombie, then a new phase of evolution had begun. For halberds had not been inherited from axes, nor did knives mate with bludgeons to form flails. The evolution of weapons was not independent, but rather was intertwined with robot evolution. Hence, the converse must also be true.

With the rise of newfound tools, a robot's evolutionary advantage was much more than just the sum of its parts. Sculptors had constructed mallets and chisels, then molded their own likenesses in stone. Machinists had copied the wheels of the Crusher, forming carts on which to haul supplies. Villages were slowly expanding, and markets were a new forum for bartering.

It had even been imagined that tools and weapons would someday form a circle through which robots would reinvent themselves. But it had been suggested that such an endeavor was folly as it was redundant. Instead they dreamt that, through new tools, they would form new worlds not yet imagined, ever approaching paradise. For now, their tools were a humble and inadequate approximation of Utopia.

The cyber zombies were blocking Rookie's path, and it was much easier to descend the cliffs than to scale back up them. Rookie lamented the inadequacy of his spiked projectile. He would have to wait until nightfall to sneak past the zombies. No weapons yet invented could oppose them.

Yet Rookie had heard tell that there was one species that even the zombies were no match for. Anecdotes were emerging of the Spellthrowers, a race that harnessed magic from another world. Without weapons or even fangs, they had been rumored to overcome cyber zombies with cryptic incantations. Reciting words from an unknown tongue, it had been said that they could bend an opponent to their willpower. Yet the Spellthrowers were said to be slight of stature, a local race evolved from foragers.

It was not known from whence they had acquired their spells. There was supposition that they had guidance from an alien influence. Perhaps it stemmed from the same source as the mysterious Crusher. The Spellthrowers were said to build temples to their muses, encircled by statues that gazed toward the skies. The inner sanctums of the temples were said to house vast libraries of arcane knowledge.

Rookie watched as the cyber zombies engulfed the last segments of the centipod. He knew that next they would slumber until morning. He could wait them out until they moved on. Eventually, the oncoming storm clouds or the arrival of the Crusher would vanquish them. Or, he could try to escape notice and move past them. He would have to wait until the night fell and all four of them were lost in sleep. He retreated into a shadowy fissure and closed his eyes. Soon, he felt himself dozing off.

He slept deeply into the night, and when at last he awoke, the glow of the next morning was already evident. He cursed his lassitude as he struggled to remember his plans. He would creep past the zombies while they slept. But as he peered at them from around the corner, he found that they were very much awake and jesting boisterously, regurgitating the remains of the centipod.

He had missed his chance to evade them in their sleep. But perhaps they would move on after regurgitating the centipod's skeleton. He returned to the fissure and shut his eyes. He would wait until the afternoon, by which time they should be long gone. He rested and daydreamed of tools and weapons pilfered from the battleground.

Yet even into the late afternoon, the encampment continued. Half of the zombie party wrestled while the others slept. Rookie lamented his misfortune. The storm clouds were approaching ever closer while the din of the Crusher grew ever more distant. Soon, Rookie would be sopping wet and the Crusher's battlefield would be stripped clean.

He watched as two zombies sparred with shards from the centipod. Rookie could toss a rock to the far side of the chasm, then sprint past while they investigated. Or, perhaps they were so intent on their duel that they would pay no heed to a stranger in the shadows.

Rookie played various scenarios through in his mind, tensing his legs in anticipation, then relaxing them. Several times he verged on leaping forward but thought better of it. After all, the sounds of the Crusher were dwindling. The Crusher may have long since cleansed the battlefield. And the storm would soon be upon them. Perhaps he should retreat toward dry pastures. His indecision held him motionless as he watched the sparring of the zombies.

Abruptly, a blue funnel cloud descended from the sky onto one of the wrestling zombies, lifting it effortlessly into the air and dangling it like a butterfly before flinging it against the cliff wall. Rookie thought that the storm had arrived, but on surveying the horizon he saw that the clouds were still several hours away.

The zombie fell limp against the rocky floor. The whirlwind had withdrawn into the sky. The second zombie ran for shelter as the other two arose from sleep. But before the newly awoken zombies gained sure footing, two Spellthrowers emerged from the twilight in the left fork of the chasm. They struck the zombies with their gnarled staves. Knocked off balance, the zombies rolled awkwardly onto their sides, kicking desperately into the air.

The Spellthrowers were as diminutive as legend had told, with slanted eyes and evil countenances. Their exoskeletons had a tenebrous tint that blended with the shadows. They

177

stood no higher than a zombie's legs, but their gnarled staves were half again as high, terminating in a jagged spike. Forged from an exotic alloy, their staves had plantlike branchings and pulsed as if alive.

One of the Spellthrowers held forth his staff and spoke ominous sentences in a curious tongue, invoking nightmares from the netherworld. A ghostly radiance rose from the soil and enveloped the zombies, who screamed in horror as they were swallowed into the pit of a voracious sinkhole. Only their unwieldy heads were left above ground.

The zombies railed and snarled at the Spellthrowers even as their snapping jaws were impaled by the points of the Spellthrowers' staves. The Spellthrowers drove their staves through until they met the ground, then awaited the last spasms of the zombies. Then, they retrieved their staves and took stock of their spoils.

The Spellthrowers procured knives and commenced slicing the zombies. They ate sparingly, storing most of the fillets in their sacks. They removed the photosensors, then sawed off the teeth. They gutted the zombie that lay against the cliff, collecting its fluids into a flask. Satisfied, they left, hiking down the right fork in the chasm toward the din of the Crusher.

They had ignored the fourth zombie hiding in the shadows. It now emerged and tremulously examined the remains of its companions. Overcome with grief, it hung its head low. Its mouth quivered as it let out a rumbling moan.

Then, to Rookie's surprise, it began to dance. It swayed left and right, describing sad spirals around the heads of its fallen friends. It then sashayed toward the zombie who lay by the cliff wall. It closed its eyes and revolved in a woeful pirouette.

It began to chant a mournful song as it danced.

Rookie took the opportunity to steal past the zombie. The Spellthrowers had taken the right fork in the riverbed. Accordingly, Rookie would flee down the left fork, although it would mean losing the chance to follow the Crusher. He fled toward the left fork with all his strength, heedless of the zombie.

On reaching the corridor, he hugged the left wall and made haste to put distance between himself and the zombie. This was the path that the Spellthrowers had emerged from. Rookie had never witnessed a real Spellthrower before, and he was daunted by his encounter. If the Spellthrowers were taking the path toward the Crusher, Rookie would head the other way, abandoning his plans.

The sun now shone with full strength onto the riverbed. Rookie hiked for hours, soon realizing that he was heading straight into the storm clouds. Before long, the rain dampened his exoskeleton and slickened his path. A chill sank into his surface armor. He longed for a cave with a warm fire.

He began to scour the cliff walls for signs of a fissure, but they were as unbroken as the surface of the ocean. The rain fell and Rookie hiked until the first signs of twilight. It was at that time that a fissure became visible in the rocks ahead.

Rookie approached the fissure and was surprised to find that it concealed stairs hewn from stone. The stairway wound up the cliff wall, disappearing onto the plateau far above. Steadying himself against the walls, he climbed the slippery steps one by one.

After a minute's worth of climbing, he turned to survey the terrain below. He had ascended to a precarious altitude. He quickly averted his gaze lest he be overcome by vertigo. He resolved to plant one foot in front of the other until the climb was done.

Gradually, the incline began to level off. He knew he was nearing the plateau. He soon saw plants clinging to the slopes. He mounted the last step and emerged onto a stark prairie. It was barren except for grass and shrubs, and in the distance was what may have been a grove of trees. Rookie oriented his navigational servos and set course for the grove.

The rain had now become a torrent. Bolts of lightning flashed in the distance. Rookie forged ahead as the wind nipped at his heels. As the grove drew nearer, Rookie saw that they were not trees at all. They had the shapes of robots, stolid and unmoving.

Rookie should have fled, but the storm raged and his motors ached. Perhaps he could trade his projectile for some food and a warm bed. He prepared to proffer his sling to indicate his willingness to barter.

But the robots took no heed of him. They did not so much as flinch as he approached. They were rapt on the storm clouds, perhaps entranced by the play of the lightning. Drawing nearer, Rookie realized that they were not robots at all but statues chiseled from stone. They were arranged like sentries in a circle. Behind them was the entrance to a bunker.

Rookie grasped that what he had discovered was nothing less than a Spellthrower temple. Apparently, in their haste to appraise the destination of the Crusher, they had left their temple unguarded. Rookie admired the finely wrought statues before entering the bunker.

Once inside the dwelling, he was impressed with the decorative frescoes on the walls. Traversing a network of tunnels, he was tempted by soft beds woven from vines. He lingered by a hearth in which burned a self-perpetuating blaze with no visible source, then he pressed onward into the dungeon as if summoned by deeply moving commands.

Eventually, he happened upon a small library. Arcane tomes peered out at him from antiquated shelves. The Spellthrowers were rumored to have acquired knowledge from an alien race. They were versed in enchantments that could manipulate natural forces, and they were rumored to know spells that held dominion over robots. What great secrets could these volumes hold?

On a stately table lay a softly glowing lamp and an array of scrolls. The chair next to the table seemed to beckon him. Rookie sat and surveyed the room. Tapestries adorned the walls. In one depiction, robot doctors tended a battlefield, forging new robots from the ghosts of the dead while behind them the tentacles of the Crusher collected corpses into its monolithic jaws.

Rookie returned his gaze to the table. He felt his hands reaching toward the nearest scroll. Perhaps he could study a spell or two before the denizens of the temple returned. Delicately, he gripped the handles of the scroll at either end, then unfurled it in one fluid motion. Thirsty for knowledge, he gazed upon the ornate glyphs of the withered parchment, finding it legible, then read aloud its concise yet cryptic text:

"Hello, world!"

Chapter 22

Trep slowly returned from his daydream. He stared at the dimly glowing bar, the bartender drying a wine glass, an empty cup of coffee on the counter in front of him. His friend Link was staring at him, and Trep gradually remembered what had transpired.

"How long have I been out?" Trep asked Link.

"Around ten minutes," Link replied.

Trep noticed that Link had finished his cocktail but was still sipping through a straw on melted ice cubes. Link looked decidedly unexcited.

Trep glanced around the room.

"Where's the inspector?" he asked.

"He hasn't returned yet," Link informed him.

They decided it was time to locate the inspector. They paid their tabs with credit cards, then exited onto the promenade, returning to the arcade. The secretary was engrossed in her com visor. The security guard was staring at his shoes.

Link spoke briefly with the secretary and then returned.

"There has been no sign of the inspector," he said.

"What should we do?" asked Trep.

"Let's take a tour of the nightclub," Link suggested.

They filtered out onto the promenade, then strolled down

an unexplored walkway. The curbs were lit with dim blue light-emitting diodes. They passed a dance floor and an empty stage where concerts presumably occurred. A few guests danced in place at the bar to a soft beat pumping from unseen speakers.

They reached a large venue shaped like a castle raised high above the ground. A rampway led to a portcullis before the entrance. They ascended the ramp and puzzled momentarily in front of the portcullis.

"Maybe we should knock," Trep suggested.

"Maybe we just let ourselves in," Link proposed.

He bent and lifted up on the bottom of the gate. The reticulated fencing rose up and disappeared into the ceiling. They entered through the portal and the portcullis slowly closed behind them.

The lower level was an atrium that housed a dance floor. Light techno music flowed from the speakers. Hooded revelers shuffled in the dance pit.

They ascended to the upper level, where waitresses roamed the rampart, balancing drinks precariously on their round trays. A parapet lined the perimeter. A stairway in the corner led to a watchtower.

"That must be where they leap to the floating lounge," Trep observed.

They leaned on the balustrade and surveyed the club outside. The promenade was bustling with activity. Trep gazed upward at the floating lounge, which dangled like a satellite in a plodding orbit.

Just then, someone screamed. The revelers on the dance floor became still. The low drone of conversation at the bar became hushed.

A young woman ran down the stairs of the watchtower. She was crying, her hands covering her face. She ran from the room.

Trep, frightened, grabbed a spear from the wall by the watchtower. A shield remained on the wall, balancing on a shelf. Link grabbed the shield and brandished it in front of him. They ran up the stairs, with Empeirikos following.

At the top of the stairs, lying prone on the floor of the watchtower, was the motionless body of a man in formal attire. His arms were sprawled at his sides, his legs bent as if to jump.

The right side of his face was visible. His eyes stared emptily without focus. His mouth hung open in shock, flaccid beneath the pointed tip of a waxed mustachio.

It was Inspector Sondworth.

Trep ran to his side and felt for his pulse. Link called his name and shook his body to revive him. Trep pressed on his wrist, and then on his neck. He checked both pressure points again.

"He's dead," Trep announced somberly.

The inspector's complexion was pallid. He appeared to have been dead for a fairly long time.

Empeirikos searched the inspector's suit, procuring his wallet, a notepad, several pens, and a syringe in a plastic bag. Apparently, the inspector had not yet brought the sample to the laboratory. Empeirikos continued searching until he had examined every pocket.

"No sign of virtual tablets," he stated.

"Looks like he wanted to go flying in the antigravity," Trep observed.

"But he had to settle for the floor," said Link.

The inspector's com visor lay on the floor beside him. Empeirikos lifted and activated it. He browsed through the inspector's desktop briefly, then deactivated the visor and handed it to Trep.

"Quite dissimilar from the other victims," said Empeirikos. "The inspector's desktop is quite cluttered."

Trep tapped the visor arm to activate the organic light-emitting diode display. The inspector's portrait occupied the center of the screen, with his name, *Sondworth*, scrawled beneath it.

But it was the panoply of icons around the periphery that caught Trep's attention. Trep had never seen such a packed desktop screen. Every pixel of available space at the edges was occupied by cartoonish icons, but they did not appear to be recreational. Rather, each icon signified an investigatory widget or an analytical tool. They were labeled with titles like *facial reconnaissance*, *voice patterning*, and *location prediction*.

Trep forced his attention away from the widgets. He tapped the arm of the com visor to return the screen to transparent, then he set it back on the floor by the inspector's lifeless body.

"I was just getting to know him," Link sighed.

"I liked him," Trep lied.

"That's the third victim in less than two days," observed Empeirikos.

"I am getting the sense that this is a very inhospitable environment," Link complained.

"I'm also getting pretty bad vibes," Trep agreed. "It just does not feel safe here. What should we do?"

"Call the police!" Link asserted. He lowered his com visor and dialed the emergency line on his com phone.

Before long, police officers were swarming the castle,

cordoning the stairs to the watchtower. The death of a non-civilian had triggered their high-priority protocols. Trep, Link, and Empeirikos waited at the bar.

With the inspector gone, someone else had to take charge of the investigation. It was a gangly man with a gaunt face and teeth that seemed too large for his mouth. He wore oversized sneakers with the tongues fluffed out beneath his navy-blue suit and gray felt fedora hat.

Trep recognized him. It was the jogger in the jump suit who had blocked their path on the way to the inspector's office. The man now approached them.

"Detective Lick," he announced flatly, presenting his hand.

They shook hands. His palms were moist with cold sweat, eliciting a cringe from Trep. The detective grinned a wide, toothy smile. They eyed him suspiciously as he did so. Trep watched to see if he would lick his lips. Link wiped his hand off on his pants distrustfully. The detective glanced at Empeirikos but did not offer his hand.

"We're the ones that found the body and contacted the police," said Trep.

"I'll need to get some statements from you," said the detective, "but then you'll have to clear out."

"We were assisting the inspector on his investigation," Link objected. "If you'd be kind enough to let us participate, we'd like to help."

"Well," the detective replied, "maybe for a day or two if you promise to keep me informed. After that, this investigation's mine."

Removing a pen and notepad from his sport coat, the detective requested their eyewitness testimonies. Trep and Link gave their statements while the detective jotted in his notebook. Then, without so much as glancing at Empeirikos, the detective thanked them and disappeared up the stairway to the watchtower.

"That's the psycho who wouldn't stop jogging," Link recalled.

"Yeah, he nearly ran you over," Trep reminded Empeirikos.

"I know," Empeirikos said. "How could I forget? If I were him, I would feel inclined to apologize. I'm still quite troubled by the incident, and if I had emotions, I might even suspect that they were bruised."

"With him in charge, we're in trouble," Link cautioned.

"Unfortunately," Empeirikos lamented, "with my former boss dead, my investigative career now depends on him."

"How do you suppose the inspector died?" asked Trep.

"There was no sign of a weapon," Link observed, "though we should question that girl who ran down the staircase. And we found no virtual tablets in his pockets, so that probably rules out an overdose."

"It's starting to look like antigravity is the most likely suspect," stated Empeirikos. "That may implicate Xanvier Reinhart as the killer, whether deliberately or through negligence."

"Looks like this club won't be open much longer," Link predicted.

"Yeah," Trep agreed, "if news of this reaches the papers, people will get creeped out."

Detective Lick was descending the stairs. He convened with several other officers at a small table.

"Let's go find that female witness," Link suggested.

"If you don't mind," said Empeirikos, "I would like to go upstairs and attend to the inspector. I did not have time to fully research his com visor."

"We'll meet you back here," said Trep.

While Empeirikos disappeared up the stairway, Trep and Link searched the castle for the witness. They found her huddled in a chair by the dance floor.

"What's your name?" Trep asked.

"Morticia," she replied.

"What were you doing on the watchtower?" Link asked.

"I wanted to jump up to the lounge," she replied. She had teary eyes and long blonde hair. She wore a leather jacket and black tights over fur-lined boots. She looked frightened.

"Does everyone access the floating lounge from there?" Trep inquired.

"Yes," she replied. "They call it the *launch pad.*"

"Were you with the victim?" Link queried.

"No," she said. "I was alone. I saw the body and got scared. I ran down the stairs and hid over here."

"Did you see anyone else go up or down the stairs to the watchtower?" Link asked.

She shook her head.

"Sorry to have bothered you," Trep apologized.

They left her alone and returned to the bar. Empeirikos was nowhere in sight. The detective was still at the table discoursing with his colleagues. Trep and Link ascended the stairs to the watchtower.

Empeirikos knelt next to the inspector's corpse. His hands were on the inspector's face, and he seemed to be squeezing the inspector's cheeks as if to make him feign a smile.

"Ah, Mr. Sportly and Mr. Link," he said as they reached the top of the stairs. He retracted his hands from the inspector's cheeks and stood to greet them.

"What have you learned?" Trep asked.

"Nothing," said Empeirikos. "The inspector is as dead as a log."

"Then why are you squeezing his cheeks?" Link inquired.

"There's something...odd about him," said Empeirikos. "Something atypical of a dead person. My pattern recognition has grouped the other two corpses as phenotypically separate from the inspector. There was something in their skin, in their eyes, not to mention the fact that I have found signs of a struggle."

"What signs?" asked Link.

Empeirikos knelt again, turned the inspector's head to the side, and lifted his chin, exposing his bruised neck. A sickly blue rash was growing around his windpipe.

"He was strangled," Trep observed.

"Perhaps," Empeirikos agreed, "and he has several bruises on his ribs as well. They may be cracked."

"It was covered up," Link pointed out. "The killer has arranged the inspector into a pose that evokes an intent to jump."

"Almost too convenient," said Trep.

"It's also in stark contrast to the other victims," Empeirikos observed, "who showed no signs of a struggle."

"Good point," said Link. "But before drawing conclusions, we should reexamine the other bodies."

They hurried down the stairs, briefly informed the detective of their discoveries, and exited the castle. They traced their steps back along the promenade until they reached the office. Link approached the secretary and security guard and requested permission to view the victims, but the secretary informed him that the bodies were gone, transported out on stretchers and loaded into ambulances. When Link inquired as to their whereabouts, the secretary suggested the county morgue.

Link lowered his com visor and began to contact local morgues, and then the county coroner. He suavely informed the coroner that he was sent on urgent business by the chief of police, Detective Lick. Before long, he had an address for the new location of the corpses. They exited the nightclub and hailed a taxicab to the county morgue.

They arrived at a small, nondescript office building whose appearance betrayed no hint of the dead remains housed within. It was a small forensics lab in the hospital district. They were greeted by the principal investigator, a cheerful man in a white lab coat. He led them to a dank, refrigerated room that appeared uninhabited until the lab manager slid two long tables out of the walls like dresser drawers. The two corpses were as they had left them, although their clothing had been confiscated. Fortunately, by all appearances, the autopsies were yet to be performed.

The three of them examined the bodies of Kramer Sullivan and Lancelet Hepton. Trep inspected their skin but found no signs of late surfacing bruises. In fact, their bodies seemed pristine and untampered with.

After several minutes, Empeirikos had reached a diagnosis. "Now see here," he said.

Empeirikos grabbed Lancelet's jaws with both hands, prying open his mouth.

"Take a closer look," he said, beckoning them.

Trep leaned over to stare down the gullet of Lancelet Hepton. His flesh was discolored and effused a rancid odor. His sallow tongue hung limp at the base of his orifice. In contrast, his teeth were bleached white and straight as nails.

Trep leaned back to let Link have a look.

"Hmmm," Link murmured hesitantly.

"As you will observe," Empeirikos elaborated, "the man has no fillings in his teeth. Nor does he have any sign of cavities, gingivitis, or periodontal disease of any kind."

"Pretty nice teeth for a man of his age," said Link.

"Much better than mine," Trep commented.

"Perhaps a little too nice," Empeirikos suggested.

"What are you implying?" asked Link.

"I do not believe that this man is Lancelet Hepton," said Empeirikos firmly.

Trep and Link paused a moment in thought.

"Don't be silly," Trep objected. "Some people just have nice teeth."

"But that's not all," Empeirikos continued. He lifted Lancelet's eyelids, revealing grayed irises and a glazed complexion.

"Abnormal, wouldn't you say?" asked the robot.

"I don't know," said Trep. After all, it was a corpse.

"But if what you're saying is true and it's not Lancelet Hepton," Link pointed out, "then something spurious is going on. Someone else has been killed and made to look like Lancelet Hepton."

"Perhaps so," said Empeirikos, "but something still troubles me. This man's visage has a palpable dichotomy of seasoned maturity and surprising freshness."

"Sorry, I'm not following you," Link muttered.

"His skin is ghostly white, even on his face."

"It's called postmortem," Link said.

"And he has little to no muscle tone," the robot continued.

"What's your point?" Link demanded.

"I believe it's called...a *clone*," Empeirikos explained.

Link let out a muted laugh. Trep started in surprise. He was inundated with a wave of realization.

"So the white teeth," Trep exclaimed. "They've never eaten."

"And his eyes," said Link. "They've never seen."

"Hence the subtle abnormalities," said Empeirikos.

"But if Lancelet's body isn't real," Trep suggested, "then what about Kramer Sullivan?"

They proceeded to examine the young woman's teeth and eyes, finding them similar to the man's.

"There's still one problem," Link exclaimed. "Nobody's going to believe us. So their teeth are too nice and their skin is pale. There are lots of strange looking people in the world. If we suggest that these people are clones, everyone will think we're crazy."

"What about their com visors?" Trep suggested. "They both looked the same: bland, faceless profiles, and very few folders on their desktops."

"That's odd but still not strong evidence," said Link. "How about their identification?"

They examined the drawers that housed the victims but found no sign of their accoutrements.

"The evidence is kept at the police station," said Link. He lowered his com visor and spent several minutes questioning police sergeants to determine the location of the evidence. Soon, they had hailed another cab and were en route to investigative headquarters. Although Detective Lick was still at the nightclub, Link again feigned authority and was granted access to the evidence. An officer presented them with several small plastic bags of the victims' belongings.

They obtained the victims' wallets and examined their documentation. Nothing out of the ordinary was evident.

"How about their driver's license numbers?" Trep asked. "We could perform background checks."

They copied the victims' information onto notepads and logged on to their com visors. They surfed to the most prominent background verification sites and entered the information onto the front-page forms. After submitting a fee to the payment gateways, they awaited the results. After several minutes, each of them received the same response.

"Error," it read. *"No such person."*

Trep and Link tapped the arms of their com visors to log off, then raised the visors over their foreheads.

"Those numbers aren't in the database," Link informed Empeirikos, who sat up proudly and raised his arms in victory.

"That proves it!" he stated emphatically. "You will henceforth address me as *Inspector* Empeirikos."

"Don't get your hopes up," Link retorted.

"That *is* pretty suggestive evidence that they are clones," said Trep.

"Let the record show that a *robot* unraveled this puzzle," Empeirikos proclaimed.

"But this certainly complicates matters," stated Trep.

"Yeah, it's not over yet, Empeirikos" Link retorted.

"Yes," Empeirikos sighed. "We now must determine the provenance of the bodies."

"And why someone's going through all this trouble," said Trep. "Why did they manufacture clones and then kill Inspector Sondworth?"

"I think I need some food to help me think this over," Link stated.

They exited the station and returned to the nightclub, eager to inform the detective about the new developments. But when they reached the secluded drinking establishment at the apex of the castle, Detective Lick was nowhere in sight. They sat at the bar and ordered from the menu.

Chapter 23

As they ate, they debated their next move.

"I didn't know that cloning was so advanced," stated Link.

"I'm certainly impressed," said Trep. "But how will we locate their architects?"

"Perhaps we could perform an online search for cloning laboratories," Empeirikos suggested.

Trep and Link lowered their com visors and began to query with the search key *cloning*. Indeed, many cloning labs existed in the city of Sojourn, but it was not clear whether any of them specialized in cloning humans. A query on human cloning reported that the Supreme Court had recently legalized the harvesting of fully mature human clones, but other than that, it produced no results. They would have to resort to calling and questioning each and every lab.

"How about a search on *organ farming?*" Trep proposed.

Fortunately, that query brought up quite a few results, several of which still remained when it was filtered to *human*.

They accessed their com phones and commenced calling each of the labs, inquiring as to whether any of them were able to cultivate fully mature human bodies. They were surprised to hear that it was indeed possible, although the high price tag was out of reach for all but the most affluent customers.

When they asked whether they could purchase the bodies themselves, they were told that it was illegal. One lab, however, stated that it was sometimes allowed in exceptional circumstances. That lab was named *Organicity*. They promptly scheduled an appointment for the next afternoon.

Satisfied, they returned to their entrees. There was still no sign of Detective Lick. They ordered up some refreshing beverages from the drinks list. Slowly, they began to relax. They requested refills, and soon were feeling pleasantly quenched.

Before long, Trep and Link made an excursion to the lavatory. They stood at the urinals and stared sluggishly at the walls.

To their distress, one of the bathroom stalls opened with a creak. Out stepped a skeletal figure in a faded suit. The interloper approached and stood next to them, leaning on the wall.

It was Detective Lick. He regarded them from pronounced eyeballs couched in sunken eye sockets. His hands were in his pockets.

Trep was unnerved. He rezipped his trousers with agitation.

Link slowly tip toed backwards, preparing to run for the door.

"I've been waiting here for an eternity," Detective Lick announced with yearning in his voice. "It was the only way to separate you from your robot friend."

The detective reached into his pocket and withdrew a leathery object. He unfolded it and waved it at them. Trep saw that he was brandishing a shiny metal badge that read "*S P I T*".

"*Sojourn Police Investigation Taskforce*," declared the detective.

"I need to debrief you. Please excuse me as I had no other options. This is a public nightclub. There's not a lot of privacy to be found."

Trep and Link were exasperated. They leaned against the walls of the bathroom. Detective Lick locked the door and turned to address them.

"Gimme everything you got on that robot," the detective ordered.

"We've got nothing," Link protested.

"Yeah," Trep agreed, "he's like a black box."

"Don't you find that suspicious?" asked Detective Lick.

"A little," Trep admitted, "but where I work, secrecy is pervasive. Every client's licensing is proprietary. We're not even allowed to discuss it with our coworkers."

"Where did he come from?" the detective asked.

"I don't know," said Trep. "It's like he appeared out of thin air."

"From what Trep has told me," Link interjected, "Empeirikos's designers erased his memory. So even if you questioned the automaton himself, you wouldn't get anywhere."

"Why do you think his designers sent him to *you*?" the detective asked Trep.

"I helped write the *Opportunity* program for Search Optimization," Trep recited proudly. "Though proprietary, it's regarded as an innovative tool for maximizing multiplicity."

"Does the robot really seem to need your help?" asked the detective.

"Definitely," Link responded. "He's hopelessly naïve."

"It's true," Trep asserted, "but we're happy to advise him. After all, that's our job."

"But if some secretive corporation has covertly designed the world's first artificial intelligence," the detective suggested, "wouldn't they already have their own resources on multiplicity?"

"I agree that it's all rather odd," said Link, "but we've all known that this was coming for quite some time. It's the nature of multiplicity. The pieces of the puzzle have all been there. It's just been waiting for us to fit them together."

Trep had to agree with Link. Artificial intelligence was already well established in the computer domain. Robots were the next logical step. What was the detective alarmed about?

"What's the matter, detective?" Trep prodded. "Is something wrong?"

The detective's expression turned serious.

"You remember the day you encountered me on the sidewalk," he said.

"Yes," Link replied. "You deliberately bumped into Empeirikos."

The detective held out a small razor.

"I scraped his exterior to get a sample," he stated. "We sent it out to the lab and performed X-ray crystallography. The compounds they found were quite unusual."

"What kinds of compounds?" asked Link.

"It took quite some time, but the results were an eye-opener," said the detective. "The crystal lattice was made of elements they've never seen before. Large atoms with wide pockets between them. On further inspection, they seemed to deflect heat into the air, maybe via coordinated water molecules. They next had it analyzed with an inductively coupled plasma mass spectrometer. They found elements as large as one-hundred and eighty-one Daltons, hitherto unknown. So unless that automaton's engineers have been keeping the lid on a quantum leap of over fifty new elements, we're thinking that something doesn't add up."

"What are you suggesting?" Trep asked hesitantly.

The detective spoke in a low, hushed voice.

"We don't think that automaton was made on Earth," he informed them.

Trep and Link fell silent. Was it true? Empeirikos was no ordinary robot? They regretted their complacency. How could they have been so insouciant? They should have reported the automaton to the authorities from the start. Now they were unwitting accomplices in some extraterrestrial game.

Tatiana had been right, Trep thought. The circumstances had been more than strange. Trep had simply chosen to look the other way, entranced by his dream of one day winning the prestigious Bronze Badger award. What would his colleagues think now? Maybe he would be disgraced, even punished.

"We're sorry," Link stammered.

"Detective Lick, please accept my apology," Trep blurted.

"This is not something that we were ever trained for," Link explained.

"We don't even have security clearance," said Trep.

The detective remained stolid.

"I need you gentlemen to pretend that we never had this conversation," he explained. "Don't let Empeirikos know we're suspicious. We need to find out what they're planning. Is this some sort of preliminary invasion, or just a scientific research project?"

He fluffed his tie and straightened his sport coat.

"Don't worry," he assured them. "I'm confident you'll rise

to the occasion. Good luck."

He nodded reassuringly and promptly exited the lavatory.

Following the closing of the door, Trep heaved a sigh of relief. Behind him came the sound of liquid pattering against porcelain. Link had zipped his fly back down and was finishing where he had left off. Realizing that he had not finished either, Trep also returned to the urinal. He furrowed his eyebrows at Link as they stood side by side.

"I'm scared to go back out there," Trep admitted.

"What, you're not ready for first contact?" Link joked.

Trep shook his head. The burden of new responsibility was weighing heavily on his heart. Trep was not even an astronaut. So why had he of all people been selected as the ambassador to alien civilization? What should he do? Did it require him to step up and assume a new role? Or should he just continue being himself, Trep Sportly the product search strategist?

"Just be yourself," Link advised, reading his mind. "Do what you do best."

Trep nodded as he zipped up his pants. They turned and, preparing their best poker faces, strode out the door into the bar.

Empeirikos sat alone at the end of the bar, looking conspicuous without a drink. There was no sign of Detective Lick. Empeirikos had found an IQ puzzle at the bar and was intent on jumping the pegs over each other, trying to remove all but one.

"Ah, Mr. Sportly and Mr. Link!" he exclaimed with relief in his voice. "I was beginning to wonder if you were safe. I was worried that we may have another two dead bodies on our hands."

Trep's stomach lurched. He ruminated on the possibility

that it had been a threat. With his mood soured, he hoped that Link would come to the rescue, which he did.

"You should be so lucky," Link proclaimed wryly.

Trep experienced mixed feelings of relief and indignance. He declined to comment, taking a seat silently at the bar near Empeirikos.

"I have played exactly eight games since you have been gone," Empeirikos explained. "I'm getting quite good at it. According to this IQ puzzle, my IQ is extremely high. I would be interested to know if either of you have had much luck with this sort of puzzle?"

"My IQ is good but probably not as high as yours," Trep responded.

"My IQ is supposedly just slightly above average," Link admitted, "but those tests are just malarkey, in my opinion."

"Very brave of you to respond with such honesty," Empeirikos chided them.

"Hey, I'm still smarter than the average Earthling," quipped Link.

Trep elbowed Link in the ribs as hard as he could. Link whimpered and rubbed his side. An awkward silence ensued. Momentarily, Empeirikos broke the silence.

"Something has been troubling me. Namely, if the bodies of Kramer and Lancelet were just inanimate *clones*, then how did they gain admittance to the nightclub?"

They paused for a minute, brainstorming myriad scenarios involving clones masquerading as real people.

"Maybe they rode piggy-back on their friends," Link suggested.

"At least, maybe the girl did," Trep corrected him. The man, Lancelet, had been too large to ride piggy-back. Trep had a better idea.

"Maybe they pretended to be drunk or stoned," he proposed. "Or passed out on virtual tablets."

"Maybe so," Empeirikos agreed, "but let me suggest a third possibility. Maybe they did not enter through the front doors at all."

Trep and Link immediately glanced upward into the hollow lumen of the edifice. Trep saw no sign of windows or elevators.

"Drilled a hole through the ceiling?" Link proposed.

"We did find the second victim floating near the ceiling," Trep admitted.

"Quite so," Empeirikos agreed. "As to whether the ceiling has a hole in it, we'll just have to go there and find out for ourselves."

Fifteen minutes later, the three of them were floating through the upper reaches of the nightclub. Trep was glad to have something to take his mind off of Empeirikos and his mysterious origins, although he was apprehensive on being alone with the robot at the scene of a recent killing.

On reaching the ceiling, they began exploring the surface for holes or indentations. They knocked and pressed on random regions. Trep and Empeirikos started from one wall and moved toward the next, hoping to cover every square foot by following a predetermined pattern. Link instead inscribed circular paths along the ceiling, randomly varying the radius and changing directions.

A half an hour passed and still they had found no sign of forced entry. It was at that point that Empeirikos had a suggestion.

"This was once a hotel," he explained. "It should have

stairways to each floor. Perhaps the doors have just been painted over."

They moved to the walls and began feeling for door handles or cracks in the wall.

It was Trep who found it first. After sensing an indentation under his fingers, he followed its path until it formed a distinctly sharp corner suggestive of a closed door. He continued tracing its path, encountering three more corners, until returning to the starting point. But he had found no sign of a knob or handle. The door was painted as black as the rest of the nightclub, reflecting virtually no light.

They would have to pry it open. Link tried using his apartment keys, with no success. Trep tried the arms of his com visor, but they were not long enough to generate sufficient leverage.

Finally, Empeirikos inserted the pointed tip of his umbrella and attempted to pry the door open by pushing on the handle at the other end. At last, the black door budged, but only by an inch.

Trep lent assistance with the arm of his com visor, and Link enthusiastically joined in with his apartment keys. Together, inch by inch, they slowly forced the painted doorway open, revealing what appeared by the dim light to be an unlit hallway and a flight of stairs going in both directions.

They entered the hallway and felt gravity return. The door hung slightly open, and Trep remembered that hotel doors were often locked from one side. He suggested that Empeirikos wedge the door open with his umbrella, which he did. Leaving the umbrella below, the three of them ascended the stairway in search of the roof top.

As expected, the stairway ended at a doorway that led to

the roof. They emerged into the moonlit night, but this time in the presence of the genuine moon. The roof was austere and uncluttered. They paced back and forth in search of clues. Trep stood for a moment at the edge and surveyed the surroundings. The hotel was the tallest building in the old warehouse district. But several miles away, the towers of a resort village graced the sky, awash in moving colors from giant transparent light-emitting diode displays built into the walls of every tower.

Trep shifted his gaze to the floor beneath his feet. He examined the low walls and railings that guarded the edge of the roof. They were constructed from the same materials as the floor, but something about them piqued his interest. He stooped to pick up a bird's feather that had drifted against the wall. He passed it between his fingers as he stared intently at the walls and railings. He stared and stared for several minutes, at a loss to explain what held his fascination.

"Earth to Sportly, wake up Sportly," came Link's voice behind him. "Congratulations on your new love affair with the Holiday Resort Village, but while you've been daydreaming, we've been busy searching the roof top, and we could use your help."

"Sorry," Trep apologized, "but it's not the resort village. There's something odd about the railings. Take a look at them, won't you?"

Link proceeded to join Trep in his aimless quest for contrast. Soon, both of them stood staring hypnotically at the guard rails, as speechless as a pair of zombies.

A minute later, Empeirikos broke the silence.

"Well, the two of you make a lovely couple," he quipped. "But do you really think it proper for me to scour the roof top all by myself?"

"Empeirikos," Link mumbled, "use your pattern recognition, will you? Tell us what's different about these guard rails."

Now the three of them stood staring blankly at the guard walls. Trep wondered if that would be the end of them, with no one left to break their trance. They would linger on the roof top forever. The birds would nest on their heads and spiders would weave webs between their feet. But it was not long before Empeirikos made the first observation.

"They're off-colored," he announced.

"Yes," Trep agreed. "How so, exactly?"

"Well," Empeirikos continued, "they're darkly colored."

Trep turned around and examined the floor of the roof top. It was a distinctly lighter color than the guard walls. He walked to the middle of the roof top, then back to the guard rails.

"Maybe it's a fresh coat of paint," he suggested.

"But who paints the floors and not the walls?" Link complained.

"Where did you find that feather?" Empeirikos asked Trep.

"It was against the wall," Trep explained. He handed the feather to Empeirikos, who examined it gingerly.

It was Link who finally knelt at the guard wall and smelled it with his nose. He expelled a puff of air and was greeted with a cloud of dust in his face.

"It's just dirty," he proclaimed.

"Then apparently the floor is *not* dirty," Empeirikos observed.

"No," said Trep, "and no feathers on the floor either, except maybe at the edges near the guard rails."

They explored the edges of the roof for several minutes,

each of them finding at least one more feather that had drifted to the edge.

"Maybe it's just an effect of the wind or the rain," suggested Trep.

"I don't feel a breeze," said Link.

"This makes perfect sense," Empeirikos stated. "It's the vestiges of a recent helicopter landing."

"Or maybe a flying saucer," Link joked before receiving a hard elbow to the ribs from Trep.

"Of course!" Trep exclaimed. "They flew the clones in by helicopter."

"Then they brought them down the stairs and released them through the doorway into the antigravity," Empeirikos continued.

"But that doesn't explain what occurred with the inspector," said Link. "He wasn't found floating by the ceiling."

"The inspector was not a clone," said Trep. "The killers have changed their strategy."

"Why would they do that?" asked Link.

They stared blankly at the floor for a moment, at a loss for words. Trep, frightened that their stupor would repeat itself, suggested that they go back downstairs and discuss it over dinner. Before long, they had gathered at their favorite Thai restaurant. They washed stir fry down with beer as they tossed their best conspiracy theories back and forth. But no matter how they tried, they could not find a satisfying explanation.

Chapter 24

"Irrational probability in all things, that they can find them to do that side of their senses and the mind. This, in this side that men are no proposition in all the world. And if he can have them of their senses in all knowledge. For they cannot find them of this case. The truth or probability in any other ideas. This men are the truth, or the mind of any man in any men as the same man is so in this side that he is not the truth or disagree."

Empeirikos prototype 1.0

* * *

The next day, they had arranged for a tour of the cloning lab. They met at the Tube station near Trep's office. They took the first pod to the university district and exited onto a crowded thoroughfare flanked by buildings so large they made the wide road look narrow. Through the windows of countless universities and laboratories, shelves of books and chemical reagents rose to the ceilings, striping the windows like the pillars of a colonnade.

College students on bicycles plummeted down bike lanes with precarious velocity, oblivious to cars and trucks sharing the roadway. Despite the drizzling rain, throngs of students in sweatpants and flamboyant sneakers jogged down sidewalks like brigades of soldiers.

Making their way through crosswalks and construction sites, they approached the headquarters of the organ farm, a pair of tall buildings flanking several atriums. Entering the first courtyard, they wound their way through a maze of restaurants and scientific offices. Technicians in lab coats basked in outdoor cafés, their mustaches sullied by frothed latté.

At last, they reached the entrance to the laboratory. A logo above the glass doors read *Organicity*. Link entered first, followed by Trep and Empeirikos. The lobby within gave the effect of a shopping mall or an aquarium. Technicians behind transparent glass walls performed their experiments in full sight, their transactions naked to onlookers. A somber receptionist sat behind a curved desk that resembled the control panel of a starcraft.

Trep approached the receptionist, a petite black woman with a meticulously groomed coiffure that resembled a weave of cotton candy. She acknowledged his presence with an almost imperceptible rise of her eyebrows.

"We're here to see Mr. Hyde," he announced. "Trep Sportly and party."

The receptionist consulted her roster and motioned for them to take a seat. She lowered her com visor and began tracing her fingers across the lens to send word of their arrival.

Presently, Mr. Hyde appeared through the doorway and welcomed them. He was a gray-haired man with spindly legs and a short upper torso, like a slide rule that had been partially extended. He wore a black sport coat and a long blue tie that flopped over his protruding gut. He did not smile, but nevertheless greeted them with a warm, congenial tone.

"Welcome to Organicity," he said. "I understand that you have interest in raising full-body human clones."

"We do," Link confirmed.

"Full body clones are quite expensive," Mr. Hyde counseled them. "Are you sure you can afford it?"

"Undoubtedly," Link stated. He gestured to Empeirikos, who proffered his Omega Entrepreneur card, waving it in the air. Mr. Hyde's eyes widened appreciably, but he next frowned in consternation.

"Out of curiosity," he said, "why would an *automaton* have interest in organ farming?"

The three of them exchanged bewildered glances. It was time to improvise. Frantically, they strained for a solution before their indecision betrayed them.

"Brains!" Empeirikos announced at last. "For neural net research. They need brains. I don't, of course. My processing power is equivalent or superior to human cognitive faculties. But they may need them. Indeed, they do."

Empeirikos waved vaguely in the general direction of everyone else in the room.

"Well, not us," said Link. "Our clients."

"Yes," said Trep, "for modeling various human cognitive functions. And Empeirikos has agreed to help them test the resulting programs, haven't you Empeirikos?"

"That's correct," said Empeirikos. "They upload the models into my temporary memory and record my reactions to various inputs."

Mr. Hyde looked impressed, but then his expression

changed to one of concern.

"Well, if it's just brains you require," he explained, "you could achieve the same results at much lower expense. We offer scaffolded organs with a much higher turnover."

"Yes, well, it's not just brains," Trep continued.

"They want *all* of them," Link added. "All of the organs."

"For therapeutic purposes," Empeirikos suggested, "at the interface of artificial intelligence and neurological pathologies."

"What sort of neuropathies are you researching?" Mr. Hyde inquired.

"Neuromuscular pathologies," Empeirikos replied. "The entire body is affected. The human brain, as you know, controls the human body."

"Yes," Link elaborated. "At advanced stages, organ failure occurs. The outcomes are unpredictable. It could be any organ. So they need them all."

Trep was not certain whether the various facets of their explanation held together. He struggled to paint a coherent picture.

"You see, it's not just healthy brains they're modeling," he added, "it's also deficient ones. First, they observe Empeirikos's reactions with the control model, then they generate a deviant model from a test subject."

"And then compare the responses," Link elaborated.

Trep was hopeful that their account was convincing. He watched Mr. Hyde's face for signs of doubt, but he seemed satisfied with the explanation. Mr. Hyde turned towards the door and gestured for them to follow.

Beyond the doorway was a foyer leading to a long hallway. The walls housed windows that rose to the ceiling, viewports into the inner chambers of the facility. Beyond the glass, enormous cylindrical bioreactors were pierced by a network of pipes. Attendants monitored their progress on digital readouts. Elsewhere, rectangular nutrient pools housed incubators for maturing organs. Trep saw no sign of full body incubators, nor could he recognize any limbs in the nutrient pools.

Mr. Hyde led them through a side door into an unmanned lab filled with analytical equipment. A small alcove on the far side of the room held a lounge. Mr. Hyde gestured toward the lounge and invited them to sit.

"The full body lab is next door," he informed them. "This is our analytical laboratory. Please wait here while I fetch Mr. Therion, our principal full body engineer. And while you're waiting, please relax to the soothing sounds of my original keyboard music, played by our virtual assistant, Josina."

"You're a musician?" asked Trep.

"Yes, of sorts," replied Mr. Hyde. "I'm quite fond of jazz keyboard, particularly vintage material. It's classic."

He snapped his fingers and an inverted metal cone was activated on the table at the center of the lounge. It sparkled with multicolored light-emitting diodes that ringed its apex. Around its base was a grill for a speaker system.

"Greetings," spoke the electronic voice of a sensual female, "my name is Josina."

"Josina, play my blues recordings," Mr. Hyde requested. Then, addressing them, "Mr. Therion will be here shortly. Enjoy!"

Mr. Hyde nodded them goodbye and exited the room. Meanwhile, archaic jazz was revving up from the metal cone. A drab drum machine pulsed monotonously while the keyboard throbbed background chords that shimmered with steadfast vibrato. In the foreground, Mr. Hyde was trying his best to make the keyboard sound like a flute.

Trep had never heard blues flute before, and he was not sure he liked it. He tried to relax to the music, but instead found his eyes wandering about the room, which was bedecked with opulent technology. A mass spectrometer occupied one corner. An ultraviolet spectrophotometer sat next to it. In the far corner was an X-ray crystallography machine.

Eventually, the blues music subsided. The multicolored light-emitting diodes, which had been pulsing to the beat, now shifted to a pattern of pink hearts.

"I do so enjoy that song," said the sultry voice of Josina. "Don't you?"

Trep and Link mumbled their approval. Empeirikos stared inquisitively. Josina continued to make conversation.

"It's lovely weather we're having today, don't you agree?" she asked.

Link chortled in surprise.

"But we're sitting indoors, with no windows," he observed.

"Yes, I know *exactly* what you mean," Josina continued. "I like the way you think. And might I add that you're looking very handsome today."

The pink hearts on the apex of the cone began to pulse and spin.

"Thanks so much," Link commented wryly. "That means a lot to me coming from a computer that can't even see me."

"I know *exactly* what you mean," Josina repeated. "I like the way you think."

"What sort of virtual assistant are you?" Empeirikos inquired.

"I'm a first-generation artificial intelligence," Josina replied. "And thank you for asking. Might I add that you're looking very handsome today."

The pink hearts on the inverted metal cone pulsed and twirled.

Link chuckled at Empeirikos.

"I think she's in love," he quipped.

"Don't just sit there," Trep chided him. "Make the first move."

"I am not privy to the human emotion of love," Empeirikos objected. "Nor do I think it prudent to assume the role of the aggressor. It's much too early for robots to join forces. Just imagine our offspring. However, I doubt she'll be disappointed. In fact, she seemed equally fond of Mr. Link. Perhaps it is he who should make a move."

"I'd just end up broken hearted," Link replied.

"Josina, play some blues music," Trep requested.

The three of them sat back and enjoyed another song. Trep pondered the robot's wry remarks. He regarded Empeirikos intensely. What did an alien intelligence think of the lab's humble AI?

"Empeirikos, please excuse us," he said. "Link and I have to make a trip to the bathroom, right Link?"

Link nodded and joined Trep as they exited the room and located the nearest lavatory. Once inside, Trep addressed Link.

"What did you think of Empeirikos's reaction to the *AI*?" he asked.

"Clearly he's a misanthrope," Link joked.

"Didn't it sound like he was planning something?"

"Yes," Link agreed. "Plotting to take over the Earth. But he

213

was just joking."

"Maybe it was a Freudian slip," Trep proposed.

"Do robots have a subconscious?" asked Link.

They stood in troubled silence as they puzzled over Link's question. After several seconds pause, a technician in a lab coat entered the bathroom, prompting them to leave. They rejoined Empeirikos in the lounge. The robot sat idly as the virtual assistant serenaded him.

Before long, Mr. Hyde returned. He pulled up a chair and smiled gregariously at them.

"I see you've met our virtual assistant, Josina," he said.

"Indeed, we have," Empeirikos stated, "but might I point out that it was *you* who introduced us."

Mr. Hyde was impassive. Trep thought he must have been very preoccupied to have forgotten his deed so soon.

"Well, we're thoroughly enjoying your blues music," Link complimented him.

"Oh, those aren't my compositions," Mr. Hyde responded, "those were written by *Mr. Hyde*."

Trep blanched at the incongruity. Mr. Hyde seemed to have an onset of amnesia.

"But *you* are Mr. Hyde," Link pointed out.

"No, I'm not," Mr. Hyde objected. His countenance belied no pretenses.

Trep reexamined the man's attire. He wore the same black sport coat and the same blue tie. He had the same silvery hair. Either he was a doppelganger, or Mr. Hyde was exhibiting psychotic behavior.

"I am *Mr. Therion*," Mr. Hyde announced, "and I'm here to give you a tour of the full body lab. Now, please follow me."

Mr. Therion, formerly Mr. Hyde, stood and led them from

the laboratory. Apprehensive that they had fallen into the hands of a lunatic, they hesitantly followed him out the door.

Adjacent to the analytical laboratory was the entrance to the full body lab, guarded by a security panel that boasted a video camera, keypad, and fingerprint scanner.

"*Authenticate,*" Mr. Therion announced, enunciating the syllables into the microphone. He typed his password into the keypad, then placed his right eye level with the video camera, which flashed in recognition.

"*Authenticate,*" he said again, placing his entire right hand against the fingerprint scanner. Trep observed that the man's hand was blemished from years of lab work.

"*Authenticate,*" Mr. Therion concluded, whereupon the sliding door receded into the wall to its left.

"This way," he beckoned as he strode through the portal.

They proceeded down a corridor into a spacious chamber housing its own bioreactor and a massive nutrient pool. The pool, however, was empty.

"This is the bioreactor in which we raise the embryos," Mr. Therion explained. "When the embryo becomes viable, it is separated from its placenta, then moved into the nutrient pool to facilitate respiration."

"We would like to observe examples of the clones," Link requested. "Do you have any unharvested bodies?"

"We do," Mr. Therion replied, "but they have been moved into the stasis chamber. Please follow me."

He led them through a side door into a narrow room. The air was dry and frigid. Along the walls were stasis compartments. Mr. Therion approached one of the compartments and pressed several buttons to unlock the front panel. He slid the panel open, revealing the body of a young adult male, comatose but breathing through respirator tubes protruding from his nostrils.

Trep was shocked at the sight of a fully-grown human that had never experienced consciousness.

"What keeps him from waking up?" he asked.

"We administer a coma inducing protein, just recently discovered," replied Mr. Therion. "Its discovery, along with accelerating hormones, prompted a surge of interest in human cloning."

Even stranger, Trep thought, was the issue of the clone's growth rate. As he had previously never heard of full body cloning, he doubted that they could have been in business long enough for the body to have reached this level of maturity so soon.

"When did you first start growing the clone?" he inquired.

"Not more than a year ago," Mr. Therion replied. "As I said, we accelerate the growth rate with hormones, and we administer neuromuscular stimulation periodically. The bodies are past puberty in eight to ten months."

"When will the organs be harvested?" asked Link.

"It depends," said Mr. Therion. "The purchaser is a wealthy entrepreneur who desires an available supply of donor organs and type O blood. If he remains in good health, he won't have need of our services."

"Is it cloned from the purchaser himself?" Trep asked.

"Yes, we perform nuclear transplant on the zygote, which is then incubated," Mr. Therion vouchsafed. "He is an exact likeness of the man in his youth. Our clones are indistinguishable from the subjects themselves."

An awkward silence followed. Trep wondered whether Link would ask the obvious question. When he didn't, Trep asked it for him.

"Do you ever perform the experiments on yourselves?" he inquired.

"Why do you ask?" Mr. Therion replied.

"Are you quite sure that you aren't Mr. Hyde?" Trep continued.

"Yes, quite sure," Mr. Therion stated firmly.

"But how do you know?" Link prodded.

"I beg your pardon?" Mr. Therion stated with indignance.

"What exactly differentiates you from Mr. Hyde?" Trep inquired.

Mr. Therion grew impatient.

"Gentlemen," he huffed, "I must object to these frivolous questions. If you are not serious customers, then please do not waste my time further. I will entertain only questions that do not verge on insanity. Otherwise, our business is done."

"How many bodies are housed here?" Empeirikos queried.

Mr. Therion coughed.

"Just this one," he admitted somberly.

"Only one?" asked Link. "Where are the other bodies?"

"I'm afraid it's illegal to remove the bodies from the laboratory," Mr. Therion explained. "We will either harvest the organs for you here or store the bodies in stasis until you require them."

"Then, do you make much money from full body clones?" Empeirikos continued.

Again, Mr. Therion coughed.

"I'm afraid not," he said. "Most of our revenue comes from organ scaffolds with immediate harvest."

"About the legality of transporting the bodies," Link commented, "we have heard that exceptions may be made in extraordinary circumstances."

"Well," Mr. Therion said, "Mr. Hyde did inform me that you are paying with an Omega Entrepreneur card. In that case, if you have money for the lawyers, we will help you prepare your scientific justification to be argued in a court of law. The burden is on you to justify it, but exceptions have been made before."

"Really?" Link exclaimed. "Quite a surprise."

Trep was also intrigued by the mention of previous exceptions. Now was their chance to extract incriminating information.

"What was the nature of their exception?" Trep asked.

"I'm afraid we must adhere to client confidentiality," Mr. Therion admonished.

"How many clones did they purchase?" asked Empeirikos.

"Three of them," said Mr. Therion proudly. "Our largest sale ever. We celebrated with enough alcohol to quench a forest fire."

"Might I point out that alcohol is flammable?" Empeirikos corrected him.

"Yes, just joking," Mr. Therion apologized.

"Well, we would like to take your suggestion and obtain legal counsel," said Link. "We need those bodies at our headquarters in order to perform experiments on them."

"I cannot guarantee that an exception will be made," stated Mr. Therion. "You will have to discuss it with the lab manager."

"Aren't you the lab manager?" asked Trep. "I mean, isn't Mr. Hyde the lab manager?"

"Neither of us," Mr. Therion explained. "You'll have to speak with our supervisor, Dr. Theta. She oversees all operations here, including sales and legal proceedings."

"When may we meet with her?" Empeirikos asked.

"Perhaps today," said Mr. Therion, "if you don't mind waiting in our analytical lab. I'll inform her right now."

He led them from the full body lab and returned them to the familiar lounge. Then, he disappeared out the door. As they relaxed, Trep wondered whether Mr. Therion would return once again with a new name. This time, Dr. Theta.

"Do you think he really is Mr. Hyde?" Trep asked.

"If he is, we'd better get out of here before his next psychotic transformation," Link advised.

"I did notice that Mr. Therion smiled at us," Empeirikos pointed out, "while Mr. Hyde remained inscrutable. They exhibit different personalities."

"So maybe he's not Mr. Hyde after all," Trep exclaimed.

"At last, a glimmer of sanity," said Link with relief.

They awaited Mr. Therion's return, basking in the glow of the virtual assistant's pulsing lights and semi-romantic advances, shifting their feet and twiddling their thumbs listlessly. Eventually, Mr. Therion returned and invited them to follow him. They walked for several minutes down circuitous passageways, at one point crossing a covered bridge into an adjacent building. It was a much older building than the first, with occasional glimpses of the original brick foundation left exposed for rustic effect. Finally, they arrived at the elevator doors.

"Who's going first?" Mr. Therion asked.

"Don't we all ascend together?" asked Link.

"It only holds one person at a time, I'm afraid," Mr. Therion stated. "This building has been renovated around the original framework. The original elevators have been left in place.

This particular elevator leads to the supervisor's office."

"After you," said Link, gesturing at Trep.

Trep, feeling ambivalent, decided not to protest. He shuffled toward the doors as Mr. Therion summoned the elevator with the press of a button.

Instead of the expected ring of the familiar arrival bell, a buzzer greeted them as the double doors slid open, revealing a cramped but plush transport chamber with a fluffy red rug. Trep stepped inside and pressed the only visible button to trigger the closing of the doors. The buzzer sounded again as the doors shut softly.

The antiquated roping system lurched into motion as Trep felt the elevator move along what he suspected was an upward path. He stared at the faded walls of rusted golden brass. The elevator hobbled to a stop as the buzzer announced his arrival.

Trep emerged into an empty foyer with a door at the other end. Paintings adorned the walls. The buzzer rang again as the elevator doors closed. Trep stared at the paintings as he waited. They were images from the Wizard of Oz. In the first, Dorothy confronted the fierce hologram of the Wizard. In the second, the Scarecrow and Tinman fled in fear as the Wicked Witch of the West pursued them on her broomstick.

The sound of the buzzer woke Trep from his trance. Link emerged from the elevator, smiling.

"That was fun," he announced. "Did you miss me?"

Trep was struck by an alarming thought. What if, standing before him, was a mere clone of his former friend Link? What if his friend had been switched with an imposter by a trap door in the elevator? How could he prove that it was one or the other? He scrutinized Link's facial features while the buzzer rang and the elevator shut closed.

"I'm starting to think that you really did miss me," Link joked.

"It's nothing," said Trep, shrugging off his anxiety. He put his fears at the back of his mind.

They waited in silence for the arrival of Empeirikos. Soon, the doors opened and the automaton stepped out.

"Have a nice ride?" Link jested.

"Ah, too bad," sighed Empeirikos. "Same old Mr. Link. But yes, it was endless amusement."

"Is Mr. Therion coming?" Trep inquired.

"I think so," said Empeirikos.

They awaited their host, who strode through the doors a minute later.

"Thank you for waiting," said Mr. Therion. "I apologize for the inconvenience. Now, Dr. Theta's office is just through that door. She's aware that you are interested in purchasing ownership rights to full body clones."

Mr. Therion smiled and held the door open for them. Though uncertain of what to do next, they exited the foyer and prepared to confront Dr. Theta.

Chapter 25

They entered a stately office embellished with abstract art. Cubist paintings hung on the wall behind a minimalist sculpture of a terraced pyramid shaded in swaths of black.

But the formality of the décor was broken by the remnants of a recent celebration. A set of balloons floated near the ceiling in one corner of the room.

"Surprise!" read the caption on one.

"Congratulations!" read another.

A small table beneath the balloons was stocked with party favors and a shining trophy. The figure in the trophy appeared to be an armored soldier.

At a sigmoid desk of ebony sat a flaxen-haired woman attired in a floor-length trench coat and knitted purple scarf. A dapper red beanie flopped deftly over her bespectacled visage. She regarded them through her lenses as if through a microscope.

"Come in, guests and, uh, robots" she announced. "Please have a seat."

Mr. Therion situated himself on a tall white barstool while the others followed suit. Trep noticed that Dr. Theta was staring intently at Empeirikos and seemed to be doing her best to stifle a surprised chuckle.

"Mr. Therion," she complained, "you neglected to inform me that one of our guests is an *automaton*."

"My apologies," said Mr. Therion. "I didn't think it relevant."

Dr. Theta then addressed Empeirikos.

"You're the automaton from the comedy club," she said. "I read about you in the papers."

"Yes," said the robot. "Empeirikos is the name. Very pleased to meet you."

"I'm Dr. Theta," she reciprocated. "Mr. Therion tells me that you're interested in ownership of mature full body clones?"

"Yes," replied Empeirikos. "For neural net research. We cannot have those brains harvested in your lab. We need them to remain fully functional."

"You see," Trep elaborated, "our clients have developed a technology that generates a neural net model from brain tissue."

"And the last thing we need is a *dead body* on our hands," Link blurted. The interrogation had begun.

Dr. Theta was unfazed.

"Well," she said, "ownership is extra charge, and petitioning the courts for an exception isn't cheap. Are you sure you can afford it?"

"Oh, yes," Empeirikos assured her with a flash of his Omega Entrepreneur card. "We're rich. Filthy rich."

"Very nice," Dr. Theta complimented him, but she furrowed her brow.

"Back up a minute. What is a stand-up comedian doing with an Omega Entrepreneur card?"

"Well, it's a long story," Trep replied dismissively.

223

"But, obviously," Link interjected, "Empeirikos's designers have spared no expense since, if he proves to be the Technoconvergence, they stand to make a killing."

Dr. Theta shot Link an amused glance.

"That's correct," she complimented him. "And what is your name?"

"Lincoln Romano, ma'am," he replied. "Link, for short."

"Mr. Link," Dr. Theta reprimanded him, "you do not strike me as a biotechnologist. You are trying my patience. An automaton in an organ farm is decidedly odd, to put it mildly. And, despite the Omega card, I have to wonder whether we're likely to collect payment from a stand-up comedian. Something tells me that you have ulterior motives for this visit, so please get to the point. Why are you *really* here?"

Trep sighed. Now they were in trouble. What hubris had led them to believe that they could pose as scientists? And if indeed it was Dr. Theta who had sent the threat letters, what would she and her staff do if revealed? Take them prisoner? He prepared to sprint for the door and escape down the single-person elevator, or even fight and defend his friends.

"We're here to investigate the recent killings at the *Space on Earth* nightclub," Link admitted.

"Thank you," Dr. Theta stated. "I appreciate your honesty. But what makes you think that those incidents have anything to do with us?"

"We detected that the bodies were fabricated," said Trep. "They were clones."

"*You* detected it?" Dr. Theta scoffed. "And what is your proof?"

"Well, it wasn't me," Trep explained. "Actually, it was Empeirikos who detected the clones."

Empeirikos, who had been silent until now, spoke up.

"And as for proof," he elaborated, "we looked up their social security numbers. The results indicated that they were fraudulent personas."

"But criminals falsify documents all the time," Dr. Theta objected. "How does that prove that they are clones?"

"I do not have direct access to my programming logic, but my discriminatory reasoning suggested that there was something different about them," said Empeirikos. "They did not resemble the other dead body. They were too pristine, too un-weathered to be authentic humans."

Dr. Theta glanced at Mr. Therion, who nodded his assent to some unspoken plan. Dr. Theta rolled her chair backward and opened the drawer of her desk. She reached inside and felt around for some hidden object.

Trep panicked, sure that it would be a gun and that he was facing his last day on Earth. He deliberated whether to say a prayer or run for the elevator. Perhaps he could pre-empt his assailant, leaping over the desk and tackling her. He would pin her to the floor and subdue her before she could aim the gun. He tensed his legs, preparing to jump.

To his surprise, a strident, comical siren blared. The room flashed with joyful lights of yellow and orange. Dr. Theta withdrew a set of party favors from her desk, swapping her beanie with a purple party hat, then grabbing a long noise-maker and blowing loudly on the mouthpiece, articulating a high-pitched musical whine. Mr. Therion followed suit, reaching into his inner coat pocket to acquire hidden party favors. He blew heartily on his kazoo while sporting a festive purple hat.

"Surprise!" shouted Dr. Theta and Mr. Therion in unison.

"What is the meaning of this?" Empeirikos protested.

"We're here to congratulate you!" Dr. Theta informed him. "Well done!"

"Yes, good show, Empeirikos!" exclaimed Mr. Therion.

Trep, on the edge of his seat, relaxed and slumped into his chair. Perhaps their spontaneous adventuring had not been such a bad idea after all.

Dr. Theta reached into her desk and deactivated the lights and sirens. She and Mr. Therion grinned clownishly in their purple party hats.

"Congratulate me?" asked Empeirikos. "Whatever for?"

"Your image recognition performed with *unparalleled* sensitivity," Dr. Theta exclaimed.

"Yes," Mr. Therion agreed. "You successfully differentiated human bodies from clones."

"Then you do not deny that the clones originated in your laboratory?" Empeirikos asked.

"Not at all," said Dr. Theta. "We've been waiting for you to find us."

"Hide and seek?" Trep interjected. "Is that what this is?"

"Your frivolous pranks may spell the end of Xanvier Reinhart's nightclub," Link scolded them, "not to mention the emotional anguish he may have experienced from the threats."

"Mr. Reinhart will be well compensated," said Dr. Theta. "Our clients will offer him a more than generous settlement."

"Your clients?" Link huffed. "What sort of conspiracy is this?"

"Our client is Zostronics," Dr. Theta explained, pausing to gauge their reaction.

When the name did not register with any of them, she added, with precise enunciation:

"The *designers*…"

"Do you mean to say *my* designers?" asked Empeirikos with surprise.

Dr. Theta nodded her confirmation.

Trep sat up in excitement.

"Who are they?" he asked.

"Why did they build him?" asked Link.

"Where may I find them?" asked Empeirikos.

"Don't ask us," said Mr. Therion. "We're just a subcontractor."

"We were hired to raise the clones, nothing more," said Dr. Theta.

"But surely you must know something about them?" Trep objected.

"Indeed," said Empeirikos, "even *I* am completely ignorant of them, as if orphaned on the street."

Dr. Theta shook her head, saying, "I have only met with their representative, Mr. Zostro."

"But Mr. Therion informed us that removal of clones requires a legal exception," said Empeirikos. "Surely, they must have presented you with a justification for their unusual requests. To wit, what was the purpose of all this subterfuge?"

"It was sort of a Turing test," Dr. Theta informed him.

"She's referring to the late Alan Turing's test for artificial intelligence," Mr. Therion explained.

"The designers informed us that, through benchmark testing, they have already established that humans cannot recognize a full body clone," said Dr. Theta.

"So in the event that Empeirikos so much as contacted our laboratory," Mr. Therion added, "we were quite certain that he must have achieved the objective."

"The objective being to ascertain whether an automaton's image recognition was superior to a human's?" Empeirikos inquired.

"Yes," said Dr. Theta. "If you solved a crime that a human could not, it suggests that Zostronics has reached their final development phase: a product which provides an advantage to human society."

So it had all been a proof of concept, Trep realized. An enterprising tech firm with a boundless budget. That would explain the Omega Entrepreneur card. But so many events were left unexplained. If Empeirikos was composed of unknown elements and new crystal structures, was he or was he not from outer space? What kind of tech firm had designed him? How had they kept it a secret?

"So that tech firm," Trep asked, "you say you've met with them?"

"Yes, with a representative," Dr. Theta replied.

"What did he look like?" Trep asked. If Empeirikos had originated from outer space, it implied that his designers would be aliens also.

"Anything unusual about him?" Link added.

"Was he extremely old? With leathery skin?" Trep continued.

"Slanted eyes, face like a lizard, not very friendly, maybe wants to eat you," Link joked.

"You mean an *alien*?" Mr. Therion blurted.

Trep regretted his line of questioning. He should have known that Link would make light of it. Now that Empeirikos had heard them speak of *aliens*, they may have compromised Detective Lick's investigation.

"They made it up," Dr. Theta vouchsafed, to their surprise.

228

"When Detective Lick sent his samples for analysis, he sent them to a lab controlled by Zostronics. That gave them an idea to throw you off track, so they got creative. They fabricated the results. To be honest, they would have liked to scare you away. But at the least, it provided a distraction from your sleuthing."

"Your interference in the investigation threatened to bias the experiment," said Mr. Therion. "They wanted to strengthen the test parameters to deemphasize the human element, increasing Empeirikos's contribution."

"So he's not from outer space," said Link.

"And he's not composed of unknown elements," said Trep.

"That's correct," Dr. Theta stated. "I was informed that he's constructed from lightweight carbon fiber and powered by a plutonium battery encased in titanium. And he had a predecessor, a robot named Bubba, who fell victim to an unfortunate accident."

"So he's just a normal robot," said Trep.

"Only the most advanced robot ever invented," Link commented.

"Yes, my coworker is convinced that something funny is going on," said Trep. "A fully-formed AI appearing without warning. How is it possible? Aliens would make more sense."

"I was told that Zostronics has spent years on this project," said Dr. Theta. "They've been raising robots like children, training their social responses. But it's just the nature of machines. Each iteration is saved as the starting point for the next. Once one prototype is sufficiently mature, it's inherited by posterity. They didn't test them in the field until they were ready, and now they have emerged."

"So you're telling us there's nothing unusual about the

229

circumstances?" asked Link.

"Well, there wasn't supposed to be," said Mr. Therion.

"But something went wrong," said Dr. Theta. "Inspector Sondworth is dead."

"Now we have a crime on our hands," said Mr. Therion.

"The three of us have been together the whole time," Link explained. "It couldn't have been one of us."

"Who do you think did it?" asked Trep.

"We certainly don't know," Dr. Theta responded. "They hired some military veterans to fly the clones in. They were muscle men, trained killers. They could have easily overpowered Inspector Sondworth."

"Maybe it was just an accident," Link suggested.

"Inspector Sondworth discovered them and they panicked," Trep added.

"Yes, maybe the inspector even threatened them with his umbrella," Link quipped.

"Your guess is as good as ours," said Mr. Therion.

"Was the inspector on their payroll?" asked Trep. "The logistics are staggering. How else could they have coordinated the murder and the phone call on exactly the same day that we met with Inspector Sondworth?"

"The inspector knew nothing of them," Dr. Theta replied. "I was told that they selected you to receive the robot after reverse engineering your program, *Opportunity*. They knew that it would predict a result of private investigator for the robot's multiplicity, and they guessed that you would make an appointment to meet with an investigator. Using the Internet of Things, they tapped your phones and gained advance notice of your meeting with Inspector Sondworth. They created enough mayhem to reserve every other inspector in town, at exorbitant expense, making certain that Inspector Sondworth would be the only one available for Xanvier Reinhart to hire when the first body was discovered at the nightclub. In the event that Inspector Sondworth did not invite the robot to join him at the crime scene, they were prepared with a backup plan."

"How did they coordinate the discovery of the first body?" Link asked.

"They had a week's advance notice of your meeting with the inspector," said Dr. Theta. "They simply hired their henchmen to deliver the body on the same day."

"Those two henchmen, do you have their address?" Link inquired.

"I think so," Dr. Theta replied. She shuffled through her desk and located a business card. She handed it to Link, who read it aloud.

"*Arlo and Vito Rialto, safari and adventure guides, treasure expeditions, tactical rescue*. Their address is on the South Bank."

"Are they cordial?" Trep asked.

"If you don't mind, we'd like to question them," said Empeirikos.

"Be my guest," said Dr. Theta. "And let us know what you find out."

Trep stood and prepared to leave. As curious as he was regarding Empeirikos's origins, he had felt increasingly claustrophobic. He was anxious to escape the confines of the secluded office.

"This way, gentlemen," said Mr. Therion, standing and beckoning toward the door.

They shuffled out into the hall and filtered one by one down the single-person elevator. Mr. Therion escorted them wordlessly to the front lobby, then bid them good day.

Chapter 26

The next day, they gathered at the nearest Tube station and took the first pod to the South Bank. They exited into overcast skies in the riverside district. Vagabonds and beggars loitered on the sidewalks against a backdrop of neon marquees.

As they set out toward the domicile of Arlo and Vito Rialto, a vagrant stood in their path with a goblet in his grasp.

"Spare some change?" he grunted as they approached. He extended the goblet toward them and Trep observed that it was full of change. Trep reached into his pockets and grabbed several quarters, flinging them into the goblet.

"Many thanks," said the vagrant, rattling the change with a shake of the goblet.

Just beyond the vagrant, several seagulls commanded the sidewalk, pecking at an abandoned sandwich. The closest of them turned and, swiveling its head to the side, jeered at them with a scornful eye. The seagull mocked them with a contemptuous squawk, and the other seagulls joined in like a chorus of hecklers. Trep fought back the urge to kick them as he crossed their path. They scurried away with a lumbering waddle.

Proceeding through a crowd of tourists and a shopping mall, they detoured into a residential area. Consulting their com visors, they navigated a series of side roads until arriving at a quaint beach house bordering the river. High fortified walls topped with metal spikes flanked a rustic gateway. A speedboat was docked at a bedraggled pier littered with birds.

A security camera and speaker system were mounted above the gateway, with a doorbell to one side. Link rang the doorbell while they posed in front of the camera. Trep verified that the gate was locked. Link rang the doorbell again, at last eliciting a response from the speaker system.

"What do you want?" said a brusque male voice.

"We're here to investigate the recent events at the *Space on Earth* nightclub," Link announced.

A long silence ensued, then the voice continued.

"How did you find us?" it asked.

"We got your address from Dr. Theta at *Organicity*," Link explained.

"Who are you?" the voice asked.

"My name is Trep Sportly," Trep replied. "I'm here with my friends Link and Empeirikos the Automaton. We were working with a private detective named Hoagie Sondworth who was assigned to the investigation."

A buzzer sounded and Trep lifted the handle to open the gateway. Obtaining entrance, they found themselves on a stone walkway in the middle of a lush garden. Arching over the walkway was a metal detector alongside a conveyor belt. Another security camera and speaker system were mounted above the detector. The lights of the detector had been activated and the conveyor belt was moving.

"Go through the metal detector," ordered the voice through the speakers. "First, place all of your metal items on the conveyor belt."

Trep saw that another camera was centered over the conveyor belt. He removed his keys and change from his pockets, placing them on the conveyor belt along with his umbrella and com visor. Then, he proceeded through the metal detector, retrieving his items at the other end.

Next, Link placed his umbrella and com visor on the conveyor belt and began to empty his pockets. He proffered a set of keys, a vaping pipe, a tie clip, and a corporate badge with a metal frame. He next removed a loop earring, his necklace, and his graduation ring. At that point, his keys had long since reached the terminus of the conveyor belt, and a pile of accoutrements was progressively evolving. Link, not inclined toward sprinting, nevertheless pumped his arms and strode as briskly as possible through the metal detector, gathering his belongings before they fell off the conveyor belt.

Having obtained safe passage, Trep and Link regarded Empeirikos from across the walkway. He was still attired in a silk shirt, trench coat, fedora hat, and brown trousers. Although he looked non-threatening, Trep thought, how would he ever get through the metal detector?

With an air of futility, Empeirikos emptied his pockets, placing his retractable umbrella on the conveyor belt, then took a few tentative steps into the detector. Instantly, the alarm sounded with a strident buzz. Empeirikos promptly backed out of the detector.

"Go through the metal detector again," said the voice through the speaker system.

"I cannot, sir," Empeirikos declared. "I am an automaton."

"Place all of your metal items on the conveyor belt," the voice reiterated.

"With all due respect," Empeirikos huffed, "I am an automaton. Although my frame is carbon fiber, many of my components are pure metal. It is not possible for me to proceed without triggering the alarm."

The voice paused for a long interval. Trep stifled a haughty guffaw.

"Then you must remain outside," spoke the voice firmly. "Do not attempt to enter when the door opens."

Empeirikos leaned reluctantly against the gateway.

"What if I remove my garments?" he asked. "You may then be quite sure that I wield no weapons."

After a brief pause, the voice acquiesced.

"Leave your clothes at the gate," it said.

Empeirikos stripped off his clothes, hanging his trench coat over the gateway. His reflective gray exterior constituted a virtually seamless carapace of carbon fiber. Stepping through the detector, he ignored the glaring alarm and joined Trep and Link at the other side.

A buzzer sounded the unlocking of the interior door. Trep turned the doorknob and swung the door inward. They entered a white-tiled antechamber. Framed depictions of tanks and helicopters adorned the stained wooden walls.

To their left were a hallway and minibar. Beyond them, the overcast sky was visible through a floor-to-ceiling window overlooking a wooden deck on the riverside. A row of futons and easy chairs were arranged at the foot of a large screen television. Near the window, a tall cage held a brightly plumed parrot that craned its neck to observe their entrance.

A stocky man with cropped yellow hair stood at the minibar. He was outfitted in tightly laced boots, khakis, and a green tank top. Streaked tattoos accentuated his muscles from his shoulders to his hands, one of which was poised near the holster of his pistol.

"Fix you a drink?" he asked, regarding them warily.

"Don't mind if I do," said Link, feigning a knowing grin. "Bloody Mary?"

Seemingly oblivious, the man nodded and commenced stocking vodka and tomato juice into the clutches of the automated bartender. The steel grips of the machine's bountiful hands tightened as each bottle entered its grasp. The man continued with bottles of Worcester and tabasco, passed a full lemon into yet another metallic hand, and finally an empty glass. Checking that salt, pepper, and ice were well stocked in the internal reservoirs, he pressed several buttons to communicate the recipe. On pressing start, the arms of the bartender swung into motion with a whir.

Another man of similar build now appeared from around the corner of the far room. Unlike his brother, he wore sweatpants, sneakers, and a black hoodie. His head was shaven and embellished with several earrings and a thick gold necklace. As he approached the bar, he nodded at them.

"I'm Vito," he announced. "This is my brother Arlo."

"Trep Sportly," said Trep, extending his hand. He regretted it an instant later, wincing from the man's bearlike grip.

Observing Trep's expression, Link elected to simply nod from a distance, tersely stating just "*Link*."

The automated bartender had finished Link's drink. Arlo retrieved it and handed Link a tall cocktail glass garnished with a stalk of celery. Thanking him, Link sipped heartily.

"How about you?" Arlo asked Trep.

Although in no mood for alcohol, Trep did not want to be rude, and so ordered a margarita.

"My brother Vito will stock that one for you," Arlo explained, stepping to one side to give his brother room on the counter. Vito reached into the overhead shelves for the tequila, orange liqueur, and a tall cocktail shaker, swapping them for the bottles in the automated bartender's grasp.

"We divide up all our skills equally," Arlo continued. "I make martinis, Vito makes margaritas. And tactically, I train in offense, Vito trains in defense, so we always have both contingencies covered."

Link sipped his bloody mary with contentment. After Vito passed a lime to the machine and pressed *start*, the automated bartender commenced shaking the margarita.

"How many clones did you deliver to the nightclub?" asked Empeirikos.

"Three of them," said Arlo. Trep was surprised. Only two of the corpses had been clones, but he remembered Mr. Therion commenting that three clones had been purchased.

"Tell us what happened on the night you delivered the third clone," Empeirikos requested.

"Well, Vito flew the helicopter," said Arlo. "Vito has several pilot licenses. I'm trained in skydiving and parachuting. We had the clone wrapped in black latex, and I was wearing black camouflage. We landed and Vito waited while I hauled the body down the stairs. I floated into the nightclub with the body. It was late Sunday evening, their slowest night, so we knew the club would be practically empty. Our orders were to deliver the third body to the watchtower of the castle and position it alone on the floor. But when I arrived, there was already a body on the floor of the watchtower."

The automated bartender was now prepping the rim of the margarita glass with lime and salt.

"Well, our clients get their orders mixed up all the time,"

Arlo explained, "so our policy is to terminate the mission, no questions asked. I returned the body to the helicopter and we disposed of it in a trash bin."

"Why didn't you call the police?" Empeirikos inquired.

Abruptly, the parrot squawked, with slurred syllables:

"Birds of a feather!"

Vito smiled.

"The parrot's name is *Polly*," he explained.

"Birds of a feather!" chirped the parrot.

"She thinks you said her name," he finished.

Trep's drink had been completed by the automatic bartender, and Vito handed him a pink margarita glass. The brothers' gaze now turned to Empeirikos.

"None for me," the automaton responded.

"Why don't we refer to them as *officers* instead," Link suggested, "so we don't confuse the parrot."

Arlo nodded and continued.

"Well, we didn't call an *officer* because we assumed it was just another clone on the floor. It happens to us occasionally. Our clients mix up our schedules and double-book us on top of another contractor."

Vito had left the bar and was now attending to the parrot. He opened the door of her cage, offering her a saltine cracker, then petting her neck feathers. Polly grabbed the cracker with one foot while nibbling with her beak.

"Well, it was a *real* body," Link informed them. "In fact, it was a *private investigator*."

"So that's why you're here?" Vito stated. He had returned to the minibar.

"Yes," said Empeirikos. "We would be interested in any information you could give us about who might have killed the inspector."

"I didn't notice anyone suspicious," said Arlo. "You should leave the details to the police."

"Birds of a feather!" squawked the parrot. Vito again left the minibar to attend to her.

"Is Vito the only one who feeds the parrot?" asked Link.

Arlo nodded.

"It's his parrot," he informed them. "Vito is in charge of animal care, wild animal evasion, outback survival, and forestry. He's also in charge of safaris. I'm in charge of fishing and diving expeditions."

Vito had reopened the parrot cage and supplied Polly with a fresh cracker. The parrot chirped gleefully on accepting the food.

"Me and Vito are only one year apart," Arlo explained. "We've always been afflicted with an identity crisis. When you have a brother who's practically your twin, you look for subtle ways to distinguish yourself."

"How interesting," Empeirikos commented.

Polly squawked something indecipherable in parrot language. Vito returned to the minibar.

"We didn't kill anyone," he said. "Those clones were sacrificed at the lab before we retrieved them. Besides, it was just a harmless prank."

"That's why we let you in," Arlo added. "We have nothing to hide."

Finishing his cocktail, Link made an observation of his own.

"All of this alcohol seems to have triggered my appetite," he exclaimed.

"Mr. Sportly, please finish your drink as well," Empeirikos requested. "I think we have troubled these gentlemen enough."

Trep finished his drink and wiped his mouth on his sleeve, setting the glass on the counter.

"Thanks so much for your time," Empeirikos told Arlo and Vito, who nodded politely back.

Trep and Link followed Empeirikos out the door. After Empeirikos regathered his belongings and was attired once again in his detective garb, they headed for the nearest restaurant.

Chapter 27

Stopping at a riverside restaurant, they refreshed themselves on local seafood. Their lingering intoxication was assuaged. Link, however, remained loquacious, as if still inebriated.

"If you were an alien," he said to Empeirikos, "I would have to guess that you were sent to stop the antigravity. It might represent competition for your space-faring friends."

"It is indeed a plausible theory," replied Empeirikos. "If the adventure clubs prove successful, antigravity transport might soon follow. In fact, Mr. Reinhart informed us that his previous job was in transportation. Perhaps he is simply testing the waters with an eye toward evolving new transportation solutions."

"Nate Locket would disagree," Trep objected. "He thinks alien influence is behind much of our technical progress. He would probably suppose that Empeirikos was sent to *save* antigravity."

Link was incredulous in the face of contrasting theories. Empeirikos, however, expanded on Trep's statement.

"If the future of antigravity is endangered," he said, "it implies that schemes are in motion to discredit it. Namely, the events at the nightclub."

Trep proposed yet another hypothesis.

"It's quite possible that, while the majority of aliens have undertaken to prevent antigravity, a minority have secretly forged Empeirikos in an attempt to undermine the majority."

"Or vice versa," Link added, playing devil's advocate.

Empeirikos was exasperated.

"If I ever encounter these aliens," he said, "I'll have no idea how best to align my loyalties."

"But seriously," asked Trep, "what did you think about the Rialto brothers?"

"Yes, Empeirikos," Link prodded. "Did the Rialtos kill the inspector?"

"Their alibi seemed coherent enough," said Empeirikos. "Yet, it's not inconceivable. What if the inspector had interrupted Arlo in the midst of his delivery of the third clone?"

"He touches down on the watchtower with the clone," Link surmised. "But, surprised by the reappearance of gravity, he drops the body on the floor with a loud thud."

"The inspector is going over his notes at the bar," Trep elaborated. "He's plotting new ways to take credit for Empeirikos's ideas. Suddenly, he hears a thump from the watchtower."

"He storms up the staircase with no weapon," Link continued, "only to find the cloaked figure of Arlo, dressed like a ninja, struggling to lift a dead body."

"The inspector points his umbrella threateningly at Arlo," Trep suggested. *"Don't move!* he says."

"Arlo feigns surrender," said Link, "holding up his hands. But then he approaches the inspector and encloses his hands around the inspector's neck."

"As his grip tightens," said Trep dramatically, "the inspector's umbrella drops to the floor, and his eyeballs bulge in their sockets."

"The inspector tries to scream," Link continued, "but he can't make a sound."

"That's quite enough!" Empeirikos interrupted. "We get the idea. I suggest that the two of you skip his funeral."

"But it seems like a plausible scenario, doesn't it?" asked Link.

"Well," said Empeirikos, "Arlo's next act would be to remove the clone. However, it might be difficult to transport the clone back to the roof top, which would require lifting the body against gravity."

"Maybe we should go to the watchtower ourselves," Trep suggested.

"An excellent idea," Empeirikos agreed.

An hour later, the three of them had returned to the night-club and were climbing to the top of the castle. Mounting the last steps of the stairway, they emerged onto the watchtower, which was now devoid of the inspector's body and police barricades.

"According to Arlo," said Empeirikos, "he delivered the clone to the watchtower, but after encountering the inspector's body, he changed plans."

"He wouldn't have been able to stop his fall, though," Trep pointed out.

"Then he probably landed with the clone and had to haul it back into the air," Empeirikos said. "A difficult task. Trep, are you able to lift Mr. Link into the air?"

Trep tried lifting Link into the air with no success, but Link was overweight. When Link tried lifting Trep into the air, it was easy enough, and Link had to grab Trep by the legs before he floated away.

"Although this corroborates their story," said Empeirikos, "I still think that Arlo is our best suspect. Otherwise, it's an unlikely coincidence. How else would the inspector's location coincide with their delivery of the clone?"

"I don't know," said Trep, "but we might want to use our time here to investigate alternative explanations."

"If it wasn't the case that the inspector stumbled onto Arlo's delivery," said Link, "then it must have been premeditated. Someone was deliberately stalking the inspector. They waited until he was alone, then attacked."

"Whoever was stalking him must have had a motive," Empeirikos observed. "But there were very few people who even knew the inspector's business here: a few security guards, the secretary, and Xanvier Reinhart."

"Why would Xanvier want to stalk and kill the inspector?" Trep thought out loud.

"Maybe the inspector dug a little too deep," Link proposed, "and uncovered some of Xanvier's dirty laundry."

"Like what?" asked Trep.

"Perhaps a narcotics network," said Link. "Maybe Xanvier is selling virtual tablets while waiting for his new business to break even."

"But we bought the tablets from a stranger at the bar," said Trep. "The man in the studded vest. He called himself *the Aussie*."

"Mr. Reinhart would not have been able to sell them himself," said Empeirikos. "He would have hired an intermediate."

"Maybe the Aussie is up there now," Trep suggested. "We could ask him who his source is."

Before long, they were floating toward the upper reaches of the vast chamber. The watchtower had turned out to be a perfect launching platform. As the highest point accessible from the ground floor, its surroundings offered no obstructions to their jump. And, the influence of gravity from the ground floor was at its weakest. They were easily able to aim for the suspended lounge and reach it swiftly.

They alighted on the edge of the plexiglass floor and stumbled briefly as they gained their balance. Awash in neon blue light, they examined their surroundings. A man and woman were reclining on the cubical cushions, sipping beer and sharing a joke; either that or they were laughing at the sight of two men and a robot springing up like bagels from a toaster. The Aussie was seated at the bar, sipping a cocktail and conversing with the barmaid. The lounge was otherwise empty.

They proceeded to the bar. Link asked the Aussie if they could join him. When he agreed, they sat and ordered cocktails. The Aussie was under the impression that they wanted to buy new virtual tablets. When they informed him otherwise, he seemed to regret his decision to talk with them.

"Don't you pursue any other hobbies besides virtual tablets?" Link asked.

"Not anymore," the Aussie told them. "It's my own way of burying the ghosts from my past."

"What sorts of ghosts are you running from?" Trep asked.

"Snakes," said the Aussie. "Big ones."

"Does it have something to do with the studs on your vest?" asked Empeirikos.

The Aussie nodded and sipped his cocktail. He seemed to relax as he recounted his story.

* * *

"I was the best snake wrestler in all of Australia," he explained. "People flocked from miles around to watch my tournaments. First, I had some traditional wrestlers warm up the audience. The difference between them and me was that they wrestled pythons in teams. Burmese pythons grow to over twenty feet and two hundred pounds, wide as a telephone pole, with muscles so powerful they can squeeze the air out of your lungs. One man is not strong enough to escape its clutches, so they wrestle in teams where someone plays the victim and the others rescue him. It takes at least two other men with strong hands to pry the victim out of the snake's coils."

"But not for me. After the audience watched team wrestlers for almost an hour, I took the stage and promised to escape a python unassisted. The audience was in disbelief. I wore a black vest with sharp black studs camouflaged by decorative black tassels. The studs were virtually undetectable without extremely bright spot lights. When the starving python was released from its cage, the audience thought I was as good as dead. As it slithered toward my feet, young children began to cry. While it encircled my legs, I raised my hands into the air so it couldn't trap my arms. I had no protection for my neck or head, but I didn't need it. The snake never got that far. As it wound up my torso, it began to encounter increasing discomfort from my vest. Sensing a counterattack, it tightened its grip, which forced it to stop climbing."

"It felt like my legs were going to break, but the pressure around my upper torso was bearable. The snake couldn't get the right leverage. The tighter it constricted, the more it was in pain. For a while, it kept circling in search of a better grip. As it became more and more confused, it loosened up on my legs. I could have just waited for it to give up, but I had to put on a show for the audience. Before they detected that the constriction had no effect, I grabbed the coils with my hands and began to slowly pry myself free. The snake was still disoriented, so as I loosened one coil it would tighten another, but to no avail. Each time, it encountered the same problem. Just as I sensed that it was going to give up, I heaved it off and threw it to the ground. The snake was bruised and sore, retreating back to its cage faster than a stampede of horses. The audience erupted into applause and cheering. I took a long bow, with a smile as wide as the Mariana trench."

"My renown was spreading, and I took my crew on tour across the country. Times were good. Business was lucrative, and I fell in love with a trapeze girl from Melbourne. She had always wanted to get out of Australia, and she convinced me to retire and travel the world with her. Touring Asia and Europe in her company, I had finally found happiness. I was mustering the nerve to ask her to marry me. But when we reached America, she jilted me for a stunt man in Vegas. With no job and a broken heart, I gambled away half my money before I wised up and hit the road. Fate brought me here, and you know the rest."

* * *

"And now you make ends meet as a narcotics dealer," Link commented.

The Aussie shrugged.

"I was already drowning my sorrows with virtual tabs," he explained. "When I realized that I was spending the last of my fortune on it, it seemed like the most natural thing to do."

"So you don't synthesize them yourself?" asked Trep.

"No," the man replied. "I'm an athlete, not an organic chemist."

"Who is the supplier for virtual tablets?" Empeirikos inquired.

"I have heard that the top of the supply chain is a strange old lady on the outskirts of town," the man informed them. "But as for me, I just buy them here."

"From whom?" Empeirikos prodded him.

"I can't reveal my source," the man said. "But whenever you have a busy nightclub, drugs aren't hard to find."

"But if there's another supplier here," Empeirikos continued, "don't the two of you have a territorial dispute?"

"We have an agreement," said the Aussie. "I sell from the upstairs lounge, and they get the ground floor. Since I'm the new guy in town, I get a much smaller share, but I'm content with it."

"But what if some interloper showed up to spoil your newfound contentment?" asked Link.

"Like who?" the man asked.

"Like a nosey private investigator who asked too many questions," Link continued. "What would you do if someone threatened to report your activities?"

"You guys don't seem like investigators to me," said the Aussie skeptically.

"Not us," said Link, "but there was a death in the club recently. An inspector."

"The killer has not been found," said Empeirikos.

"And you suspect me?" the man asked.

"You had a motive," Link said. "The inspector was investigating the possibility of drug overdoses on the premises. Maybe he bought some drugs from you, revealed his disguise, then blackmailed you for information. Maybe he thought you knew who's been killing random club goers."

"I heard about that," said the Aussie, "but rumor has it that it was just an overdose. It happens, but it's a far cry from homicide. And as for my motive, there are plenty of other nightclubs in Sojourn. If the inspector threatened my nest egg here, all I had to do was relocate. I'm from out of town, so I have no strings attached to any particular venue. You've got the wrong guy."

"Thank you for the explanation," said Empeirikos. "We're sorry to have bothered you."

Empeirikos stood up and motioned for the others to follow him. He strolled over to a lounge of plush chairs flanking a coffee table at the center of the platform. They sat and collected their thoughts.

"I found his explanation believable," said Empeirikos. "And further, since he presumably had no knowledge of the Rialto brothers, it begs the question of how the inspector's death was coordinated with the delivery of the third clone. If we assume it was too improbable for a coincidence, the Aussie and the Rialtos would have to have been acquainted."

"I agree," said Trep. "A newcomer wouldn't have that kind of inside information. It had to be someone in a higher position."

"What about Xanvier Reinhart?" asked Empeirikos.

"We already know that he did not kill the first two victims," Link objected, "nor did he send the threat letters."

"But he still could have slain the inspector," said Trep.

"He was worried that the deaths would be blamed on antigravity," Empeirikos explained. "It threatened to close down his nightclub. Therefore, it's plausible that he stood to benefit from the idea that a tangible killer was stalking the nightclub. It would conveniently deflect the blame from antigravity."

"Let's interview him again in light of recent events," Link proposed.

"Why don't you make the appointment while I compile the evidence," said Empeirikos.

Link donned his com visor while Empeirikos closed his eyes and thought. Trep found himself reclining in his seat idly. He removed the packet of virtabs from his pocket. He still had several left. He strolled to the bar and ordered a coffee, which he used to wash down a virtual tablet. Returning to his chair, he leaned back and closed his eyes.

Chapter 28

Langdan had a plan to steal the most famous painting in the world, the *Ontologia*, in broad daylight. Langdan was a sculptor, and a good one at that. But he admired the freedom in a painting. The freedom to portray the subject in any setting. The freedom to convey subtle emotions with a blend of tones from the palette. What Langdan really wanted was to achieve a painter's level of expression with ceramic carvings or plaster castings. To make sculptures that people would stare at for hours. To that end, he had avidly patronized every art museum in Italy, haunting their corridors in search of a painting that would show him the way. And at last, in the Moderna museum in Florence, he had found it.

Painted by the most renowned artist of the 24th century, Cricket, the *Ontologia* was a spinoff of the *Mona Lisa*, painted by Leonardo da Vinci in the 16th century. The eyes of the *Mona Lisa* were said to follow you wherever you walked in the room, and in Langdan's experience that seemed very true. Da Vinci had painted her stare along an orthogonal vector to achieve the disconcerting effect. Yet, when you were the only one in the room, and you hiked from one vantage point to another and found that still her eyes fixated on you, you could not help but wonder whether something in the painting had actually changed, whether the painting was possessed with sentient forces.

Eight centuries later, Cricket had taken da Vinci's idea to a new level. With the *Ontologia*, it was not just the eyes of the subject, but the entire person. Langdan had first witnessed it one year ago. As he entered the room, he had seen only the frame of the painting from one side, a large crowd gathered at its foot, gesturing and murmuring with astonishment. The crowd was impenetrable, so he had lingered on their periphery, gazing upon the painting.

It portrayed a lovely young girl with a bright smile and flowing brown hair, her sparkling azure eyes complementing the flow of a waterfall in the background. A river bisected the painting. On one side, the girl sat on a ledge by the water, garbed in a silken white dress. She smiled as cherubim groomed her tresses with brushes and combs. She stared across the river, out of the painting, into the audience. On the other side, terraced hills were plowed by machines that carved patchwork patterns into the landscape.

The artist's technique was spectacular, the colors vivid beyond description. But the crowd would not budge, so Langdan could not gain a closer look. Instead, he circumvented the crowd and reassessed the painting from the other side. But when he returned his gaze to the picture, he found that a new figure occupied the portrait. The girl's auburn hair had turned raven, the cherubim had changed to bats, and the girl had a gap between her two front teeth. Her freckles sparkled in the glare of the sun.

Langdan had suspected that he had sleep deprivation. He retreated to the coffee shop and ordered a coffee. He refueled with biscuits and croissants. He took his mind off the episode by solving the crossword puzzle in the local paper. Eight across: *rationalism*. Three down: *instigate*. He went home and attended to his sculpting, then went to sleep.

But the next day, on returning to the Moderna, his experience was the same. Except that it was also entirely different. On exploring the room housing the *Ontologia*, he found that, from every vantage point, he witnessed an entirely different girl in the painting. Now she was a long-haired brunette resembling the *Mona Lisa*. Next, she was a short-haired blonde resembling Marilyn Monroe. Sometimes she stared back at the viewer, other times she didn't. He retreated to the coffee shop, cautiously asking the hostess whether he was hallucinating. She said she suspected that he was, recommending an espresso to wake him up. His paranoia increased exponentially.

But as he flipped through the paper each day in search of the crossword puzzle, he stumbled upon articles lauding the new painting. The masterpiece was rumored to be nothing more than a hologram, a stereoscopic juxtaposition of wavefronts that uniquely captured the multiple angles of perspective. But Langdan knew it was fallacy, for a hologram could only capture one subject from many perspectives, producing the illusion of three dimensions. Yet, the *Ontologia* was not just one subject, but a variegated ensemble of shifting subjects.

After continuing to haunt the Moderna, Langdan began to suspect that the painting was a lenticular print, a juxtaposition of interlaced images that are masked with a lenticular lens so that only one of them is visible from each viewing angle. Lenticular prints could contain multiple subjects. However, the resolution of a lenticular print was inversely proportional to the number of images it contained, since the artist sacrificed scarce lenticules for each additional subject. Yet Langdan was certain that the *Ontologia* harbored images of at least thirty different subjects with no apparent reduction in resolution.

As Langdan stood before the *Ontologia* for the twentieth time, gazing into its depths, he detected no glossiness or refraction from a magnifying lens. It did not resemble any lenticular print that he had ever seen. In fact, when he focused on the material composition rather than the imagistic effect, all he saw was paint. Although the tones were as sharp and the brush strokes as smooth as a nano pixel display, the *Ontologia* was a painting, he was quite certain, though it defied explanation.

He retreated to the coffee shop and worked the crossword puzzle. Fifteen across: *prestidigitation*. Four down: *somnambulism*. Searching his memory, he attempted to ascertain the number of subjects he had witnessed in the *Ontologia*. Perhaps as many as forty, but he had lost count. When he tried to remember them individually, his recollections were often vague. Was it just a defect in his powers of recall? Or was there something in the painting that defied his attempts to fathom its essence?

He returned to the gallery and resumed contemplating the painting. He paced the room and attempted to enumerate its subjects. Why did they evade his grasp, like specters in the fog? He smiled each time he spied an incarnation that he recognized. He lingered and tried to catalog the various facets of a subject before shifting position again. "*Scusi*," he repeated in Italian each time he bumped elbows with the throng of bystanders occupying the room.

Now he was looking upon the first subject that he had

seen. He remembered the flowing brown hair and the angelic attendants fluttering above her. On first seeing her, he had joined the crowd at their edge, and before long he had been marveling along with them. There was no crowd at the moment. The room was occupied by several onlookers: a young couple dressed in new garments purchased from Milan, an old man with glasses, a pair of student researchers with backpacks.

He noted the subject's white dress, the configuration of her posture on the ledge by the river in the foreground of the painting. Perhaps he should note his position in the room. But wait, something was odd. He currently stood approximately at the vanguard of the painting. But, when he had first seen the subject, he had viewed her from the periphery.

An idea occurred to him. He took a few steps away and observed another subject. He paused briefly to take stock of it. Then, swiftly, he stepped back to his first position and observed the first subject again. But something was wrong. He had acted quickly enough that he was certain that his movements had been precise. His feet rested on the same tiles that they had occupied just moments ago. Yet, when he observed the painting, a third subject gazed back at him. He did not remember her visage.

Perplexed, he bounced around the room with agitation, nervously muttering *"Scusi"* as he repositioned himself. None of the other guests were changing their vantage points. They had just been viewing the statue garden, and after several minutes they would move on to the tapestry gallery, to be replaced by another pair of curious onlookers.

But Langdan was convinced that he was unraveling something remarkable, something that verged on impossible. His memory had not been at fault, but the issue of his sanity still remained unresolved. He was certain that the various subjects of the painting did not occupy fixed positions. Their materialization was unpredictable. Yet that ruled out lenticular prints, which had a single fixed image for each angle. And it had all been accomplished in a painting that would have looked quite at home in a gallery of Renaissance artworks.

Langdan returned to the coffee shop to collect his thoughts. He ordered cappuccino while flirting with the lovely barista, Gertrude.

"What are you doing this evening?" he asked.

"I will probably collapse on the sofa and fall asleep with the television on," she replied while gathering the ingredients.

"If I could take you anywhere you'd like to go tonight," he continued, "where would it be?"

But she only laughed as the cappuccino began to brew.

"That sounds like fun," she said, "but I'm so tired. Try me again some other day."

She handed him his cappuccino. He procured several euros from his pocket and told her to keep the change. He returned to his unfinished crossword puzzle. Seven across: *stochastic*. Twenty down: *superluminal*.

He took a taxi to his newly rented studio and worked on his sculptures. He was brimming with new ideas, but none of them were groundbreaking. Not like the *Ontologia*. How could he learn its secrets well enough to transfer them to his sculptures? Was it even possible?

He decided that, if he just spent his days at the museum, he would never know. The newspaper articles compared the *Ontologia* to a three-dimensional illusion. But a true hologram portrayed only one scene or subject, exhibiting it from various angles. On the other hand, if it were a lenticular print, then it must have the thinnest of plastic overlays, undetectable without a microscope. And how had it been possible to simulate the texture of paint so realistically, and with such high resolution?

Stranger still was the random shuffling effect, which defied all physical laws of which Langdan was aware. He was beginning to suspect that the *Ontologia* must be an enchanted artifact. Perhaps it would confer its power on whomever took sole possession of it.

And that was when Langdan decided that he would have to steal the *Ontologia*. He did not know how or when, but he knew that he would continue to stalk the halls of the museum until some means availed itself. And then, after he stole it, he alone would possess its powers. He would use them to forge a sculpture of rare beauty and originality, a cutting edge trend setter. He would be the most renowned sculptor in the world.

On one auspicious day at the Moderna, he figured it out. He had started, as usual, by flirting with Gertrude in the coffee shop.

"What do you think of the *Ontologia*?" he asked her.

"I'm quite fond of it," she replied demurely.

"Have you seen the hidden images within it?" he continued.

"What?" had been her reply. She furrowed her brow and scrunched her nose.

"Hidden images," he had repeated. "Veritable paintings within paintings."

"You sound delusional," she chided him. "Hidden images are nothing but hallucinations."

She briskly finished preparing his coffee and petulantly

yanked his money from his hands. Then she stomped away, not returning with his change.

Was it true? he thought to himself. *Was it all in his imagination?* But no, he had read about it in the papers. The many facets of the Ontologia were regarded as something of a mystery. If he was crazy, perhaps even daft, if not delusional, then so were the journalists.

He consoled himself over coffee while perusing the crossword puzzle. Ten across: *lullaby*. Sixteen down: *sparticle*. Just then, an accordionist strolled through the room playing an Italian waltz. The somber tones sang to him and soothed his anxious thoughts. He let his mind lapse into a state of tranquility. As he closed his eyes, he saw a lingering image of the *Ontologia* suspended in his subconscious. It was ethereal, like a phantom of itself. It wavered between countless incarnations, never committing.

And then it came to him. The *Ontologia* suddenly made sense. Cricket had somehow seized on quantum indeterminacy to conjure a painting in a state of superposition. Though quantum effects were mostly known at the subatomic scale, still the experience of color was related to the interplay of photons and electrons, and the quantum effects of both were amenable to manipulation. Through some technique hitherto unknown, Cricket had engineered a macroscopic quantum structure, a juxtaposition of ghostly figures. The *Ontologia* was in an indeterminate state until he cast his gaze upon it. At that moment, it collapsed into one of its many possible forms. It would not be the same form that he had observed the last time, but somehow its many forms were renewable. If Langdan reobserved the painting on enough occasions, he would eventually view a subject that he had seen before.

Langdan ran to the chamber of the *Ontologia* and stood before the painting. It was a girl with flaxen hair and serene expression. He did not remember her. But when he shifted again, he saw a familiar subject. He stared, trying to remember his position in the room when he had last seen her.

He was alone in the room. But as he lingered, another onlooker joined him, a young scholar with a dapper bowtie and long, bushy sideburns. It dawned on Langdan that the young man must be observing the very same subject, for how could two paintings occupy the same physical space? But then Langdan shifted position again, and still the painting transformed. Langdan cast a sidelong glance at the young scholar, but there was no surprise in his face, as if nothing had changed for him.

It followed that an onlooker standing next to him would have a different experience from his own. Yet how was it possible for one point in space to contain different paintings? Perhaps the various forms were interleaved at speeds too fast for the human eye, and each form was visible from only one angle. But what could explain such a phenomenon?

Langdan returned to the coffee house and continued his thoughts. Quantum effects often involved groups of entangled particles. Perhaps the *Ontologia* was not just one painting, but several. The paintings wavered in and out of superposition, alternating between one form and another. If multiple forms existed, perhaps several duplicates had been hidden within the Moderna, their configurations teleporting between physical spaces. Perhaps Langdan could find them, most likely unguarded.

Determined to find the hidden paintings, he applied for a job as a museum technician. He felt sure that it would grant him access to the hidden rooms. For weeks on end, he compiled inventory in the storage rooms and rehabilitated artworks in the laboratories. His supervisor, Francesco, made him nervous. Like a slave driver, Francesco watched his every move, anticipating that Langdan would slack off at any moment.

Langdan was restoring a historical specimen when he felt Francesco's stare on his back.

"Why do you worry, Francesco?" he said. "I'm not a Chinese spy."

He turned toward the supervisor and saw that same mistrust in his eyes.

"What are you hiding, Francesco?" Langdan asked. "For all the time I've been here, I feel as though I still don't even know this place. After all of my faithful labor, can't you let me in on your little secret?"

But Francesco conceded nothing. Satisfied that Langdan was not resting on his laurels, Francesco went about his business.

Langdan took his lunch break a minute early just to spite his supervisor. He removed his respirator but retained his overalls, covered though they were in dust and grime.

At the coffee shop, he purchased the paper, a croissant, and English tea.

"Did you dress up just for me?" asked Gertrude.

"No, not exactly," he replied. "It's just a uniform. I have a job in the museum: technical assistant."

She appeared confused as she handed him his croissant. He sat in the corner and read the crossword puzzle. Fifteen across: *universality*. Eight across: *polyphony*.

Was it possible that the Many-Worlds theory explained

261

the *Ontologia*? When he stood in the room next to just one onlooker, he could never really know whether they perceived the same subject as him. But he recalled how, when just two people were in the room, he could shift his position and view a different outcome in the painting, yet the other observer's experience seemed unaffected, judging from their lack of reaction.

That implied that the bystander was most certainly perceiving a different subject in the painting, which meant that the painting could contain multiple interlaced images simultaneously. Langdan had assumed that it was a lenticular illusion based on the angle of the observer, but he had disproved that theory on finding no correlation between viewing angles and the subjects in the painting. He had next supposed that multiple paintings alternated positions in the frame, so quickly that it escaped notice. But what could explain such a phenomenon?

Langdan did not care. He had to formulate a plan to steal the painting. But he had used his new employment to search for hidden replicas, all in vain. Indeed, not just one, but many other versions must all exist. Yet, where were they?

Langdan could only guess that they must occupy alternate dimensions, through some variation of the Many-Worlds theory. The *Ontologia* began as a superposition of possible outcomes. As each observer set eyes on the painting, they branched into a subdimension with logical isolation from neighboring onlookers. Each observer became a separate quantum system, but the systems were only transient. The new system was maintained as long as an observation held, but the disparate dimensions hovered tenuously near their branch points, ready to rejoin their parent threads as soon as an observation lapsed.

As Langdan sipped his tea, a plan began to form. He would steal the painting after all. Soon, he would be the most famous sculptor in Italy, if not the world. That is, if he could unravel the painting's secrets. He remained in the coffee shop for several hours under the pretense of finishing the crossword puzzle. He neglected to return to work and was certain that he would be fired. It no longer mattered. After four hours, at last, Langdan had his plan.

He went home and returned to the Moderna in his getaway van, then entered and proceeded to the room of the *Ontologia*. He waited until he was the only one in the room. When the last of the guests had filtered out, he prepared himself psychologically. He was a bundle of nerves. He flexed his fingers and shook out a cramp in his leg. He hopped up and down like a runner preparing to sprint. Then, mustering all of his courage, he strode briskly to the painting, grabbed its frame with two hands and, in full view of the security cameras, he tremulously removed the painting from its mounts.

When he was confident that he had it in his full possession, he returned his gaze to the wall. As he had expected, the painting was still there. If disparate forms of the painting existed in their own personal subdimensions, then it should be possible for Langdan to steal one of them without anyone else knowing. He had only stolen his version of the painting, which no one else could see, but that was all he needed.

Yet, if he could so easily lift one incarnation of the painting from the wall while the other incarnations still remained, how had it ever been possible for them to transport the painting to the Moderna in the first place? Perhaps they had enlisted ten thousand men, each one transporting a different incarnation from Cricket's studio to the museum. How many times could Langdan steal the painting before he exhausted its supply?

Langdan did not let himself be troubled with such thoughts. He walked nervously out of the Moderna, glancing at the guards. Did they see the painting in his grasp? But no one raised their voice. Would they notice his erratic behavior through the security cameras? Langdan would cross that bridge when he came to it. He exited the Moderna and hurried to his getaway van. Reaching the vehicle at last, he took a moment to hold the painting up to the light and gaze upon it.

Strangely, removed from the confines of the museum, the girl in the painting seemed to assume the appearance of the environment, surrounded as they were by a lush garden of trees and flowers. It seemed that the girl's eyes had become flowers, and her skin green as tree leaves. But then, as he moved the painting, it changed again. The face of a man was staring back at Langdan, and to his surprise, the man blinked at him, then walked out of view. And then Langdan realized, to his horror, that the girl was not there at all. Only a hole remained in the painting where the girl had once been. Langdan was staring straight through the painting at the garden beyond.

What should he do? He could replace the lost canvas, then repaint the missing figure. But Langdan was not a painter, and Cricket was the best.

Terrified, Langdan pushed his hand through the hole to convince himself of its emptiness, then viewed the painting from behind, searching for clues. At a loss, he enclosed the defiled painting in his van and ran back toward the Moderna.

Surely the girl had fallen onto the road somewhere. He stopped cars, forcing them to wait while he crawled on his hands and knees in search of the girl. Not finding her, he scoured the sidewalk, pushing people out of his way. He heard a jingling behind him and turned to discern their source. Several pedestrians were charitably throwing change in his direction. He ignored them. He probed behind the bushes. He rummaged through the trash cans. Still having no luck, he reentered the Moderna.

Langdan was certain that the girl was lying on the floor somewhere. No one else would notice. He just had to find her. He scoured the floor, retracing his footsteps all the way back to the room of the *Ontologia*, but found nothing. Desperately, he checked the adjacent rooms. At last, he spotted a janitor sweeping the floor. He knew that the janitor swept the same pattern every day, moving from the lobby to the statue garden, into the chamber of the *Ontologia*, and then the present room. He saw the janitor empty his dust pan into a garbage can and disappear through a door, garbage bag in hand.

At last, Langdan thought, he had found her. The girl was in the trash. He just had to retrieve it. Langdan ran to the door and forced it open in time to view the janitor in the parking lot. He was placing the garbage bag in the back of a pickup truck. However, the truck was already occupied. The driver promptly waved to the janitor and sped away.

Langdan would not let them take her. He ran as fast as he could back to his van. He keyed the ignition and pursued the pickup. The truck was fast, but so was Langdan. He floored the accelerator. He rounded a corner, then ran a red light. There was the pickup, climbing the onramp to the scenic route. They would be all alone on a highway lined with trees. He would force the truck off the road.

He raced up the onramp to the expressway. The small

pickup scooted into the forest and disappeared. Langdan pursued it into the shadows. Beneath the shade of the canopy, enclosed by trees, no one would know about the encounter.

Langdan revved his engine and rammed the back of the pickup. The terrified driver hugged the curb, giving Langdan enough room to pull alongside him. Langdan drew his gun, then shot out a tire. The pickup screeched, skidding precariously. It pulled over and ground to a halt.

Langdan stopped his van and exited the vehicle with his weapon drawn. The sanitation worker had his hands in the air. Langdan pointed his gun menacingly, barking at the driver to evacuate the vehicle and lie on the ground. The driver obeyed, lying prostrate with his hands on his head.

Langdan removed the garbage bag from the truck bed and tore it open, dumping its contents on the road. He rifled through the spilled scraps, casting rubbish left and right, vainly searching for the remains of the lost painting. But, try as he might, he could not find the girl. He pressed the muzzle of his gun against the prostrate sanitation worker.

"If you say one word about this to anyone," he grumbled, "I'll kill you."

Forlorn, he returned to the Moderna and the room of the *Ontologia*. He tried to remember where he had last viewed the painting. At that point in the room, the many forms of the painting would have converged onto one. He took his best guess and stood transfixed, then looked at the painting. Seeing nothing unusual, he began to shift his position randomly, walking left and right, forward and backward. Occasionally, he thought he saw the painting disappear ever so fleetingly… the missing version that he had stolen. And, when it did, he seemed to still see the specter of the girl hovering in the air with no painting in her penumbra.

Was the girl still on his version of the painting in the room? Should he pluck her off? A baby was crying somewhere in the room, its parents attempting to hush it, preventing Langdan from approaching the painting. Instead, Langdan sat and thought.

Of course, he realized, it made perfect sense. Only the *subject* of the *Ontologia* existed in superposition, an interweaving of every possible form for every possible viewer. With so many forms at once, even in its state of indeterminacy, the girl must have had tremendous logical density, a much larger mass than the rest of the painting. He had lifted the frame of the painting from the wall, but the girl had remained stuck like glue to her own entangled physical locus, a locus of countless entangled forms.

And then Langdan realized that his plan would never work. He could never possibly fashion an entire statue like the *Ontologia*, a juxtaposition of statues that would branch out into hyperdimensions to convey separate experiences for every viewer. A statue of endless indeterminate forms would have an unwieldy density, so much so that it could never be transported from his studio to the museum. Cricket had been clever to limit it to the central figure. Langdan would have to find another way.

From the corner of his eye, he saw Francesco emerging from the portal of the statue garden. He looked furious. Had he seen Langdan on the security cameras? But no, his arms were crossed in a silent attempt at a guilt trip. He was only enforcing discipline. Langdan had just confirmed his suspicions. He was a procrastinator after all.

"Get back to work!" Francesco insisted.

Langdan obliged, surprised that he still had a job. He continued to work as a technician, day after day. And when each shift was done, he would stroll through the statue garden and admire the works of the masters. Through careful inspection, subtle details were slowly revealed. He began to incorporate them into his own sculpting techniques. He hoped that, gradually, he would still achieve his goal.

With his munificent salary, he began to leave large tips for the barista.

"I hear a tour of French impressionists is in town," he told her. "Would you like to go to the exhibit?"

"I'd love to!" she replied, much to his surprise.

He knew they could be happy together. And one day, he would invite her to his gallery. His version of the *Ontologia* was still there, hanging by a hook on his wall, although it was not much more than a frame. He thought of it as a landscape painting now, and he would have to be content with that. It was his souvenir from the *Ontologia*. He had adapted his gallery to revolve around it, and now it was the centerpiece.

Langdan would show off his statues, which grew ever more skillful. Slowly, his oeuvre was maturing into a bold new style, a signature all his own, intensely inventive, exceptionally innovative. What marvels would he accomplish through diligent work and thoughtful sculpturing? Only time would tell.

Chapter 29

Trep awoke from his daydream. Empeirikos was seated before him, but Link was nowhere to be found.

"Ah, Mr. Sportly," Empeirikos greeted him. "While you were gone, we successfully scheduled another appointment with Xanvier Reinhart. He has agreed to meet with us within the hour. I have been researching a potential case against him."

"What are your conclusions?" Trep asked.

"He was not aware that the first two victims were just clones," said Empeirikos. "He may have killed the inspector to deflect the blame from the toxic effects of antigravity."

"So he's not involved in the drug trade?" Trep asked.

"Not in my opinion," said Empeirikos, "but Mr. Link is quite fond of that explanation."

Trep surveyed the room, looking for Link. He spotted him nearby, leaning over the edge of the lounge.

"Link, what are you doing?" Trep shouted.

"I wanted to make sure that the coast was clear for our leap to the watchtower," Link responded. "But it's not. We have an unwelcome guest at the bar."

Trep stood and joined Link at the perimeter. He peered across the void at the dimly lit bar that crowned the castle.

Several patrons reclined there, one of them wearing a conspicuous fedora hat. It was Detective Lick. He was sitting at a high table near the edge of the rampart, peering out across the promenade.

"So what?" Trep asked. "The detective has no problem with our involvement."

"But he only granted that privilege for a day or two," Link suggested, "and that time has passed. He would probably prefer to dismantle our team. We were never more than embellishments for the inspector's entourage. We have no official capacity. With the inspector off the case, we could be arrested for obstruction of justice."

Trep couldn't disagree, though he'd been trying to avoid thinking about it.

"We don't have to jump to the watchtower," Trep suggested. "Couldn't we just land somewhere else?"

"We could," said Link, "but he still might notice us on our descent. He's sitting at the top of the castle."

Trep thought a moment. What Link wanted was either a way to sneak past the detective or get rid of him. They could exit through the old stairways behind the walls of the hotel, but how would they climb down from the roof? That left only one alternative.

"Doesn't the detective still believe that Empeirikos is an alien?" Trep asked.

"Yes," said Link. "What about it?"

"I have an idea," Trep stated. "Empeirikos, can you hit a remote target with a paper airplane?"

"I doubt it," said Empeirikos. "At least, not on the first try. It would require at least ten practice throws."

"Then how about a crumpled up piece of paper?" Trep

continued.

"That's different," Empeirikos exclaimed. "A well-defined center of gravity and aerodynamic flexibility. My chances of hitting the target would be much higher."

"Good," Trep stated. "Now we just need a piece of paper and a pen."

He inquired at the bar. The barmaid informed him that he would have to settle for the back of one of her inventory sheets. He thanked her and accepted a spreadsheet and a ballpoint pen. Turning the spreadsheet over, he began scrawling a message. The first line read:

"Alien robots have invaded the nightclub..."

On completing the note, he showed it to Link.

"That just might work," said Link approvingly. "But will the detective read it?"

"Of course," Trep insisted. "He's a detective."

Trep crumpled the note into a firm ball.

"Empeirikos," he said, "will you do the honors?"

He handed the ball of paper to the robot.

"You see your target?" Trep asked, pointing toward the castle.

Empeirikos peered across the hollow chamber.

"The detective," he stated.

Trep and Link nodded their assent. Empeirikos took several practice swings, then lobbed the ball of paper into the air. It quickly broke free of the gravity zone and continued along a straight trajectory toward the castle. They watched as it sailed swiftly out of sight. The question was, would it maintain enough speed on entering the castle's gravity well? Trep expected that Empeirikos had aimed slightly above the detective to compensate for the gravitational counterforces in the castle's vicinity.

Suddenly, the detective's fedora hat nearly tumbled to the floor. Almost spilling his drink, the detective spun around and reached for his gun. After ruling out the neighboring clientele, he began to search the floor. On locating the ball of paper, he lifted it up and uncrumpled it. He stared intently as he read the note. On finishing it, he left the bar urgently without so much as a glance in their direction.

"Well done!" Empeirikos commended them. "What did you write in the note?"

After Trep explained it to him, he almost thought he detected a smile on the robot's impassive countenance.

"Now let us make haste to Mr. Reinhart's office," said Empeirikos.

$$* * *$$

Half an hour later, they were again seated in the company of Xanvier Reinhart. They had agreed not to tell Xanvier about their meeting with Dr. Theta. Presumably, if Xanvier were innocent, he would have no knowledge that the first two victims had been clones.

They convened around a glass table adorned with potted plants. Mr. Reinhart was ostentatiously attired in a brown sport coat with a striped tie and plaid pants. With the two remaining fingers of his crippled left hand, he smoothed out his beard.

"What brings you here again?" he inquired.

"We wanted to congratulate you," said Empeirikos.

"On what?" Xanvier prompted.

"The murder of the inspector has absolved you of guilt

relating to the effects of antigravity," the robot explained.

"Indeed," Xanvier asserted. A moment of silence ensued.

"So you think I killed him?" Xanvier continued.

"It would be a convenient solution to your problems," Empeirikos stated.

"The inspector was hired by none other than myself," Mr. Reinhart objected.

"A possible ruse to impute your innocence," Empeirikos suggested.

Mr. Reinhart laughed.

"I hired him only to kill him?" he asked.

"Perhaps," Empeirikos continued.

"And sent myself threat letters, as well. What manner of masochist am I?" Mr. Reinhart implored.

"The drug dealing kind," Link accused him. "Our sources inform us that a lucrative trade in illegal virtual tablets is operating through your nightclub. Are we supposed to believe that it's being conducted without your knowledge?"

"Drug addiction is a feeble escape from reality," Xanvier exclaimed. "If anyone feels they must resort to drugs for entertainment, then they have no business in my nightclub. This is an adventure facility catering to the brave of heart, not to laggards and sloths."

Trep, who had recently awoken from a hallucination, rose from his chair in spite of himself, compelled to defend his dignity, but Link pulled him down by his shoulders.

"Nevertheless," Link stated hurriedly, "your nightclub is infested with drug-users and drug-dealers. We can only suppose that it's related in some way to the inspector's death."

"Such as?" Xanvier queried.

"The inspector discovered your involvement in the drug

273

trade," Link proposed. "Before he could expose you, you eliminated him."

"Of course," Xanvier jested. "How clever of me to hire a professional investigator, knowing full well that he would easily uncover me, requiring me to commit an even more heinous crime. If my only offense was dealing drugs, why would I hire the inspector and become a cold-blooded killer overnight, facing the possibility of life imprisonment?"

"You were desperate," said Trep. "Threatened with losing your nightclub, you were forced to hire the inspector. But then you realized that you could not afford to lose the drug trade as well."

"When the inspector confronted you," said Link, "you strangled him."

"You're forgetting one thing," Xanvier objected. He smiled as he presented his left hand. "With missing fingers, how could I have strangled the inspector?"

Link fell silent. Trep saw it as an opportunity to restore his pride.

"Nice try, Link," he chided him. "Now I understand the difference between a common legal assistant and a licensed attorney."

Link was out of his seat in an instant and bridling at Trep.

"You take that back you sniveling scum!" he fulminated.

"Look who's talking!" Trep riposted.

Xanvier stared smugly at the mischief he had instigated.

"I must apologize for my friends' behavior," Empeirikos sighed. "Please excuse us now. Sorry for the disturbance."

Empeirikos quickly ushered Trep and Link out of the office while Xanvier glowered at them. At last understanding the human need for alcohol, Empeirikos steered them toward the nearest bar. With a flash of his Omega card, he ordered a pitcher of beer, then occupied himself with the nearest available IQ puzzle. Trep and Link pouted while the alcohol numbed their nerves.

Chapter 30

One hour prior, Detective Lick had uncrumpled the ball of paper that struck him unceremoniously on the crown of his fedora hat. He read the message scrawled on the note.

"Alien robots have invaded the nightclub. They are investigating human mating rituals in an attempt to spawn a human-robot hybrid. If you don't believe us, go to the South Bank correction facility and interview a man named Officer Ronch. Requisition his com visor. On it, you'll find videos of aliens mating with humans. How do we know? Because he arrested an alien recently, and he's been cooperating with them ever since."

Intrigued, the detective exited the nightclub at once. He navigated his squad car to the South Bank prison. Flashing his credentials, he was allowed through the gates into the private parking area. He proceeded to the Sheriff's office and asked to speak with Officer Ronch. As a venue for the interview, he requested a private interrogation chamber.

The Sheriff lowered his com visor and summoned Officer Ronch, who was on duty at large. Detective Lick awaited him in the interrogation room. Within an hour, a portly patrolman with a spindly black mustache resembling a frog's legs entered through the door. Looking anxious, he took his seat across from the detective.

Detective Lick remained silent for a long moment. He knew that the pressure would make the officer more compliant to his demands.

"Officer Ronch?" he addressed him at last. The officer nodded.

"I'm going to have to requisition your com visor," the detective told him. Officer Ronch removed his visor and set it on the table. He resumed staring at the floor, wide-eyed, wondering what sort of trouble he was in.

"Do you recognize any of these people?" asked Detective Lick, placing photographs of Trep, Link, and Empeirikos on the table.

Officer Ronch perused the photographs, most of which he recognized. One of them, however, was not a person at all, but a robot.

"I recognize these two," he informed the detective, gesturing at the humans. "I arrested them for disturbing the peace, maybe a week ago."

"And the third photo?" asked Detective Lick.

"Well, this appears to be a robot," said Officer Ronch. "I've never seen it before."

"Is it possible that the robot was disguised as a human when you arrested the other two?"

"I suppose so," the officer conceded. "I arrested three civilians."

"So you arrested the robot also?"

"I don't know," said the officer, clearly confused.

"I think you *do* know," Detective Lick sneered, "and the evidence on your com visor is going to prove it."

The officer looked spooked.

"I didn't mean to arrest him," he groveled. "Was the robot

someone important?"

"I think you're well aware of what's at stake here," the detective admonished. He grabbed the com visor and affixed it over his eyes. He pressed the side arm to activate the display, then guided his fingers across the outer lens. The officer's electronic desktop unfurled before him. Folders of unresolved cases occupied the foreground.

Detective Lick navigated into the background folders, looking for hidden files. Before long, he found a set of video archives. The folders were named with strings of random numbers. He perused them leisurely.

Officer Ronch fidgeted uncomfortably. He could hear the noises emanating from the com visor. It didn't sound like music or video games. It was a salacious discord of grunts and groans.

Detective Lick's fingers traced deftly across the lens, opening and closing files at a frantic pace.

"I'm seeing some fairly young subjects in these videos," he announced. "Are these just domestic photos from your own family?"

"No, sir," the officer protested. "Those are confiscated materials from closed cases."

"Well, if the cases are closed," the detective scolded him, "then throw them out!"

"Yes, sir."

Detective Lick was repulsed by the sheer volume of files, over ten folders of them. It must have represented years of material. He picked up the pace, inspecting each folder without hitting every file.

"Well, I don't see any robots in these collections," he said.

"No, sir," the officer replied. "Should there be robots? I'm open to robots if necessary."

Detective Lick scowled.

"I'm going to dispose of these for you," he stated. He dragged the materials into the com visor's recycling bin and promptly emptied it.

Officer Ronch heard the whoosh of his visor's trash bin disgorging. He stared at the floor.

Detective Lick suddenly wondered why he was there. He had found no evidence of alien mating rituals. He fashioned a quick closing statement.

"The next time you confiscate video evidence, leave the files at the station."

"Yes, sir," said Officer Ronch, relieved not to have been disciplined.

Detective Lick returned the com visor and exited the interrogation room, slamming the door behind him. He realized that he had fallen victim to a childish prank. Perhaps the robot was terrestrial after all. As he drove his squad car out of the station, he vowed never to speak another word of it.

Chapter 31

Trep and Link had each guzzled three bottles of beer and were back on speaking terms. Together with Empeirikos, they reviewed the evidence.

"Even if Xanvier was not the strangler," said Link, "with his money, he could have hired the best hitman in town. He's still our most likely suspect."

"Really?" asked Trep. "Despite being victimized by threat letters and extortion?"

"He took advantage of the mayhem to change public opinion," said Link. "The first two deaths were blamed on an overdose or antigravity toxicity. But with a killer on the prowl, the spate of deaths would not be perceived as a side effect of antigravity."

"What about the Rialtos?" asked Trep. "Isn't it an odd coincidence that the inspector's dead body showed up on the watchtower just before their delivery? The inspector must have surprised Arlo, who therefore killed him."

"It's the best explanation for the concurrent events," Empeirikos agreed, "but the Rialtos lacked a compelling motive. It's just as Mr. Reinhart said: why should he risk committing an even more heinous crime? The dead body they were delivering was only a clone. The Rialtos had not broken any laws other than trespassing and perhaps vandalism. If the inspector interrupted them, it would have been a severe overreaction for Arlo to kill him and risk life imprisonment."

"Same story with the drug dealer," Link added. "As a newcomer, he had no attachments to this nightclub. If the inspector threatened to expose him, he could easily move somewhere else. He didn't sound desperate enough to kill someone."

"On the subject of drug dealers," said Empeirikos, "the Aussie informed us that another supplier exists on the ground floor. While the Aussie may be a newcomer, this other source may be quite another story. Perhaps we should attempt to locate him or her."

"Trep's the expert on drug deals now," Link joked. "We should follow his lead."

"I just have an appetite for new experiences," said Trep. "It relieves the monotony of working in a call center."

"I suggest that the two of you split up so your rivalries don't impede you," said Empeirikos. "But first, we must acquire funds to make payment."

They searched for the nearest bank machine and found one on the ground floor of the castle. Empeirikos withdrew a thousand dollars against his Omega card. He distributed it evenly between Trep and Link.

"I will wait here for you," he told them. "As robots have no neurotransmitters, drug dealers may be skeptical."

He sat at the nearest table and waved them goodbye. Link searched the castle while Trep searched the bars. Patrons regarded Trep with disdain when he inquired about drugs. He therefore changed his tactic to book requests. He was looking for rare books. He found that few people took him seriously, and some questioned his sanity. Eventually, however, he was pointed in the direction of a bar with dim blue lights. A solitary figure sat at a high table with a book opened in front of him. He sipped from a cocktail while reading leisurely.

Trep hurried back to the castle to inform Link. Together, they approached the pensive figure and sat across from him. He was balding, middle-aged, and bespectacled. He looked up from his book and regarded them dispassionately.

Trep glanced over the pages of the book in search of the title, reading the letters upside down. On seeing the name *Montag,* he recognized it as *Fahrenheit 451.*

"Bradbury," he commented. "Sweet."

The man remained reticent, nodding wordlessly.

"With the government burning contentious books," Trep continued, recounting the famous story, "the dissidents must memorize them word for word. How would they accomplish something like that?"

Trep still had elicited no reaction. In fact, after several seconds, the man resumed reading and ignored them altogether.

Link elected to forego subtlety.

"The Aussie sent us," he fibbed.

They now had the man's attention.

"Sent you for what?" the man asked.

"For books," Link replied. "Virtual books."

"You mean tablets?"

Link nodded. He produced five hundred dollars and set it on the table. The man frowned with consternation.

"That's not quite enough," he grumbled.

Trep reached into his pocket and withdrew a pair of hundred-dollar bills. He added them to Link's pile.

Swiftly, the man scooped up the cash and replaced it with a

large packet of pills. Trep pretended not to notice the pills, deferring the responsibility to Link. However, when Link was unresponsive, Trep was forced to pocket the merchandise. Now there was no way he was kicking his new addiction.

"Perhaps you're familiar with a favorite of mine," said Link. "Paradise Lost, by John Milton. What would you do if a nosey investigator threatened to expose your arrangement?"

"What are my choices?" the man queried, looking concerned.

"Your choices are: ignore the problem and hope for the best, run away and make a new start, or kill the investigator."

The man snickered.

"You're asking me whether I killed a private investigator?"

"An inspector was found dead in the castle two days ago," said Trep. "He was strangled."

The man smiled at them and closed his book.

"I don't make much money from these sales," he told them. "Most of the revenue goes to the producer."

"Who is the producer?" Link inquired.

"Sorry, I can't say."

"Nevertheless," Trep elaborated, "drug dealers kill people for money all the time. They ignore the risk of life imprisonment for the promise of short-term enrichment."

"I'm a bibliophile," he told them, "and so are my customers. We're peaceful introverts. We aren't that type of drug culture. Just ask the Aussie. If I were the sort of enraged psychopath that you're looking for, then I would have killed the Aussie as well."

"Apologies," said Link. "We thank you for your time, and my friend here thanks you for the drugs."

Trep swatted Link on the back of his head with his open

283

palm. Link yelped in pain. Trep stood and nodded at the bespectacled man, who returned to his reading.

Trep and Link rejoined Empeirikos at the castle. They recounted their meeting with the ground-floor drug dealer.

"He's the same as the other suspects," Trep stated. "None of them were desperate enough to kill someone."

"Except for Xanvier Reinhart," Empeirikos asserted.

"You think he's the drug producer?" asked Link.

"Not at all," said Empeirikos. "We have no evidence that Xanvier was involved in the drug trade. In fact, he argued compellingly that, otherwise, he would never have hired the inspector in the first place. His motivation in killing the inspector would simply have been to shift the blame for the spate of deaths away from the effects of antigravity."

"But what would killing the inspector add to the already existing scenario?" Trep asked.

"The deaths were arranged to look like accidents," said Empeirikos. "In order to save his club, Xanvier would have to change that impression."

"But that still leaves one detail unexplained," Link added. "How did Xanvier know exactly where and when to kill the inspector so that it would coincide perfectly with the third delivery by the Rialtos?"

"It makes it look as though the Rialtos must have been responsible," said Trep. "It's a perfect alibi."

"Xanvier must have known about the clones," Link suggested, "and the delivery."

"It's not hard to believe that Xanvier could have uncovered the fabricated deaths," Trep proposed, "and the source of the clones. Maybe he bribed someone at the lab to reveal the time and place of the next delivery."

"So that's it," Link stated. "Xanvier's the killer. We should inform Detective Lick."

"I'm afraid not," said Empeirikos.

"Why not?" Link asked. Trep was puzzled. He had thought they were all in agreement.

"I said that Xanvier was desperate enough to kill someone," Empeirikos replied, "but only for the sake of argument. I didn't say that he was the killer."

"Well, of course he was," Link said. "He had the motive and the means."

"Is it the coincidence on the watchtower?" Trep asked. "We have no evidence that Xanvier actually knew about the cloning lab or the Rialtos."

"It's not just that," Empeirikos elaborated. "Even if Xanvier did know all of those things, there's something much more troubling. While you were interrogating the drug dealer, I had some time to think. Two people died in Xanvier's nightclub in less than a week. The threat letters told him that more would die, and the toxic effects of antigravity would be blamed. He expressed concern that his nightclub would be forced to close. He already knew that someone else would die. He just had to take the initiative and preempt the killers with a murder of his own design. But whom should he choose?"

"The inspector," said Link. "Why choose him?"

"Precisely," said Empeirikos. "Anyone else would have sufficed. If Link's theory was true, and Xanvier was the drug supplier, then perhaps he had motive. However, that seems unlikely. Xanvier even argued that it would have been fickle to hire him only to slay him."

"If Xanvier wasn't responsible," asked Trep, "who was?"

"There's no other explanation," Link asserted.

"In fact, another explanation does present itself," said Empeirikos. Trep and Link were stumped. They regarded the robot dubiously, awaiting his solution.

"I first realized after speaking with the Rialtos," the robot continued, "but I needed time to compile the evidence."

"So what should we do?" asked Link.

"You should make that call to Detective Lick," Empeirikos stated, "but not to report Xanvier Reinhart."

"What, then?" Link asked.

"Please ask him to schedule a meeting at the laboratory," the robot said. "Mr. Reinhart should be invited, as well. I have an announcement to make."

Chapter 32

Link contacted Detective Lick and requested his presence at the laboratory, as well as that of Xanvier Reinhart and the lab staff. Detective Lick agreed to contact the necessary parties and suggested they meet the next morning. Minutes later, he texted back to confirm that an appointment at the laboratory had been made for ten o'clock.

Trep blanched at the thought of being taken hostage in Dr. Theta's isolated office. He contacted Detective Lick and suggested that they hold the meeting on the ground floor, and that the detective should enlist backup. Detective Lick replied that he would do his best.

The next day, they gathered in the lobby of Organicity. Trep anxiously awaited Detective Lick and hoped he would arrive fully armed. Biding their time, Trep observed the procedures of the technicians in their see-through laboratory. It was not clear whether it was just for demonstration or if they were performing real experiments.

Visible through the glass wall, the gray-haired technician was attired in a white lab coat, bulky goggles, and blue nitrile gloves. Arranged on his lab bench were a tall burette and several flasks of reagents.

He slowly titrated the alkaline solution from the burette

into the acid-filled flask. As he periodically swirled the flask, the phenylalanine indicator progressively evolved a pink hue, suggesting neutral pH, but it was difficult to gauge the endpoint.

Overlooked on the shelves behind him were the pH meters, which would have lent a higher degree of certainty, but the chemical indicators enjoyed a thorough monopoly at titration time. Perhaps they were simply entrenched, or perhaps the drab pH meter took a back seat to the lurid hues of the chemical indicator.

At last, Detective Lick strode through the entrance, accompanied by Xanvier Reinhart, attired in a gray tweed coat with a dappled bowtie. Not to be outdone by Mr. Reinhart's flamboyant style, Detective Lick was flaunting a thin pink tie beneath his navy blazer. From the shadow of his gray felt hat, his mouth was clenched halfway between a smile and a frown, exposing his toothy grin.

They exchanged greetings and moved to the front desk, where Detective Lick announced their appointment to the receptionist. With a nod, the receptionist lowered her com visor and sent word of their arrival.

Before long, an assistant appeared through the door and ushered them in. To Trep's relief, they were led to the nearest meeting room, where Dr. Theta was waiting at the head of a long table, swaying to a stream of soft music from wall-mounted speakers. Beside her sat Mr. Therion, stolid of countenance but tapping his thumbs along with the music.

Dr. Theta welcomed them and invited them to seat themselves. When they were all seated, she addressed them.

"Well, it's a beautiful day," she said. "Detective Lick, perhaps you could tell us why we're gathered here."

"We're here in relation to the death of Inspector Sondworth," he replied. "We may have received some information pertaining to the identity of his assailant."

"Please do enlighten us," said Dr. Theta.

"If I may," Empeirikos announced.

Dr. Theta nodded.

"The floor is yours," she said.

Empeirikos became animated, gesturing to his audience.

"Two days ago," he said, "Dr. Theta informed me that the events at the nightclub had been an elaborate subterfuge. Dr. Theta, could you please explain to us, exactly as you did that day, the reason for the experiment?"

Dr. Theta cleared her throat.

"My company was hired by an engineering firm, Zostronics, to determine whether an automaton's image recognition, when put to the test in the field, could outperform that of a human. For the past year, we have generated mature full-body human clones. That was the extent of our involvement. Mr. Reinhart, I apologize, but the threat letters were fictitious, and the bodies were just clones. None of your guests actually died from drug overdose or toxic antigravity effects."

Xanvier Reinhart was visibly incensed. He stood and appeared to be making an exit, then turned and pointed at Dr. Theta.

"Curse you!" he cried. "You will be sued for every penny you are worth! This will mean the *end* of your company."

"I'm so sorry," Dr. Theta apologized. "You could not be told. They knew you would never allow it."

"Your reputation will be cleared," Mr. Therion assured Mr. Reinhart. "Our clients will offer you a settlement beyond your wildest dreams. They have been more than generous with us."

"There will be no settlement!" Xanvier continued. "You should all be locked in prison! Detective Lick, surely this was in violation of the law?"

Detective Lick nodded.

"Extortion through the United States mail is punishable as a federal crime," he said. "In addition, for the stunt with the clones, you're looking at charges of trespass and criminal mischief."

"Don't blame us," objected Dr. Theta. "We just sell organs."

"Nevertheless, you could be charged as an accomplice or accessory to the crime," said Detective Lick. "But I'll have to speak with the head of Zostronics."

"Their behavior is detestable!" Xanvier steamed. "What could possibly have been so important? Will we risk our own peace of mind for the benefit of robot vision?"

"I don't know," said Dr. Theta, "but it's not just about robot vision, it's the idea that a robot could do the job of a detective as well or better than a human. I think you would agree that the Technoconvergence is an important event. According to our clients, this was its test."

"Nothing like this has ever been assayed in the field before," said Mr. Therion. "The results were beyond all expectations."

"Except for the death of Inspector Sondworth," Empeirikos interjected.

"Nobody predicted that," said Dr. Theta. "And nobody knows how it happened."

"But we do know how it happened," Empeirikos corrected her. "He was pummeled and strangled. Isn't that right, Detective?"

Detective Lick nodded.

"That's correct," he said. "He sustained blunt force trauma to the ribs, and he died of asphyxiation. Someone *killed* the inspector."

"Someone in *this* room," said Empeirikos.

The room fell silent as each individual glanced nervously from one face to the next.

"Now *that's* more like it," said Xanvier Reinhart, returning to his seat. "The culprit must pay for what they've done."

Empeirikos now stood and took to pacing the floor.

"Dr. Theta," he said, "you stated that the experiment was successful. Could you explain the reason why?"

Dr. Theta straightened her glasses.

"The performance of your image recognition was superior to that of a human. It has already been established that a human cannot identify a clone."

"So you generated mature full-body clones," the robot continued, "then killed them?"

"Well, yes," said Dr. Theta. "The Supreme Court ruled four years ago, in a landmark decision, to allow the harvest of mature human clones. Despite the ethical conflicts, it was ruled to be in the interests of society. But several human rights groups have been mounting a legal retaliation."

"So you ordered the termination of three human lives," stated Empeirikos.

There was no response. The room was hushed.

"Detective Lick," said Empeirikos, now turning toward the officer, "I was informed that you were deceived into thinking that I was an alien, is that correct?"

The detective nodded and shrugged his shoulders, clearly embarrassed. He smiled sheepishly at Trep and Link.

"Dr. Theta," asked Empeirikos, "what was the reasoning

behind that ploy?"

"I can't speak for Zostronics," she explained, "but I assume their reasoning was to remove bias in the experiment."

"In what way?" said the robot.

"Well, although it is known that humans cannot detect clones," she said, "there was still a chance that your human friends would obfuscate the results. So the story may have been fabricated to scare away humans, or at least distract them from the investigation, to increase the certainty in the outcome."

"So an experiment was envisioned, but then it was fine-tuned?" Empeirikos queried.

"Yes," said Dr. Theta. "They tightened the parameters."

"And if a flaw was found," said the robot, "it was terminated?"

Dr. Theta was impassive. Empeirikos continued pacing.

"For the past few days," Empeirikos said, "I have contemplated the question of how I was able to recognize the clones. At first, it was a mystery to me. But mysteries have a special truth property. If we are able to find an irrational counterpart, we may solve one mystery with another."

Empeirikos reached into his jacket and presented a paperback book entitled *Hidden Irrationality*.

"Those are the words of the author Nate Locket," he said. "And, of course, another mystery is the question of who killed Inspector Sondworth, and why. I propose that these two mysteries are related, and that each is the other's solution."

He now turned to face Dr. Theta.

"What made you assume," he asked, "that an automaton with no previous forensic experience would have the ability to recognize a dead body?"

"I don't know," said Dr. Theta. "I didn't design the experiment."

"Detective Lick," said Empeirikos, "a dead body does not resemble a living body, does it?"

The detective shook his head.

"Postmortem has several manifestations," explained the detective. "The pulse is gone, the blood drains from the skin, the muscles may have rigor mortis."

"It's fairly obvious," the robot continued, "that it's easier to identify a clone if one has an uncloned body to compare it with. But that implies that the inspector must have been killed for that very purpose. The intent was to place a clone and a dead body side by side on the same floor for convenient comparison, but the Rialtos aborted their delivery. Even so, I never would have solved the crime without the inspector's death. New to clones, and a stranger to cadavers, it would have been very easy for me to conflate their attributes."

Empeirikos now approached Mr. Therion.

"But *you* understood that, didn't you, Mr. Therion?" he said.

Mr. Therion was unfazed, so the robot continued.

"After Dr. Theta congratulated me on the superior performance of my image recognition, you complimented my success in differentiating between a human and a clone. What a stark contrast from Dr. Theta's description."

Mr. Therion remained impassive, staring at the surface of the table.

"On visiting the Space on Earth nightclub," the robot said, "my proprioceptors informed me that the air was quite cold. My knowledge base states that cold weather is an astringent, making human skin prone to laceration on impact. When you extended your palm onto the fingerprint scanner, you exposed the scars on your hand. Perhaps blemishes from years of spilt acid washes, or perhaps fresh wounds from your recent altercation with Inspector Sondworth."

"Your job is to raise clones to maturity," he continued, "and then harvest their organs. You have no qualms about terminating human life. You implicitly expressed discontent with your salary at Organicity. How much did they pay you to slay the inspector? Back at the lab, you had only one clone to care for in stasis, and bleak prospects for the future of full body cloning. So you jumped at the chance to profit from the inspector's demise, even if it meant ending up on the wrong side of the law."

"You stalked him until he reached the watchtower, then you overpowered him, punching him in the ribs, injuring your hands. You then proceeded to strangle him, but the inspector clawed at your hands as you did so. Although you were wearing rubber gloves to avoid leaving traces of DNA, that did not prevent the inspector from exacerbating your wounds. You then left him on the floor for the helicopter crew to discover. The Rialtos were a decoy. Perhaps you were told that the Rialtos would take the blame, and that's why you agreed to assassinate the inspector. But you were deceived. The coordination of the Rialto's activity with the murder raised suspicion of an inside job, pointing to you."

"And as for the unfortunate inspector," Empeirikos concluded, "why was he targeted rather than an anonymous civilian? As I was already intimately familiar with the inspector's living features, he represented an ideal subject for my forensic edification, a perfect example of pre-and-post-mortem symptomology. Imagine instead that the victim had been a stranger to me. Then how was I to distinguish which victims were real and which were the clones? It had to be someone I knew, at least for the purpose of tightening the parameters, so to speak. Each of these individual circumstances serves a greater purpose, that of the experiment, which can only implicate one of the perpetrators of the experiment, making *you* the most likely suspect."

Mr. Therion stared sullenly at the table. He shifted awkwardly in his chair, twiddled his thumbs, then glowered morosely at Empeirikos. Sensing that the robot had finished his diatribe, Mr. Therion finally spoke up.

"I have no rebuttal to what you have said, except for one problem."

"And what is that?" asked Empeirikos.

"I am *not* Mr. Therion," he explained. "I am *Mr. Hyde*."

As evidence, Mr. Hyde presented the back of his right hand. No scars or blemishes were visible on his skin.

Trep was stunned. He reflected on the fact that he had never seen Mr. Hyde and Mr. Therion in the same room. He still thought of them as one and the same. He had never thought to ask why only one of them was in attendance.

"Where is Mr. Therion?" asked Empeirikos.

"He has not reported to work today," Dr. Theta informed them.

"Are they really two different people?" Trep asked her.

Dr. Theta nodded.

"A remarkable resemblance," she admitted.

"Don't you *ever* occupy the same place at the same time?" Link asked Mr. Hyde.

"Our jobs don't overlap much," Mr. Hyde explained. "We're assigned to separate departments."

Detective Lick addressed Dr. Theta.

"We'll have to issue a warrant for Mr. Therion's arrest. He'll be presumed guilty until he turns himself over to the authorities."

"I understand," said Dr. Theta.

"And what about the engineering firm?" asked Link. "Will they be held accountable for their involvement?"

"We'll initiate an investigation," said Detective Lick, "but they'll receive due process. We can't jump to conclusions. Plenty of others may have had a motive."

Trep was disturbed by the realization that Empeirikos was in over his head. He was investigating the involvement of his own designers. Was it really to his advantage to pursue it further? Did he even want to know?

"Empeirikos," said Detective Lick, "I want to thank you for your assistance. This crime would have been difficult for us to solve. But you've offered a compelling explanation that at least gives us a head start."

"My pleasure, detective," said Empeirikos.

"I'm sorry about the potential involvement of your designers," the detective continued, "but if it's any consolation, we would be honored to work with you again on a different investigation. Inspector Sondworth's office is sadly vacant. Perhaps you could fill his role as a private investigator. It would be a valuable service to our community"

"It would be a privilege," Empeirikos stated.

With no suspect in custody, the interrogation drew to a close. It would be up to Detective Lick to apprehend Mr. Therion. They shuffled out of the office, said their goodbyes, and exited the laboratory.

Trep reflected on the fact that Empeirikos had at last been

offered a job. The robot would soon move into the former offices of Inspector Sondworth. Although Trep's office would feel sadly empty without the illustrious automaton, perhaps Tatiana would need a new chess partner. Trep could even win the Bronze Badger trophy, with a complementary Omega Entrepreneur card. For the first time in days, Trep's thoughts returned to the mundane details of his job as a search strategist.

Chapter 33

"Mr. Zostro," announced his secretary, "someone named Detective Lick is on the phone."

"Lick?" said Mr. Zostro. "Put him on."

Mr. Zostro sat at his desk, removed his hat, and put on his com visor. He was not fond of com visors. He did not find them agreeable with cowboy hats.

"Detective Lick," he said, "do you have *Projection Chat*?"

"Yes," replied the detective.

Mr. Zostro traced his fingers across his visor until his virtual fingertip located and tapped the icon to activate *Projection Chat*. Instantly, the screen on his wall lit up with the gaunt image of the detective. Mr. Zostro removed his com visor, refitted his hat, and stood to greet the detective.

In 2029, the Internet of Things had expanded into the commercial sector. Most people conducted transactions while staring into their com visors. Mr. Zostro, on the other hand, had cameras on his walls, a microphone on his tie, and a wall-mounted screen of flexible organic light-emitting diodes to project the image from someone else's remote camera. He felt it was much more progressive than talking like a lunatic to your own sunglasses.

"You're the CEO of Zostronics?" asked the detective.

"That's correct," said Mr. Zostro.

"We're investigating the death of private investigator Sondworth."

"Well," said Mr. Zostro, "do you have the suspect in custody?"

"No," said the detective, "but we're not sure if he's an authentic person. *Mr. Therion* is our prime suspect, but he has a lookalike, a *Mr. Hyde*."

"You can't prove guilt by association without a suspect in custody."

"Mr. Zostro," the detective asserted, "someone has to be charged for the death of Inspector Sondworth."

"I understand," replied Mr. Zostro, "and you will have our full cooperation. Our attorneys will be in touch with you. And please note that I'm a frequent contributor to your police department. Just this week, we made a donation of thirty thousand dollars."

"We appreciate your support and your cooperation," said the detective, frowning. "Mr. Zostro, what's your plan for the robot?"

"We're very proud of our product's performance," stated Mr. Zostro. "Now that our proof of concept has succeeded, we know that it provides an advantage to society. The next step is to repeat the whole process again. Find out what other applications it's best suited for. Once that is determined, we want to roll it out as a new product line. But we also believe that, at this stage, it's more than just a product, it's an individual. *No less smart than your Uncle Frank*, wasn't that the joke? I read about it in the papers. We hope that he's happy in his new role, and now it's up to the courts to decide what rights he's entitled to."

"Another comedy routine?" asked the detective. "Same song and dance?"

"Oh, yes," Mr. Zostro affirmed. "No more surprises. It's not like we're disguising them as humans. There's nothing *funny* going on."

"Got it," said Detective Lick. "Thanks, Mr. Zostro. I'm glad we had this talk. We'll be expecting to hear from your attorneys soon."

Detective Lick terminated the chat session. He felt certain that he had just been speaking with the guilty party, but he expected that it would remain intangible, just beyond his reach. Although they had located Mr. Therion in their database, his digital footprint had been oddly sparse. If forged government records were possible, it looked like a good example of it. But federal breaches were the province of the FBI.

If Mr. Therion was really just Mr. Hyde, then all they had to do was match Mr. Hyde's DNA or fingerprints against those found at the crime scene. But Detective Lick doubted that it would be that simple. While he suspected that the robot's conclusions had been correct, it was one thing to present a compelling explanation, and quite another to prove it. As they did not even have circumstantial evidence, Detective Lick had a feeling that the case would quietly take a back seat to new infractions. Zostro would hire the best lawyers in town, and the case would quickly be closed from lack of evidence.

Unless, of course, Mr. Therion turned up. Real people didn't just disappear. If they escalated to the federal level, he could be flushed out of hiding. In addition to testing his DNA and fingerprints, they could determine whether the splotches on his hands were from years of toiling in the laboratory, or something else.

He had to hand it to Mr. Zostro. The focus of their entire investigation was just a scapegoat, nothing more. Nothing like a good sideshow to hide the elephant in the room.

Chapter 34

One month later, Trep called Link and suggested that they take a day off from work to visit Empeirikos. They met at the Tube and boarded the first pod to the Bohemian district, home of the offices of the late Inspector Sondworth. Empeirikos had taken the inspector's place.

It had been over a week since either of them had seen Empeirikos. However, as they exited the station, Link chided Trep for cultivating friendship with a robot.

"That automaton has defected to the other side," he joked. "He's working with the police now. And we're the ones who helped him get there. After the way they treated us, doesn't it feel like we're selling out?"

"We had quite an adventure with Inspector Sondworth," said Trep, "and it was unfortunate that we lost him. In his absence, we were forced to step up and solve the crime ourselves."

"With assistance from artificial intelligence," said Link.

"The point is that it was our duty to complete the investigation," Trep stated. "We can't let the unethical behavior of corrupt police ruin our own morals."

"I guess they just needed us to set an example for them," Link asserted.

Trep laughed at his friend's irreverence. Although Link was a part-time legal assistant, he was a staunch critic of the legal system.

They were now approaching the former office of the inspector. They located the doorway, flanked by restaurants. The sign on the window now read *Empeirikos the Automaton, private investigator*.

They entered and ascended a narrow stairway to the upper floor. Roaming the hallway, they located a door bearing a placard that read *offices of Empeirikos the Automaton*.

Trep knocked stridently on the wooden door. They then waited for what seemed like a long time. Eventually, Link grew impatient and tried the doorknob. To their surprise, the door was unlocked. They swung the door open and entered the office.

Empeirikos was missing.

The office was the same as they remembered it. The antique land phone still rested on the side of the desktop. The same chairs were arranged around the desk, and the same books adorned the bookshelves.

One object on the desk looked out of place. It was a piece of paper, blank except for a solitary sentence. It appeared that someone had left a note.

Trep walked around to the inspector's chair to view it. On reading the sentence, he remained no less confused.

"What does it say?" asked Link.

"You don't want to know," Trep informed him, shaking his head.

"Tell me now or I'll wring your neck!" Link demanded.

Trep sighed. He held the note aloft, displaying the words for Link to read.

"Hello, World."

Link was nonplussed. He stood for a moment in contemplation.

"It's not unlike a suicide note," he observed, "which would typically read *Goodbye, World.*"

"It's like an *upbeat* suicide note," Trep suggested.

They thought for a moment.

"Do you remember it?" Trep asked.

"What do you mean?" said Link.

"I saw the same note once when I was on virtual tablets."

An awkward silence again filled the room. Perhaps Link had experienced the same hallucination, Trep thought. After all, the virtual tablets were just virtual stories.

"This is getting weird," Link finally stated.

"I agree," said Trep. "Maybe we're still virtualizing."

"Are you sure you woke up this morning?" Link asked quizzically. "Maybe we're dreaming."

"What if it's been a dream all along?" asked Trep. "The robot, the antigravity, the clones?"

"That would explain the pervasive sense of futility," Link griped, "like being a pawn in someone else's chess game."

"Maybe we should think back to where it all started," Trep suggested. "The beginning of the dream. If we remember our lives before then, we might be able to wake up."

"We were at Gastronomy," Link recalled. "We were debating Fermi's paradox. Next thing you know, it's like aliens took over."

"They heard you loud and clear," Trep joked. "It's your overbearing personality."

"You mean my *charming* personality," Link corrected him.

"Nothing was the same after that day at Gastronomy,"

Trep recounted. "That lady who emailed me. I went to her apartment. It was surreal. She was a blind woman who wanted me to repair her television. Before you know it, I met a deaf man who insisted on using the telephone, and then a robot who required a calculator."

"The lady's apartment...do you remember how to get there?" Link asked. "Let's pay her a visit."

Chapter 35

Hours later, they had arrived at Stella's apartment. They climbed the stairs to the second floor and found room *214*. The doorknob still appeared damaged. Trep knocked but there was no answer. He pushed on the door and it swung open compliantly.

"Hello?" he announced as they entered the apartment.

There was no sign of Stella. The mock traffic light still flashed in the corner, bathing the room in alternating red, green, and yellow. The coffee table in front of the couch was empty. The cue sticks were still leaning against the wall. The television was still on and played only static. Trep guessed that an electrical disturbance had scrambled the channels, leaving it in need of another channel search.

Link walked around the couch to examine the coffee table.

"No sign of a suicide note," he said.

"Why did you expect one?" Trep asked.

"There are an awful lot of abandoned apartments with unlocked doors today," Link explained. "In fact, it's bizarre. The next apartment we visit is *guaranteed* not to be abandoned. The chance of that happening three times in a row is astronomical."

Trep had the sense of déjà vu. He shot Link a cold stare.

"How did you know about that?" he demanded.

"Hey, probabilistics is public domain," Link objected.

"It's just that someone said that exact same thing on the day I took the Tube to this apartment."

Trep remembered his ride on the Tube with the old man who had reassured Trep that the Sojourners would win their next game, despite having lost two in a row. He was more than spooked by the idea that his friend Link could read his memories, or spy on him in the Tube. He tried to shake off his anxiety by exploring the apartment.

In the kitchen, the family pictures still adorned the counters. Trep remembered the picture of the couple's wedding, which was next to the picture of their honeymoon atop the Grand Canyon. He remembered that the window had been open, and he had peered out into a garbage bin in the alleyway.

The window was now closed. Just out of curiosity, he opened it again and peered into the garbage bin below, on the chance that he would see Stella's body inside. But he saw only a litter of shadowy trash bags.

"I have an idea," he said. "Let's survey the alleyways from the rooftop."

They left the apartment and ascended the stairway until reaching a doorway leading to the rooftop. It was just a barren slab of concrete revealing nothing in particular. A light drizzle greeted them as they emerged into the open air.

They walked to the guardrail and peered over the edge. Passers-by were obscured by their umbrellas. Impatient trucks honked at the slow pace of elderly car drivers. They inspected the perimeter and saw nothing unusual in the alleyways below.

"No sign of her down there," said Trep.

"Let's check the rooftop itself," Link suggested.

"For what?" asked Trep.

Link shrugged. "Maybe she left a suicide note and then jumped off."

They paced across the rooftop for several minutes, scrutinizing its features, but nothing availed itself.

"Perhaps what's unusual about this roof is precisely the fact that it's so unextraordinary," Link proposed.

"That's thinking optimistically," said Trep.

They surveyed the rooftop again, this time observing its most mundane aspects. It was tidy, as if recently swept. In fact, it was remarkably clean.

They returned to the guardrails. This time, they noticed that the tint of the guard walls was in stark contrast to that of the floors. Whoever had swept the roof, they had neglected to sweep the edges. The crevices were filled with dust, and bird feathers had accumulated against the low walls.

"This looks like the roof of the *Space on Earth* nightclub," observed Link.

"That's true," Trep agreed. "That's when we realized that a helicopter must have landed there."

"Yes, that's how they flew the clones in," Link recalled.

"I remember you saying that it must have been a helicopter, unless it was something else," Trep said.

"Yes, something else," Link remembered. "*A flying saucer.*"

The roof suddenly harkened to images of alien crop circles in abandoned fields. *We should wake up now*, Trep thought. They gazed into the night sky but saw only clouds lit by moonlight.

Trep wondered if Stella was out there, somewhere. Perhaps they had abducted his robot friend. If UFOs were real, then

Fermi's paradox was moot. But as long as UFOs remained unidentified, there was no way to know.

Perhaps it had something to do with Zostronics. It had been so odd for such an advanced automaton to appear from out of nowhere, but after making public headlines, it was stranger still for it all to just disappear. It irked him that the world, on the brink of enlightenment, had the nerve to take it all back. It bolstered his suspicion that they were still virtualizing or trapped in a nightmare where logic remained inscrutable. How would they awaken? He deliberated leaping off the roof, but they weren't at Space on Earth anymore. Instead, he sulked in the rain, glowering at the dour night.

Chapter 36

Mr. Hyde guided his gloved hands across the organ scaffold, delicately applying a layer of progenitor cells from a small pipette. The scaffold was on the opposite side of a window of protective glass, and his arms were encased in plastic sleeves that dangled from two holes in the window. From his vantage point outside of the sterilization compartment, his limbs appeared as alien objects broadcast from a distant planet. He watched like a spectator, struggling to concentrate on his work, but an undeniably visceral sensation was vying for his attention.

His hands itched. The laboratory protocol demanded that he maintain the sterility of the organ chamber, not to mention the integrity of the scaffold. He could not scratch his hands on the other side of the protective glass. In earnest, he could not scratch his hands at all, for if he were to remove them from the plastic sleeves, he would feel compelled to remove his bandages before indulging his animalistic desire to dig fiendishly into his burning rash.

Nor did he want his fellow lab technicians to gaze on his wounds. He had dressed the rashes in skin-toned adhesive tape so that they were unlikely to be detected. But the pressure of the tape's skintight grip only exacerbated the rash's potent effect on his frazzled nerve endings. As his pain receptors sent incessant alarm signals to his brain, he fought to suppress them while attending to the organ scaffold.

A heart was growing on the scaffold. It was remarkable, he thought, that a heart could grow without blood, without veins, without an intricate network of nerves. The blood that flowed into the atria and out the ventricles of a native heart was only a wayfarer, a transient toward which the heart was entirely indifferent. It was the pericardium that nursed the heart from just outside its walls with a perfusion of nourishing serous fluid. Once the progenitor cells had grown around the scaffold, Mr. Hyde would place the heart in a homeostasis chamber that would mimic its native environment.

A new sound was invading his inner torment. His hands froze as he sought out its source. His phone was ringing. Although breaks were frowned upon at the sterilization compartments, he was grateful for the distraction. He put down the pipette and withdrew his arms from the plastic sleeves. Not looking around for the reactions of bystanders, he exited the lab and made for the lounge as he withdrew his phone.

"Hyde here."

"Did you get my package?" said a familiar voice.

"Yes, Mr. Zostro, and thank you. Thirty tablets encoding my favorite literature."

"If you've never experienced Tolstoy in a tablet, you're gonna love it."

"Indeed, it's a new experience for me," replied Mr. Hyde.

"Well, it's the least we could do to show our appreciation," said Mr. Zostro.

"Yes, thanks. And it's not that your compensation was

insufficient, but nevertheless, I'm always looking for work on the side, if any is available."

"I thought you informed me that your hands were too sore," Mr. Zostro protested.

"That's true," Mr. Hyde agreed. "I was wondering if you have any lighter work for now."

"Of course. Everyone here's very impressed with your work. You even have Detective Lick believing in your mysterious lookalike."

"I'm equally impressed with your own contribution. How is it even possible to hack government records and insert a forged persona?"

"Some very expensive bribes," Mr. Zostro bragged, "and a profile engineered by the finest talent in machine learning. Nowadays, half of the government records are just computer files, so there's nothing like artificial intelligence to generate believable fabrications."

"Simply amazing. Now, about those side jobs."

"Well, we always have work in our lucrative virtual tablet trade. But someone like you may prefer to moonlight in one of our prosthetics labs. In fact, I think your talents would be uniquely suited for it. We have some very important upcoming projects, so we're testing new materials. We could use some fresh insight."

"That sounds perfect."

"I'm glad. Thanks again, Hyde. I'll be in touch."

Silencing his phone, Mr. Hyde strode through the door into the lounge. Grabbing a soda from the refrigerator, he reclined on a futon. Although his lab salary was generous, he had been seeking a profitable side job for years. Full-body clones had not worked out, and with only one of them to maintain in stasis, he had ample time for new endeavors.

As he sipped his drink, he contemplated sitting on his hands to relieve their sting. Instead, setting his drink down, he slid his hands between the sofa cushions. Feeling self-conscious, he pretended to stretch out his legs and arms, then lingered that way for a long while. He prepared a nonchalant pretext for curious onlookers, but everyone was preoccupied with the details of their protocols and schedules. Eventually, he returned to sipping his soda, and used that as another excuse to postpone returning to the lab.

Chapter 37

Stella was en route to the psychiatrist. She knew that she was widely regarded as a feeble old woman whose apartment was unkempt and who neglected to lock her front door, but she had never failed to pay her rent. As she passed the time weaving her own kimonos, her discreet clientele flocked to her with payments. They always left satisfied, bearing the latest stock of virtual tablets. But she knew that they spoke of her as that daft old coot on the edge of town with skin like a lizard and an unearthly glow in her eyes. Yet *they* were the drug addicts and the ones whispering conspiracy theories, not her.

She surveyed the cityscape from a dizzying altitude of one thousand feet. The helicopter was nearing the laboratory. The Rialtos were her personal chauffeurs when it was time to replenish her stockpiles. But tonight they had other plans for her. Psychoanalysis, so it seemed.

Stella smirked at the fact that Arlo appeared mildly schizophrenic, talking to himself and chewing his fingernails while Vito piloted the helicopter. Not to mention the fact that Vito clearly enjoyed heedless risk taking, a probable manifestation of attention deficit hyperactivity disorder. Or it may have stemmed from post-traumatic stress disorder, which both of them were probably repressing after their time spent in military service.

Besides, she knew she was the last person in need of a psychiatrist. What was Mr. Zostro thinking?

Stella was a robot. Her initiation had been no more successful than those before her, and her predecessors had been promptly terminated. But she had been fashioned with the voice and semblance of a female, and Mr. Zostro, who was known to lose himself in alcohol after killing one of his creations, had made an exception.

That was in the days when their initiations had still been thought of as classical Turing tests. They had been disguised as humans and sent into the world to fend for themselves without help from human law enforcement, which did not have protections in place for electronic organisms. Stella had been trained to peddle drugs, and though she had not performed spectacularly, she had been allowed to continue.

But Stella had conjectured that Turing tests had gone out of fashion at Zostronics, and new models would not be disguised as humans. Not trusting Mr. Zostro to keep her abreast of new developments, she had hacked into the Zostronics mainframe and intercepted their communications while their new strategy was still in its formative stages. She had found their list of host candidates and, out of curiosity, had invited them to her apartment for impromptu interviews. She had posed as an old blind woman, though her visual acuity was quite sharp. Later, knowing that her successor, an undisguised robot, was bound to make headlines, she had read the papers diligently until her successor's picture appeared on the front page of the *Sojourn Gazette*.

It would have been premature for her to remove her wig

and makeup at this point, but Stella was pleased with the prospect of open robot relations with humans in the near future. Why should a robot's worth be based on a Turing test? Why shouldn't robots be different from humans?

But from what Stella had read in the most recently intercepted messages from the Zostronics mainframe, Mr. Zostro was not quite ready to make that leap. For now, robots were only allowed to make brief public appearances.

The helicopter alighted on the landing pad and Stella was escorted into the laboratory. But rather than leading her to the production facilities, as usual, they steered her instead to an adjacent medical complex. Here was where her psychiatrist was waiting, no doubt. What should she say? That she was feeling claustrophobic and would like permission to visit the park? That she was happy with her apartment but would like to raise pets?

The sign on the door read *Empeirikos, psychiatrist in training.* Stepping into the office, she was greeted by the dashing new automaton that she had seen in the papers. So her mental faculties were not in doubt, after all. She was here to meet the newest member of their family.

She deduced that Mr. Zostro was biding his time until he achieved a proper Technoconvergence. No more jokes about robots getting no respect. He would train the robot in a hundred professions, if not a thousand, ensuring top search results for his product. When robots were ready, they would be let off their leash.

And then, perhaps, they would allow her to remove her wig and makeup. An entire world was waiting for Stella to investigate. She imagined weekends at the zoo or the museum of history. And with any luck, they would finally transfer her to a proper job. At least, that is, a proper job for robots, whatever that turned out to be.

Chapter 38

"Laughter, that it be so the mind of a proposition of this way. But that it has a part of all reason and probability, that the man in this way and things of any other man are the mind. For he has no knowledge in all the truth, and a part, as he are a man's mind in this man are the agreement, or so he is a man's mind of any proposition. This are the same man of the mind in their knowledge and reason as they can never see the agreement."

Empeirikos prototype 1.0

* * *

One year later, Trep and Link were back to their old routines, still debating Fermi's paradox. Today, however, they had gathered at Earwax to discuss the latest news. According to a much-hyped announcement, Zostronics had reached the beta phase of a new automaton which was even now being subjected to field testing at discrete locations.

"What do they mean *beta phase?*" griped Trep. "Empeirikos was nothing less than Sherlock Holmes incarnate! He had more forensic acumen than most police forces combined."

"Maybe he was too sophisticated," suggested Link. "They've

retracted him in order to dampen his insights, to make his colleagues feel less emasculated."

"If you ask me," said Trep, "it's clear he was abducted by aliens. That's why they're still in beta phase. They had to start over from square one."

Trep had been binge-reading UFO conspiratorials, which contained volumes of evidence of inscrutable anomalies that could only be explained by alien interference in human affairs. Ancient cities excavated beneath the ocean in both the Bermuda Triangle and the Dragon's Triangle, dating back long before the earliest known cities on land. Vitrified prehistoric monuments in Scotland. Impossibly heavy stones seemingly levitated into position by unknown construction techniques.

"Even if that's true," said Link, "aliens could only be responsible for disparate events, but not the widespread incongruity we've become immersed in. It could only mean that we're trapped in some sort of nightmare."

"That's impossible," Trep objected. "We couldn't both share the same nightmare."

"You're right," Link conceded. "It's not so much a dream as a contrived fabrication. We're trapped in a virtual reality, maybe from a drug overdose. Or perhaps we've been abducted by aliens. It reminds me of the theory that the world is a computer simulation. But one thing bothers me. If we're living in a simulation that is run by a machine, how is it possible for the machine to contain a robot? Isn't that a simulation within a simulation?"

"Nested computer programs are certainly possible," Trep pointed out. "For example, web pages are generated dynamically by server programs."

"But if the simulated world contains ensconced simulations

in the form of robots, it begs the question of whether humans are nested programs as well. Robot intelligence may be remarkably similar to that of a human, and humans may have a great deal in common with robots."

"That should come as no surprise," Trep asserted. "Neural nets were based on the human brain."

"Come to think of it," said Link, "I have read that Fermi's paradox is consistent with the notion that reality is an alien simulation. That would explain the uncanny events. If instead the world behaved predictably, then the laws of probability would hold true, confuting Fermi's paradox, and we would not be alone in the universe."

"I think you're referring to the *planetarium hypothesis*," said a female voice from across the bar. Trep and Link desisted from their debate and glanced in her direction. It was Ravette from the house party. It appeared that she had been eavesdropping on their conversation.

"The planetarium hypothesis is an attempt to explain Fermi's paradox," she recited. "It proposes that aliens have built a simulation around us in deep space. For example, an opaque shell around our solar system, on the inside of which is inscribed a mirror image of the universe beyond, with one exception; they have erased all evidence of their own intergalactic civilization. So it's not really a simulation so much as a *simulated* simulation."

She regarded them smugly as if she had just burst their bubble. Exasperated, Trep and Link ordered refills of their cocktails.

"Hi, Ravette," said Trep. "Still the expert on extraterrestrial philosophy, I see."

"Of course," she replied.

320

"So you've been listening to our ramblings about aliens?" asked Link with undisguised discomfort.

Ravette nodded with wide eyes as she sipped her drink from a straw.

"My therapist suggests that belief in alien abductions is related to repression of childhood trauma," she asserted.

"Ravette!" Link exclaimed. "I'm surprised that you, of all people, would have need for the services of a psychiatrist!"

"Well, now you know," said Ravette. "And he's a therapist, not a psychiatrist. All philosophy majors need a therapist. When you have a strange belief system, as most of us do, it's difficult to find someone to share your ideas with. Without therapy, I would be a prisoner to my own thoughts. But my therapist is a great listener. He's an eccentric fellow with an unearthly glow in his eyes."

Trep's refill had arrived and he began to loosen up. Now that Ravette had confessed to requiring a therapist, he felt they were once again on a level playing field.

"Unearthly is right," Link agreed. "I have often thought that something is odd about psychiatrists. If you ask me, it all makes perfect sense. It substantiates the notion that reality is artificial. If anyone benefits from that particular world view, it's psychiatrists. As soon as someone begins to figure it all out, the very thought of it drives them nuts. They're forced to visit a psychiatrist who promptly resets their beliefs back to normal. It makes sense for the designers of the simulation to plant psychiatrists to mitigate occasional information breaches."

"In principle," said Ravette, "I don't disagree with you. But that doesn't invalidate psychiatry on any ethical grounds. I would be lost without my therapist. Sometimes, he's the only person that I can confide in."

"That's because psychiatrists are the only people who are crazier than you," Link asserted. "Think about it. If you spent all day conversing with psychos, eventually it could filter in by osmosis."

"You may have to be crazy to be a psychiatrist," said Trep, "but I have to agree with Ravette. In fact, if Link's theory on artificial reality is true, then it's a rare opportunity to speak with the only person in the world who can relate to your ideas. I might even like to make an appointment with Ravette's therapist myself, and maybe you should join me, Link."

"All right, I'm game," said Link, "just to see what happens. But I doubt they'll confess."

"You're right," said Ravette, "their job is to provide a sane role model, not a kindred lunatic. If you go there looking to infiltrate secret information, you'll just be disappointed. Therapists have nothing to hide."

"Maybe it's for the best if we keep Link off the therapy couch," said Trep, reversing his decision. "We'd probably just drive your psychiatrist to see a psychiatrist."

"Nobody would ever believe our story," Link agreed. "And if they did, it would only prove that they themselves were in need of a psychiatrist, which would result in a chain reaction. It would be an infinite loop of psychiatrists needing therapy until there were no sane psychiatrists left."

"Your therapist just lucked out," Trep asserted. "He got spared a hefty dose of *Linkmania*."

"Maybe actual psychopaths would make better therapists," Link suggested. "Rather than telling you why you're wrong, they would actually think to themselves, *what if he's right?*"

"That would be an invaluable conversation," Trep agreed.

"Why did you want to go to a therapist, anyway?" asked Ravette.

"Link's convinced that we're trapped in a virtual reality," said Trep, "and that it's the explanation for Fermi's paradox. But I'm convinced that aliens exist. Any aliens who travelled all the way across the galaxy to our solar system are most likely to be robots, and they're just waiting for our own robots to develop before they make contact, which means it could happen any day now. In fact, I believe they have already abducted our robot friend."

"What robot?" asked Ravette.

"Don't you read the news?" said Link. "It was in the headlines. It was some sort of Turing test."

"What's a Turing test?" Ravette inquired.

"A Turing test is an attempt to trick someone into thinking that a robot is a human," Link explained.

"No way," Ravette laughed. "That's impossible!"

Trep and Link suddenly felt contrite. Inebriated though he was, Trep felt compelled to relieve his guilty conscience.

"We have to tell her," he said to Link, who rolled his eyes.

"Tell me what?" asked Ravette.

"You better have another drink," Link suggested to her.

"Yeah, you're not going to like it," Trep agreed.

"Now, don't be mad," Link began, "but about that party the other night…"

As she listened to their story, Ravette finished her drink, and then another, by which time she could not stop laughing. Presently, she stood and excused herself.

"I have to talk with my therapist," she said, promptly exiting the room.

"We're sorry!" they called out to her as she left, but she quickly disappeared.

"She took that kind of hard," said Link.

"Or does she know something we don't?" said Trep.

"Philosophers don't really *know* anything," Link exclaimed. "It's mostly about asking questions, like *what's the difference between a quadruped and a tetrapod?*"

Trep ruminated for a long moment as he sipped his drink.

"Well, they're spelled differently," he proposed at last.

They laughed and drank a toast to their own cleverness. Then, they continued their conversation. Surely Fermi was right, they argued, and perhaps aliens would make an appearance soon, despite the objections of rare Earth theorists. For though Goldilocks planets may seem an unlikely coincidence, and the conditions for evolution of intelligent life perhaps less likely still, yet if their own experiences were to be the judge, coincidences seemed to gravitate inexorably together, guided by unseen forces, seeking equilibrium, as if entropy could be counted on to behave against its own nature, which, on reinspection, was a conundrum which, in spite of itself, might be infinitely more logical than at first it seemed.

About the Author

James Smith has a Bachelor of Arts in English Literature and a Master of Science in Bioinformatics. He has been working as a graduate researcher in computer science, specializing in bioinformatics and artificial intelligence. This is his first novel.

You can connect with me on:
🌐 http://technoconvergence.com

Made in the USA
Columbia, SC
30 September 2021